HEART OF THE SHADOW

HEART OF THE SHADOW

LEGACY OF THE SHADOW'S BLOOD™ BOOK 6

E.G. BATEMAN

MICHAEL ANDERLE

DISRUPTIVE IMAGINATION

Copyright © 2021 LMBPN Publishing
Cover by Fantasy Book Design
Cover copyright © LMBPN Publishing
A Michael Anderle Production

LMBPN Publishing
PMB 196, 2540 South Maryland Pkwy
Las Vegas, NV 89109

Version 1.00, November 2021
eBook ISBN: 978-1-68500-601-3
Print ISBN: 978-1-68500-602-0

THE HEART OF THE SHADOW TEAM

Thanks to our JIT Team:

Diane L. Smith
Paul Westman
Rachel Beckford

Editor
SkyHunter Editing Team

CHAPTER ONE

Lexi pulled back the animal hide that served as a door to Jonathan's tent, then dropped it when she caught a face full of sand. She blinked the grit from her eyes and spat it out. Swiping her mouth with the back of her hand, she grimaced before glancing at her companion's amused chuckle. "What?"

Jonathan raised an eyebrow. "Did you expect a result different than the previous fifty times?"

Lexi shook her head. "I think I preferred it when you wouldn't speak to me." It was the wrong thing to say, and she knew it the moment the words left her mouth.

Jonathan narrowed his eyes. "You behave in ways I don't anticipate. I could almost believe you're real."

If the walls had been solid, Lexi would have banged her head against them. "Not this again. I'm real, and on some level, you know I am. Otherwise, you wouldn't have saved me from Boris." She gave an involuntary shudder thinking about the giant beetle-like creature, whose steely-shell exterior had been hiding hundreds of hungry babies waiting to feast on Lexi's desiccated corpse. So much for friendship.

Jonathan was still talking. "I would have continued to believe you were real if you hadn't announced that you are my daughter. You overplayed your hand, my evil friend." He shook a finger at her as though admonishing a child.

Lexi tried to be a few steps ahead in any conversation. If she said the wrong thing again, it was likely he'd clap his hands over his ears and shout as though banishing an unwelcome vision. However, hiding out from this storm was frustrating for them both.

"Trickery. It's always trickery with you. How long has it been since I was taken in by your lies?" He looked at his feet. "You bided your time, didn't you? Well, shame on me."

Lexi guessed it had been a long-ass two hundred years.

They'd been having the same conversation for weeks. Jonathan admitted that as a shadow mage, he could see straight through demonic glamours. Therefore she wasn't a glamour, but he had convinced himself that she was the Darkness, disguised by some other form of magic.

Lexi reached for the tent flap again, then jerked her hand back before making the same mistake. She attempted to divert his thoughts and stop them from spiraling again. "We've been stuck in this tent for two weeks. What kind of storm lasts for two weeks? The only good thing is the critters stay away, too."

"You wanted to meet the others, and this is the safest way to get through the canyon." He sat on a cot and pulled on his boots. "Although in truth, I expect I'll be introducing them to a figment of my imagination."

"Where were you heading to when you found me?" Lexi asked.

"I sensed someone using magic near the demon gate and thought the Darkness was making another assault on the portal. Now, I doubt that what I sensed was real. We would surely have met one of the others by now since they should also have felt the magic."

"It's ridiculous that we can't translocate without drawing the attention of the Darkness." She couldn't believe the mages were barely using magic beyond the lowest levels. "Surely, hopping to the other end of the canyon would be worth the fight at the end?"

Jonathan grimaced. "You could do that, but I'm afraid I'd have to insist you put some distance between us before you attempt it. Our fights can last for years, and immortal or not, stab wounds hurt."

She repressed a sigh of relief when he spoke as though she was real. "I know, 'using magic will draw the Darkness,'" Lexi parroted the statement Jonathan had repeatedly made since he had saved her. "It just seems unfair. The council made you all-powerful, then sent you over here where you can't use that power for fear of being consumed by the thing you came to destroy."

Jonathan shrugged. "They didn't know the trials we would face. No one did."

Lexi's anger at the injustice spilled out in a rush of words. "You're awfully forgiving. I was *horrified* when I heard what they'd done to you. They shouldn't have done it, and I don't understand why they sent you at all. With a portal that couldn't be breached from the other side, they had effectively sealed the thin place. Why did they have to send thirteen of you through?"

"Do you think we haven't driven ourselves crazy asking the same questions? Most of us have gone mad. Excuse me, I have to step out." He covered his face and walked through the tent flap.

Lexi turned away from the wind that blasted in as the supple hide dropped back into place. *My father looks younger than I do.* She chuckled at the thought, shaking her head in disbelief. He was over two hundred years old but had stopped aging in his late twenties.

She wandered around the tent, studying the walls. What she had first thought was a pattern in the hide was where he had been marking off the days: four lines with a strikethrough were repeated thousands of times. She calculated three-hundred and sixty-five days multiplied by two hundred years. Over seventy thousand days. She shook her head at the thought. At first, he had appeared to be in control of his faculties, but telling him she was his daughter had shifted him over the edge of a mental precipice she couldn't have known he was teetering on.

She wondered how long it would be before she needed to count off the days like this to stay sane. She had made her choice —to sacrifice herself so Scott could free her sister from the demon. Lexi smiled at the thought of Azatoth gone and Alicia free, of Betsy able to return from fae with her son, and Bryan free to leave the maze. She hoped that Scott was getting on with his life, but she didn't think so. She knew without a shadow of a doubt that he would be trying to find a way to get her back, and while she didn't dare to hope, she did.

The tent flap opened and Jonathan re-entered. He wasn't alone.

A tall, Black man who was built like a linebacker stooped to enter behind him. "It's a miracle we saw each other in this storm." His accent was African, but she couldn't identify which part.

Lexi was thrilled. Finally, someone who could confirm that she existed!

The man closed the flap behind himself and glanced briefly at Lexi, then turned to Jonathan, waiting for him to remove the gauze from his face and shake the sand out of it.

Jonathan indicated Lexi, who was sitting on the lurid green couch from her dimensional pocket. "There. Tell me, Akeem. Do you see her?"

The man stared into Lexi's eyes, then turned to Jonathan. "I'm sorry, my friend. There is no one here but you and me."

Lexi launched to her feet. "What? You looked right at me!"

Akeem ignored her, facing away.

Jonathan looked grief-stricken. "Why do I fight it, Akeem? Clearly, I am lost to the Darkness."

Akeem smiled sadly. "So it would seem. Perhaps it would be less painful just to accept it."

Lexi narrowed her eyes. So that's what he was playing at.

Lexi pulled on the man's fur-lined hood to get his attention. When the hood dropped, a demonic face grinned at her from the back of his head. "What the hell is *that*?"

Akeem stepped away from her, turning his face toward Jonathan. "Open yourself to it before the denial of the inevitable drives you insane."

Lexi grabbed the big man by his arm and spun him around. "Look at this. Jonathan. You can't trust him."

Jonathan gasped. "Akeem, you've joined with the Darkness. No!"

The man turned his face back to Jonathan. "What are you talking about? Are you hallucinating?"

Jonathan backed up until his legs touched his cot. "I don't know. I... I..." His voice trailed off; he was paralyzed by indecision.

Lexi realized that this was why shadow mages lived so far apart. They couldn't trust each other or themselves. She pulled her katana out of her dimensional pocket and advanced on Akeem. She couldn't kill him, but she could mess him up.

Fuck this rule denying magic. I'm going to create a hole fifty feet deep and bury him in it!

He moved quickly for such a big man. He waved a hand as he advanced on her, and her katana was gone. All thoughts of magic left Lexi as his hands gripped her throat and he forced her back onto the couch. She beat at his hands ineffectually in an attempt to loosen the chokehold. Her vision blurred. He couldn't kill her, but he probably had worse plans for her than a hole in the ground.

Then Jonathan was there, trying to drag the big man off her. However, Akeem was stronger. The larger man's head jerked to the side as the demon face on the back of his head snapped its teeth at Jonathan.

Lexi called a weapon from her dimensional pocket into her hand and thrust it into Akeem's belly. His hands fell away from her throat, and she saw something horrific: the blade had continued through Akeem's gut and slid between Jonathan's ribs.

It was torn from her grasp as they staggered backward together and landed on Jonathan's cot, smashing it as Akeem's weight drove the blade deeper into Jonathan's body.

A wheeze burst from Jonathan's throat as Akeem's unconscious body drove the air from his lungs. He was still coughing and spluttering when Lexi yanked the blade out and rolled the huge man to the side.

Jonathan wiped an arm across his face to remove the white chalky substance that was all that remained of the demon possessing Akeem. "Lexi, help me up."

She froze before holding out a hand for him to grab. It was the first time he had called her by her name. When she had helped her father to his feet, they inspected the back of Akeem's head. All traces of the demons except the chalky powder had left him.

Jonathan shook his head. "My mind is clear. I don't understand why I feel different."

"I do." Lexi wiped the bloody sword on Akeem's coat.

A few minutes later, Akeem regained consciousness and sat up with his head in his hands. "I'm so sorry, my friend. I don't know how I allowed myself to become so lost." He turned to Lexi. "What did you do?"

Lexi showed him the sword. "This is Harpe, the weapon used by Perseus to kill the gorgon Medusa."

Akeem blinked. "Your weapon is magnificent."

Lexi snorted. She was sure she'd once heard Dick say the same words through the thin walls of the condo.

She turned to share the thought with Scott, and the smile left her face. These were the times she missed him. From the moment the portal had closed, she had been unable to sense him through their bond, and her dimensional pocket was no longer connected to his.

She hoped that whatever he was doing, he was safe and well.

CHAPTER TWO

Scott dragged his fingers through his oily, unkempt hair. He didn't care about how he looked anymore, but his scalp had become itchy in the last few days. He wasn't surprised after being in some pretty unsavory places over the last month. He dropped a ten-dollar bill on the bar and turned to survey the room. It was a dive, dark and dingy with a funky smell. It represented the hopelessness he felt.

He wasn't there out of choice. He was looking for a magician, which was the name Kindred gave to people with a small amount of natural sorcery but needed to bolster it with witchcraft or some other form of magic. This man had proven difficult to find. Scott had been going from one seedy bar to the next for weeks.

As he waited for his drink, he cast his gaze around. The patrons looked anywhere but at him. They knew he was Kindred; he didn't hide it. He knew what they were, too: weres, unseelies, vampires cruising for willing meals—or unwilling if the former weren't available. There were even a few minor demons. In short, the dregs of supernatural society. Some got up and left, unhappy with his scrutiny.

Coins hit the bar behind him and he turned to face the barman, who stared at him with loathing as he placed a shot glass beside Scott's change. "Whatever business you've got, get it done. You're losing me custom."

The mage squinted through gritty eyes and pointed at the barman. "Maybe I should make *you* my business." He knocked back the Scotch. He'd lost count of the drinks he'd had during the nights. "Do you want to be today's business?"

The barman poured him another, then dropped his gaze and moved to the other end of the bar.

"That's what I thought." Scott grabbed the glass and headed for an empty booth in a dark corner at the back of the bar. The place was disgusting. The floor was so sticky his boots peeled loudly away from the floor with each step.

A spiky-haired man in a long, camel-colored coat appeared in the booth on the bench opposite him. "You look like shit, and you've developed an interesting taste in drinking establishments."

Scott blinked slowly. "I've been looking for you."

The magician gazed around the dump. "You should aim higher. Also, I told you I'd find you when I had news."

Scott shrugged. "You were taking too long."

The man frowned. "You asked me to get you access to a demon of comparable size to a human. It took some work to find a suitable match. I'm doing this as a favor for Albin. Don't make me regret it."

Scott hadn't slept well for months, and he knew he'd been drinking way too much. He held up his palms, a peace gesture. He didn't have time for this. "Have you got it?"

The man held out a hand. In his palm sat a silver dollar.

"That's it?" Scott reached for the coin.

The man closed his fingers around it. "Are you sure you want to do this? There's a time limit, and you do not want to be stuck over there."

Scott narrowed his eyes. "Are you going to give it to me or not?"

"Fine. Let's do this." He pushed the coin across the table. "Use an east-facing wall. That's important."

Scott nodded and tapped the coin with a fingertip. He felt the magic within it. It was what he'd been looking for. The coin disappeared into his dimensional pocket.

His companion sat forward. "Um—"

"The money's in your pocket," Scott interjected. He stood and slipped out of the booth.

His companion called, "Good luck."

Scott turned back, but the bench was empty. He headed out of the bar and walked down the busy street, contemplating calling Dolores or Dick. He knew he should. They could help him, or more likely, talk him out of it. He didn't want that...or maybe he did.

I'm going to wimp out if I'm not careful.

He paused at the entrance to an alley, then looked up. The predawn sky was dark on one side and glowing red and orange on the other.

Sun rose in the east.

Now was as good a time as any. He knew he should speak the words to make himself sober, but he wasn't sure he'd be able to go through with it sober. Besides, he liked the buzz. It hid the numb feeling of going through the motions he'd been experiencing since Lexi had stepped backward through the portal and disappeared.

Scott turned down the alley. A cat sitting on a dumpster hissed as he passed. He paused and met the cat's gaze. Sometimes a cat was not a cat. This one, however, was. It was annoyed that Scott had interrupted its breakfast, something furry that was still moving. "Don't worry, your meal is safe."

Scott continued to the end of the alley. He took the coin from his pocket and slammed it against the wall, where it stuck. He stepped back, not knowing whether this was going to work. The coin slowly turned, gathering speed. Within moments, it was spinning while red sparks flew from the edges. The bricks around the coin wobbled. The effect of the magic grew until the portal was seven feet high and four feet wide. The coin continued to spin, then slowly moved away from him as that whole section of wall curved in and became a tunnel.

Drunk and without a plan, he stepped in.

As he walked through the tunnel, it got progressively darker. He didn't realize he'd reached the end until the ground underfoot became soft and springy. The place stank of brimstone and death. He hadn't even considered how he was going to subdue the demon long enough to harvest its essence.

He spoke the words that enabled him to see in the dark and was glad he had done so. He was standing in a clearing in a swamp. Several large bipedal demons lounged on the ground around him. They raised their heads when he appeared, and a few climbed to their feet.

"I suppose I should be sober for this." He whispered the spell.

With clarity of mind came an adrenaline rush. Scott plucked a luminescent stone from his dimensional pocket and flicked it up above his head. It hovered in the air for a moment before lighting up the space.

A cacophony of howls assailed Scott's ears as the demons covered their eyes at the unexpected brightness. He reasoned they might never have been exposed to such brightness. Retreating splashes and thuds told him that most were running away. He hoped not all of them would run. He didn't want to have to chase them.

Only three had remained. They were all at least a foot taller than him, with taloned hands and slimy-looking moss covering their humanoid bodies. They held one arm over their faces to block out the direct light.

Scott considered that being drunk might have been preferable after all. At least he only had to worry about one taloned hand each. Their legs were as thick as tree trunks, and their toes ended in sharp, curved talons that clicked against each other as they crept toward him. They wasted no time. As one, they descended upon him and would have caught him if he'd still been standing there. He cast a shadow illusion as he translocated and blasted a bolt of energy into the back of a demon's head. It dropped silently to the ground.

They grabbed for the shadow mage but stopped and turned to where he was standing behind them.

Damn! Fast learners. Scott blasted another. The demon dodged and was only grazed. It howled but didn't stumble.

The mage translocated several times in the next few moments, leaving shadows of himself around the clearing to confuse the creatures. He threw an energy ball at the remaining demon, but it dodged, and he hit the injured one. That finished it off.

There was only one left, and that was all he needed. This one was smarter. It was sniffing the air. Scott could deceive its eyes, but he wasn't sure he could deceive its nose. Scott tried the translocating trick again, but everywhere he moved, the demon anticipated him. A deep pulsing sound drew his attention—the tunnel. His time was almost up.

Scott grinned and muttered, "What would Lexi do?"

Lexi spoke from behind the demon as it faced him and moved closer.

"I'm starting to think that big lummox is smarter than you."

The creature turned toward the voice, as Scott had anticipated. Unfortunately, he hadn't anticipated being momentarily stunned by his own illusion. It was like she was really there: the wry smile, the casual way she held her katana, her other hand on her hip as though she was bored and supremely confident. The creature had spun and swiped its black talons across Scott's stomach. The mage doubled over.

The demon glanced at the Lexi glamour as she continued, "Well, that was pathetic."

Scott put a hand out toward the creature. "Sleep."

It dropped to the ground.

The illusion of Lexi stood over the unconscious demon. "We'll need to work on this in your next training session."

He groaned at the pain, then smiled, ignoring the tears welling up in his eyes. "We will," he promised as she faded.

Scott pulled a small tin box out of his pocket and opened it as he spoke. Dark mist spiraled from the sleeping demon and poured into the box.

Scott's gaze swiveled between the demon's essence and the pulsing, wavering tunnel. The moment the box snapped shut, he bolted for the tunnel. He felt it closing behind him as he ran with one hand pressed to his wound.

The end was just a few feet away when the little box slipped out of his hand. He didn't stop. While it was still falling, he kicked it out of the tunnel and stumbled the last few steps into the alley.

The tunnel collapsed, and the coin dropped to the ground. He stooped to pick it up, but it disappeared before his fingers closed around it. Scott dropped his hands to his knees, then gulped air and tried not to throw up when he saw the mess the demon had made of his stomach. He grabbed the box and used the last of his strength to translocate to the condo.

He appeared in the bathroom, bent over as pain from the wound across his stomach wracked him. He pulled off what was left of his shredded t-shirt, the movement making him grip the edge of the washbasin. The small tin containing the demon's essence tumbled out of his hand and hit the floor, but it was magically sealed and didn't open. He wasn't concerned. Instead, he watched blood trickle out of the deep claw marks.

He reached into the medicine cabinet and pulled out some bandages, which he soaked in cool water and soap. His vision narrowed to a pinprick and he dropped clumsily to the floor, but he refused to let himself faint. He muttered a spell to take away the pain, then another to heal himself as he drew the dressing across his abdomen. He watched as the bleeding stopped and the torn flesh showed signs of healing.

He closed his eyes as the room spun.

CHAPTER THREE

S cott woke up to Dick tapping his cheek.

"Scott! What the hell happened to you?"

The mage's hand went to his abdomen. The skin was smooth. "Nothing."

"I beg to differ." Dick scoffed. "It smells like a vampire buffet in here, and it looks like the ER on a Friday night."

Scott sat up. His blood-soaked t-shirt and the bandages lay beside him. A sizable puddle of blood was drying on the floor next to the washbasin. "You're referring to that?" He took a few moments to think of a plausible excuse. "How upset would you be if I counseled you to forget this? Oh, wait. You wouldn't be upset because you wouldn't remember."

Dick gave him a withering look.

Scott frowned at his stomach. While the scars had healed, dark streaks remained on the skin.

That was odd.

He held his hand above them and muttered a spell. Thick green liquid bubbled up from under the skin.

Dick put a hand over his nose and mouth. "Dear God! What's that smell?"

Scott raised his eyebrows. "Its claws must have been poisonous. I didn't think of that." He grabbed his bloody t-shirt and mopped up the gunk, then glanced at Dick. "What are you doing here?"

"Your neighbors are sensitive to the smell of blood," Dick reminded him. "The twins are climbing the walls in there. Although if they catch *that* smell, I'm sure they'll be cured of their thirst."

Scott got to his feet. "You shouldn't have come in. You know she's having us watched."

Dick folded his arms and leaned against the wall. "Are you going to tell me what you've been doing?"

Scott shrugged. "Nothing. Just a bad day at work."

"Really? That's not what your cell phone says."

Scott narrowed his eyes. His cell phone was spelled to return to him if someone else picked it up.

The vampire smirked. "I'm not stupid. I didn't touch it. It's on the floor over there. You received a text a minute ago."

Scott grabbed the cell phone and checked the screen.

Big Bad: Are you coming into work today or what?

Scott cast his gaze over the rest of the floor.

"Looking for this?" Dick held the little metal box just out of Scott's reach. "I tried to open it before I woke you up. I can't get into it. I assume it's sealed with magic."

Scott didn't answer. He put out a hand, palm up.

Dick rolled his eyes. "Fine." He dropped the box into Scott's hand. "So, what is it?"

The mage disappeared the box into his dimensional pocket. "Essence of demon."

Dick's jaw dropped. "Did you do it?"

"Not *that* demon." Scott sat on the edge of the tub. "Az is too strong to be held in a little box like this. This is a lesser demon.

We're only going to have one shot at it, so I'm experimenting. I can't fuck it up when I make a move against her."

"How's it working out so far?" Dick pointedly stared at the bloody handprint on the washbasin.

Scott scoffed. "I could make some improvements, but I have the essence of a demon. It's the farthest I've gotten. Now I need to find somewhere to put it."

Dick smirked. "I might be able to help with that. How about you get to work now? The last thing we need is your boss showing up here."

———

Azatoth sat with her feet up on the desk, scanning reports and flipping each page behind her onto the floor as she went.

Scott stood in the open doorway, loathing the demon. "Are you ready?"

The demon scanned two more pages before looking at him. "Am I walking out of the office? No, so I'm not ready. You're an hour late, and you look like shit. Where have you been?"

"I ate something that disagreed with me," Scott lied.

Azatoth eyed him skeptically. "You should kill them first so they can't disagree."

Scott narrowed his eyes. "What?"

"But then there's no wriggling, and that's half the fun." The demon grinned maliciously but then frowned as she reached for a packet of antacids on the desk. She popped a couple of the tablets then returned her attention to her task.

Scott sighed with irritation and turned his attention to Nora's desk beside Azatoth's office door. He gazed in disgust at the gray, reanimated corpse of the secretary, typing stiffly at the keyboard. The phone rang, and Nora stared at it with her head tilted as though she were trying to remember what she was supposed to do about it.

Azatoth's voice came from behind him. "She's just not the same anymore."

"She's dead, so yeah, you could say that." Scott turned to face the demon and found Lexi staring at him. The demon looked exactly like her. Not the way Alicia did as her twin. She'd glamoured her hair and clothes to look like Lexi's.

Scott didn't move. He just stared, seething at the demon's audacity. He was angry at himself for the surging feeling of loss that came so easily to the surface. He dropped his bag on the floor and crossed his arms, indicating that he intended to stay there until she removed the glamour.

"Fine." Azatoth sighed and the glamour vanished. "I thought it would make you feel more comfortable."

Scott worked to move his jaw, which had frozen in anger. "More comfortable than the other twenty times you did it? Thanks, but I hate it."

"God, you're *so* boring." The demon rolled her eyes. "I don't know how Lexi put up with you. I bet she had way more fun working with me than you. I feel like the kindest thing I could do is put you out of your misery." She walked toward the elevator.

Scott still hadn't moved. "Do it, then."

Azatoth turned and walked back. "Sorry, Scotty. I'm keeping you glued to my side. You want her back and I *need* her back, or that portal open. If anyone can make that happen, I think it's you. You or your irritating friends."

The door to the conference room opened, and Millicent stepped into the hallway. She called to Azatoth, "Glad I caught you." Her expression was not happy. "Things are getting out of control in Las Vegas. I think we need to get the wards back up."

Azatoth raised an eyebrow. "Oh, we do, do we?"

Millicent stepped back, suddenly unsure of herself. "Obviously, it's up to you. I meant to say, every criminal element in the supernatural world knows the security is down and thinks it's a free-for-all. The casinos are losing money hand over fist. They're demanding we either deal with it or let them put their own wards up."

The demon raised an eyebrow. "Sounds like fun. I should visit." She gave Scott an evil grin. "You've got an empty bedroom, don't you?"

Scott clenched his teeth. The last thing he wanted was for the demon to be hanging around his neighborhood. He'd burn Lexi's bed to a crisp before he let the demon near it.

Millicent's shoulders drooped in defeat. Scott was amazed. He thought the stick up her ass should have prevented that.

Azatoth also noticed the woman's demeanor and rolled her eyes. "Fine. I'll think about it."

"Thank you." Millicent forced a smile for the demon. "Have a nice day." She headed back up the hallway.

Azatoth watched the mage walk away and muttered, "I think she's fallen out with me. I wonder if I should pull her guts out." The demon frowned, then took an antacid from her pocket and popped it into her mouth.

Scott didn't like Millicent, but the idea of casually killing her was more than he could bear. He snorted. "I don't think it's you she's fallen out with."

As if on cue, Eric stepped out of the room and frowned at his mage. "Please stop wandering off. We need you in here."

Scott turned to the demon. "How's your new cabal working out?"

"It's working fine, and it's not a cabal. It's the Kindred High Council. Show some respect." Azatoth headed toward the elevator. "Come on, then."

Scott retrieved his bag and joined her, keeping the smile from his face. The demon's council wasn't working out well, and he knew it. The stronger mages who would eventually have made their way to a place on the council were reluctant to perform some of the spells she was demanding of them, such as trying to burn a hole through the universe to get to the demon realm where Lexi and the Darkness were trapped. The mages they'd freed from the Hollows were proving to be so mentally unstable as to be a hazard anywhere near magic.

Azatoth stood facing the wall for a few moments, then turned to face him. "Well?"

He looked at her. "Well, what?"

"Call the elevator. Do I have to do everything myself?"

Scott noted the ID hanging around her neck. She could have done it. He grabbed his card and waved it at the wall. The elevator doors opened, and they stepped in.

Scott hated being in enclosed spaces with her. He stared ahead while she leaned against the wall, using the corner of her ID card to dig dirt out from under her nails.

"I hate these stupid little boxes," Azatoth complained. "I'm the fucking CEO of this company. I should be able to travel to the archive without using the elevator."

"Have you had any luck assigning someone else as the head curator?" Scott inquired.

Azatoth growled. "I've tried three times this week. The security guy prints the ID card with no problem, but the moment the employee puts the lanyard on, the words disappear from the card. It's infuriating. I was surprised it didn't accept you. I thought… Well, it didn't work, so never mind."

Scott knew what she was thinking. Because of his connection with Lexi, whom the archive *had* accepted, she thought he might be able to take over and bring some order to the place. Since Lexi had gone, no one could find anything.

In truth, Scott felt the archive must have accepted him in some way because he never struggled to find a book. Sometimes he'd deliberately pick the wrong one to make it less obvious. "It seems the archive doesn't want a new head curator. Perhaps it's a good sign, a sign that she's okay."

Azatoth gazed ahead, her eyes unfocused. "She's immortal,

but that doesn't mean she's okay. There are a lot of ways someone can be alive and not okay. Immortality is a curse."

The elevator doors opened, and they stepped out.

A noise to Scott's right drew his attention. A gnarly-looking elf was leaning against a wall at the opposite end of the hall, smoking. The elf saw them, and the cigarette disappeared immediately.

Scott narrowed his eyes. The corridor was a dead end. There didn't seem to be any reason for the elf to be there. However, there were dark fae all over the building now, strutting around like they owned it. The staff were aware that things weren't right. They whispered about it in the staff restaurant; although no one was inclined to investigate after the first few people had gone missing.

Scott was amazed that people still turned up to work.

Azatoth stared at the odious little man, but she didn't approach him. She just smiled. "This is a no-smoking building. There are smoking areas outside beside the bike racks. Or you could pop off to whatever greasy little swamp you came from. If I catch you smoking in here again, your guts will be decorating the hallways." She led the way into the archive, shoving another antacid into her mouth as she went.

The demon went to Devon's chair and put her feet on the desk. Scott went into the stacks. He walked past Devon's engraving equipment, untouched since the man died, then past the aisle with the thesaurus portal. He had previously tried to re-enter the mirror inside the portal, but while he could still go to the little room inside the book, the portal to the past had disappeared. It was just a mirror now.

Scott supposed a point in time could only be visited once before it became fixed. It made sense that a second visit would undo whatever you did the first time you went back. He continued to the section on fae realms, grabbed several books, and returned to the front desk. "What did you mean when you said immortality is a curse?"

The demon poked at the holographic puzzle on Devon's desk. She tried to spin the wheels on the barrel-shaped object, but her finger went through it. She slammed her hand through it, frustrated that she was unable to touch it. "If I ever figure out how to touch this thing, I'm going to smash it."

She turned her attention to him. "You probably think it took me two hundred years of slipping through cracks in the realms to get here. In truth, the travel itself took around fifty years, mostly because I didn't know where I was going. The rest of the time was spent recovering from what I had to do to myself to get out of that horrific dimension. If you're lucky, Lexi might find better ways. She could return just in time to see you die of old age. I hope that gives you more motivation to find a safer, faster path for us to get her out."

Azatoth stood. "Have you got everything?"

Scott nodded.

"I've got a meeting. I'll see you back in the office. Bring coffee." With that, the demon marched out of the archive.

Scott walked around the desk to the holographic device. He knew the puzzle had not been solved in the fifteen years it had been sitting on Devon's desk. It was similar to a Jefferson disk, or the *DaVinci Code* cryptex, but it was twice the size and rested in a cradle. The shiny brass panels were inlaid in the rosewood. He wondered if the numbers had been engraved by Devon himself.

Scott knew Azatoth had seeing-eyes all over the building and might have been watching him at that moment. If so, it wouldn't be for long. The spirits in the archive kept interfering with the demon's seeing balls, rendering them useless—something else that infuriated the demon. He placed a finger near the device and swept down. The wheel spun. If she *was* watching, that would annoy the hell out of her.

He smiled and headed out.

CHAPTER FOUR

Lexi blushed under Akeem's scrutiny.

The big man tilted his head this way and that and sighed. "You can't deny she has her eyes." He screwed up his eyes to blur her image. "Maybe your nose, but not so ugly."

Lexi turned away. "Okay, that's enough. You've been staring at me and making comments about my face for two days. Any more, and I'll have to charge you for a front-row seat."

"She definitely has Amelia's spirit." Akeem turned to Jonathan. "How do you feel?"

"I feel..." Jonathan shrugged. "I don't know. I've had two hundred years of nightmares about hearing her scream and seeing her pulled away from me through the gate. Now I'm supposed to believe that she didn't die but was thrust into a strange world she wouldn't have understood. I wonder if she was frightened, calling for me."

Lexi could only give him what little truth she knew about her mother, although she wasn't sure if it would make things better or worse. "When she was found, she had no memory. She didn't even know her name. They called her Elizabeth. I don't know if I look like her. I don't remember her." She almost told him about

Alicia but decided to see how he coped with the news about her mother first.

Jonathan stared into the middle distance, and probably the past. "It seems too fantastical."

"I know." Lexi shrugged. "I'm sure there's some way to prove it when we get out of here."

Akeem chuckled, but it was a sad sound. "There is no way out of here."

Lexi was defiant. "Mortimer did it." The two men shared a look. She was beginning to get a bad feeling. "What am I missing?"

Jonathan asked his friend, "How long has it been since you last saw Philippe?"

Akeem rubbed his chin. "I haven't seen him since we all last saw each other."

"Fifty years, then." Jonathan shook his head. "I hope he's faired better than us."

"He'd better have," Akeem stated. "He has the glass."

"Ah, Boston."

Lexi frowned in confusion. "Glass? Boston?"

Neither man would be drawn further on the subject, but Jonathan explained, "Philippe saw Mortimer escape and described it to us. You can choose if it's what you want. I decided many years ago that I would much prefer to stay here."

Lexi's jaw dropped. "I can't believe it was so bad an option that you would choose to stay in this place."

Jonathan grimaced. "Let me put it a different way. Philippe saw Mortimer *begin* to escape. When he passed by a few years later, he was still in the process of escaping. It wasn't pretty."

Lexi narrowed her eyes. "Did he dig his way out?"

Akeem shuddered. "I'm going to let Philippe explain it. I don't think my stomach is up to it. But, the storm has passed. Now seems as good a time as any to visit Philippe."

They traveled for two days, setting up camp at night. They took turns watching out for the hideous creatures that inhabited the place. Lexi found it curious that the creatures didn't come into the tent at night, although they remained close by.

Lexi grinned as she walked beside Jonathan. "Are we nearly there?"

Jonathan narrowed his eyes at her. "Must you keep asking that?"

Lexi snickered. "We've got a lot of catching up to do. Wait until I start sneaking out to meet boys."

Akeem chuckled, then pointed. "You see that tree in the distance?"

Lexi surveyed the barren landscape ahead of them. "How could I miss it? It's the only landmark around here."

The big man explained, "That's Philippe's tree."

Lexi smirked. "Is that like a status thing over here?" She turned to Jonathan. "Do you have a tree? Is it bigger than Philippe's tree? Will I inherit it? No, wait, you won't die. Where do I get my own tree?"

Jonathan sighed. "Dear God."

When they got close enough for Lexi to see the tree's details, she blinked in surprise. "Is that an oak?"

Akeem nodded. "It is."

Lexi blinked. "That thing must be huge."

"Last I saw, it was at least two hundred feet," Akeem confirmed. "I think it might be bigger now."

Lexi sniffed as they approached the tree. "That smells like barbecue." Her stomach gurgled and her steps quickened as she walked around the massive trunk to find a man sitting on a log with his back to them. He faced a fire and was turning what appeared to be a giant spider on a spit. Instantly, her appetite left her.

"So, my old friends have arrived. I sensed you approaching this morning." He turned and raised an eyebrow. "I see you bring a fair damsel." He narrowed his eyes, looking from her face to her unhealing wound. "And a puzzle."

Jonathan made the introductions. "Lexi, this is Philippe."

The Frenchman stood and offered his hand.

Lexi grasped his hand, but instead of shaking it, the man kissed her knuckles. That worked out well for Lexi because he didn't see Harpe appear in her hand. In fact, he didn't know anything before she brought the blade down and sank it into his back.

He howled and toppled face-first to the ground.

Jonathan gaped as she pulled the blade free and wiped it on the man's jacket.

"It seemed like the quickest way to ensure he wasn't infected by the Darkness," Lexi explained.

The man at her feet wheezed, "You could just have asked."

Lexi glanced at him. "You might have lied." She pointed at the fire. "Your mutant spider-thing is burning. You know you don't have to eat, don't you?"

The Frenchman shrugged. "I prefer to eat. It makes me feel more like the man I was before they changed me."

"It's getting dark." Lexi turned to Jonathan. "We should make camp soon."

Philippe looked at the dusky sky. "We should climb. It's safer to be in the treehouse at night."

"You've got a treehouse up there?" Lexi couldn't see more than a few inches into the dense foliage. She returned her gaze to his face. "And you're inviting me in after I stabbed you?"

Philippe reached up and pulled down a ladder made of vines, then climbed into the tree. Lexi went up next and grabbed Philippe's offered hand. Her jaw dropped as she found herself in a small entrance hall. This was no shack built into the tree; the whole tree was a house. A spiral staircase of interwoven tree limbs curved into the branches above. To her right was a small sitting room. The tree's branches were woven into an armchair and a small bookcase. A tall lamp stood beside the chair with a glowing rock cradled in the branch at the top. To her left, branches formed a large table with two benches along either side.

Lexi found her voice. "I thought you couldn't do magic here?"

Philippe returned her shocked look with one of glee. "It took one spell one hundred and fifty years ago on an acorn I found in my pocket. It was a spell of protection with a few other things thrown in, and it was the last magic I performed until the tree grew. The acorn became a tree that protects me and enables me to perform a little magic safely."

Lexi was impressed. "I wish I'd had a coffee bean in my pocket when I came over."

Akeem put his hand to his heart. "Coffee."

All three men gave sighs full of longing.

"So, what brings you to the tree? Or did you just come to stab me?" Philippe grinned at Lexi.

Lexi blushed. "Sorry about that."

Phillipe waved off her apology. "It's all right. If you'd had any ill intentions toward me, you wouldn't have gotten anywhere near the tree."

Jonathan answered, "Lexi has chosen not to stay with us. Can you take us to the fissure tomorrow?"

Philippe's eyes bulged. "I hope you're not considering leaving that way."

"Maybe." While she didn't understand what they weren't saying, their concerned expressions weren't lost on her. It seemed unlikely that leaving the realm that way was an option. "What's the problem?"

Jonathan frowned. "I think you have to see it for yourself."

Akeem muttered, "Philippe described it to me. That was enough."

Lexi raised an eyebrow. "Why haven't you been there?"

Akeem shrugged. "Philippe hasn't revealed the place to any of us. It's safer that way. You've seen what can happen when we're taken over by the Darkness." The big man chuckled. "Now we have the demon-killing sword. I think a poke from that every now and then will keep us honest."

Philippe nodded. "I'll take you all tomorrow. It's a day's ride from here."

Lexi tilted her head in curiosity. "Ride?"

Akeem put up his hands. "No. I'll walk. I'm not getting on one of those things."

"That's a no from me, too." Jonathan folded his arms.

"It's perfectly safe." Philippe shook his head. "Fine. If we're walking, I need to feed them in the morning before we head out." He yawned. "I'll leave you to turn in." The Frenchman headed higher up the tree. Lexi transferred her couch from her dimensional pocket and settled down.

CHAPTER FIVE

S cott stepped through the door into Dolores' apartment.
The little fae smiled but remained silent until he'd
finished checking himself for bugs. At his nod, she asked, "Any
news?"

"Nothing yet. I think we've managed to map the route Az
took to get here. She's sketchy on the details, but many of the
realms aren't in the same position in relation to each other that
they were before. They might not be usefully aligned for another
thousand years. We haven't found any demon realms that could
make the journey shorter. We're moving onto fae realms next."

Scott pulled Dolores's consciousness into his dimensional
pocket, where she studied the whiteboard with demon realms
listed and crossed out. She wandered over to the corkboard,
following the trails of thread from pin to pin. She stopped in
front of a circle that indicated a dimension labeled 7624.

She grabbed a black marker and drew a cross through it.

Scott sighed. "I thought that one was a good possibility."

Dolores shook her head. "We looked into it. It doesn't run
close enough for another six thousand years. "

Scott grabbed another pen and drew crosses through three

other circles. "Which means this, this, and this won't work either. Shit!" He contemplated throwing the pen in frustration but deliberately placed it on the desk instead.

Dolores glanced through the books he'd chosen from the archive. "Excellent choices. I've already been through the copies at the Seelie Court. There's nothing here that runs anywhere near a demon realm. It should take at least a week for Azatoth to work through them."

"Here's hoping the Order comes up with something first." Scott put an arm on her shoulder, and they moved their minds out of the dimensional pocket.

Dolores patted his hand. "I hear you've been moonlighting on the spell. Any progress?"

Scott's cheeks warmed and he shrugged. He felt like a failure. "Nothing yet. I can't find a way to move Az into an inanimate object. The spell just doesn't seem to work that way."

The French doors at the back of the apartment opened, and Dick wandered in. "What about your little box of evil? Can't you just shove her in a magic box and yeet it into another dimension or the fiery pits of hell or something?"

Scott shook his head. "She's much too strong to risk something like that going wrong."

Dick nodded. "Then let's try out the one you've got and see if it works."

Scott narrowed his eyes. "Try it out on what?"

"Haven't you told him yet?" The vampire took a decorative bowl from a side table. "Can we use this?"

Dolores rolled her eyes. "If you must."

The vampire grinned. "Splendid. Don't worry, you'll get it back. This way." Dick led the way to the back of the apartment, which was once again a little derelict fishing shack on the shore of a lake.

Scott stared at the little jetty that led out to the water. "You have got to be kidding." Wrapped tightly in a fishing net was an alligator. It was unusually still. "I assume it's bound by more than just the net."

Dolores nodded. "Of course."

Scott sighed. "This feels immoral. Where did you find an alligator around here anyway?"

"Well, that was your doing," Dolores told him. "As is their taste for fae."

Scott remembered the lucky chip helping when he'd had a body to dispose of and blushed. "Ah…"

Dick patted the mage on the shoulder. "We'll just see if it works. If it doesn't, you can take the essence back, drop the gator into the lake, and return the essence to the foul creature it came from."

Scott thought for a moment. He loved animals and this felt shitty, but if it meant getting rid of the demon, he would do it. He approached the alligator and sniffed. "Tallow?"

Dolores nodded. "Just as Caleb used."

Scott took a small blade from his pocket and poked the alligator with it. He wanted to tell it he was sorry.

He put the box into the bowl and dripped the blood on top of it, then carefully placed it beside the alligator. He kept his gaze firmly on the beast's eyes, looking for a sign that it might regain consciousness.

The mage muttered the incantation he'd found in the book beneath the Chelsea Hotel, then winced when the box lid sprang open, cracking the bowl.

Dick whispered, "Oops. Sorry, but it was an ugly bowl."

Dolores spoke through gritted teeth. "My grandson made it."

Dick raised his hands in a conciliatory gesture. "My bad."

Scott returned to stand beside them.

The alligator moved, rocked its head this way and that, and opened its eyes. They were pure black. It dropped its head and closed its eyes again.

Dick looked from the alligator to Scott. "That means the demon is inside it, right?"

Scott nodded.

"So, it worked." Dick clapped him on the back. "We can get the demon out of Alicia. Then we can concentrate on finding a way to get Lexi back."

A deep groan came from the alligator. It thrashed, straining against the net.

Scott turned to Dolores. "Isn't it supposed to be asleep?"

The fae shrugged. "I'm not sure it still counts as a creature of Earth, so the magic might not work on it the same way. What is that noise?"

The three of them stepped closer to the alligator.

Dick furrowed his brow. "It sounds like gurgling. Maybe we gave it indigestion?"

They took a few more steps.

Dolores was about to take another step, but Scott placed a staying hand on her arm. "Is it getting bigger?"

Dick's eyes widened. "We should get back. I think it's going to—"

The alligator exploded, covering Scott in chunks and guts.

He turned to Dolores, who was also drenched in gore. Dick wasn't at his other side. Scott did a one-eighty and found him standing at the cabin door.

He shrugged. "You can't expect me to get blood on Gucci."

Scott turned back to the exploded alligator and waved a hand. "Reveal."

A dark cloud of demonic essence rose from what was left of the alligator. He quickly placed a shield around the essence and directed it back into the little box, then snapped it closed and looked down at his clothes. "Well, that was a failure."

Dick came back. "Not necessarily. We learned a lot. It didn't explode immediately. If we can work fast enough, we could get the demon out of Alicia and yeet it into Hell."

Scott considered that. "We'd have to work pretty damn fast. Also, we'd need to find something of comparable size to a human."

Dick flashed an evil grin. "How about Eric? He's the same size as a human. It's a risk I'm willing to take."

Scott snorted. "Don't think I haven't considered it. But what if Azatoth got back here? Any dimension that we're capable of sending it to, she could just come back from. The essence could bounce from human to human, exploding people until it runs out. What if it divided and made everyone in the world evil? I don't want to end the world. If we use the spell without knowing the implications, at the very least, we could show our hand too soon and lose any hope of destroying it."

Dolores patted his arm. "Perhaps you should clean yourself up, dear." She was already de-gored. They walked back to the shack. "What is the council up to now?"

Scott stood outside the door, drew the alligator remains off himself, and cast them into the water before he stepped into the apartment. "I don't know what the latest plan is, but it's not going well. Which reminds me, Project Vegas is having an impact. Just this morning, Millicent was flapping about the situation. The supe security organizations have been bugging Kindred. Can we do something to give Az a nudge in the right direction?"

Dick looked delighted. "We're working on something. I'll see how that went after Dolores and I visit the Order."

Scott's face brightened with hope. "Any sign of contact?"

Dolores smiled sadly. "Not yet. It should be soon. The Order has been able to communicate with the realm roughly every fifty years. We're coming up on one of those fifty-year windows. As soon as we're able to contact her, I'll let you know. I hope that making contact might help with Limpet's efforts too."

Scott sighed. "How is he?"

"Exhausted, but he's a trooper. He found a few more uncharted realms. Here are the coordinates and the estimated number of *Limpets* to surrounding realms." She dropped a sheet of paper on the desk. "If he'd gone through with her, they would probably be halfway home by now."

Scott smiled. They'd begun plotting out realms but realized there was no scale to measure their distance from other realms. The Limpetscale had been Dick's idea. If a realm overlapped Earth, it carried a Limpet number of zero because it could be reached with a fae door or a demon portal. If it couldn't be reached by those methods but could by a thinner demon, it had a Limpet designation of one. If various combinations of magic and a thinner demon could reach a realm, such as the thin place in the tower at Emmersley, it was a two. There were worlds Limpet could sense but couldn't break through to. Those were threes. They estimated that a shadow mage's magic plus a thinner demon would probably reach most realms, but that wasn't available to them.

Dolores checked the time. "I have a few people I wanted to talk to about some very old fae magic, but they've all got interests in the casinos, and they're livid about the situation in Las Vegas. Of course, they blame Kindred, so they're refusing to listen when I talk about a legacy mage who needs our help. It's completely lawless there right now with the wards still down."

Dick nodded. "I've noticed some of the casinos are hiring mercenaries. We'll get those wards back up. I have my best people on the case."

"I'm glad of it. From what I saw this morning, the council seems to be finding it a distraction, too. Good luck."

Scott left the apartment and entered the coffee shop. As he waited in line, his consciousness hopped into his dimensional pocket and updated the board with the new realms Limpet had found. It was getting harder to put them in relative positions on the board. He was going to have to move to a 3D model. As he considered that, his attention was drawn back to the coffee shop and the TV on the wall in the corner.

The news anchor looked serious. "The heist resulted in the loss of several hundred thousand dollars worth of stock from the Las Vegas Gucci store. Two young women were seen in the area. Officers are working to track them down, but they have no leads at this time."

Best people? Scott rolled his eyes and collected the drinks before translocating to the lobby of the Kindred building.

The elevator reached the executive floor and the doors opened.

Nora stood in front of him with a vacant expression in her milky eyes.

"Holy shit!" Scott nearly dropped the cups in fright.

CHAPTER SIX

As the zombie secretary shuffled into the elevator, Scott stepped around her, making sure he didn't turn his back to her. She creeped him out. He stepped backward out of the elevator. He could have sworn he saw her lip twitch into a smirk. The doors closed, then disappeared, and he was left staring, eyes narrowed, at the wall.

Nora had appeared at her desk a few days after Lexi had dispatched her. The secretary was the only member of the cabal Azatoth had bothered to bring back. He had assumed she had been reanimated by voodoo, but now he wondered if Azatoth might be controlling her directly. He found the demon's powers unfathomable.

He made a mental note not to assume Nora was an empty vessel, which gave him another idea. *Could* she be a vessel? Could Azatoth be moved into *her*? She already smelled so bad he figured no one would notice if he doused her in animal fat. He turned to find Millicent staring at him.

The woman's glare could sour milk. "You're paid to work, not stare at walls."

"I'm fairly certain I'm not paid." Scott turned his back on her and walked into the demon's office. He turned to close the door and realized Millicent was entering the office behind him.

Scott put the drinks on the small meeting table. The books he'd taken from the archive appeared in his hands. He laid them beside the cups.

"You asked for me?" Millicent asked Azatoth.

Scott glanced at the two of them. "You want me to wait outside?"

"Not necessary." Azatoth turned to Millicent. "I've been thinking about your request. You can put the wards back up."

"Great. Thank you. I'll get right on it." Millicent dashed out and closed the door behind her.

Scott was curious. He moved the coffees and books to her desk. "Why the change of mind?"

She glanced at the books. "I'm hoping we can get through these a little faster than the last batch, and the constant interruptions about problems in Vegas are getting on my nerves."

Scott took a sip of his coffee, then took out his notepad and pen. He began drawing a table with the names of fae realms scribbled in the first column.

Azatoth tapped her pen against the desk. "I don't know that you need to be so thorough."

"I just want to keep notes on them in case I need to refer back." As Scott turned the page, the notepad caught fire with a poof.

Scott stared as the flames died out, leaving a perfect circle in the middle of the pad.

Azatoth grabbed a book opened it without looking up. "Let's move this along, shall we?"

"Fine!" Scott returned to the book.

After an intentionally fruitless afternoon of researching fae realms, Scott returned to Vegas and rapped on Dick's door. He knew it was risky. He was being watched. Everyone who knew Lexi and could be located was being watched. He'd been keeping his distance from the vampire while in Vegas, but sometimes, he just wanted to see some friendly faces.

"I'm a little busy, Scott. I'll see you later." Dick's voice was high, and hushed mutterings took place behind the door.

Scott flicked a finger at the door. It swung open but stopped when it wedged against something behind it.

Rosa poked her head out. "You can't come in. I'm...naked."

Scott folded his arms and smirked. "How could you possibly be naked with all the Gucci clothes you've got in there?"

Rosa gave him an awkward smile. "Oh. You know about that?" She pulled the door back for him to enter.

Scott rolled his eyes. "I do now."

Rosa scowled. "Dammit."

The mage chuckled. "It wasn't hard to guess."

Dick called from the living room, "Naked? Really? You couldn't come up with something more believable?"

"I panicked! I'm not very good at lying." Rosa grabbed a bundle of coats and headed upstairs.

Ruby walked out of the kitchen with six shoe boxes. "Never put Rosa in charge of lies and deceit. That's my department." She headed upstairs behind her sister.

Scott shuffled into the living room. Boxes were piled everywhere, like a little city with narrow pathways left to allow them to get around the room. "You can stop them from ransacking every high-end store in the city. The wards should be back up by tomorrow."

Dick's face brightened into a smile Scott hadn't seen for weeks. "Did you hear that, darling?"

"It's about time." Albin's disembodied voice came from a speakerphone somewhere in the room. Dick scattered shirts and coats and scarves until he found his cell phone. "I'll see you tomorrow, then."

Dick went to the bottom of the stairs. "Kids, Daddy's going out tomorrow, and you may never see him again."

Ruby ran halfway down the stairs. "What are we supposed to do with all this crap?"

Dick shrugged. "I don't know. Give it all to the needy and desperate."

She smirked. "You've got enough clothes."

Dick straightened his cufflinks. "You're asking to be grounded, young lady."

"I'd like to see you try." Ruby flounced back upstairs.

Scott laughed. The ease with which the three of them had settled into a family unit was remarkable, and it was nice to see. He wished he felt like part of it. They tried, but nothing truly felt like family since Lexi had gone.

Scott called up the stairs, "Are you girls living here now?"

Ruby's voice came down. "Just until we've shifted the Versace stuff. Our apartment is wall-to-wall boxes and clothes racks."

Limpet arrived through a portal in the wall as Scott surveyed the stolen goods. A second later, Marcel's head popped up from a pile of Gucci underwear on the couch. He barked and launched himself at the little demon, licking his face and rubbing against him.

Scott grinned. "Hey, little guy! How did it go today?"

Limpet ignored him. He jumped onto the pile of underwear and curled up to sleep.

A moment later, there was a knock on the door. Dick froze, and Ruby appeared at vamp speed next to him. Both of them stared frantically at the piles of stolen goods.

Scott sighed and used the spell he normally used to make his luggage invisible in hotel rooms. The hall was suddenly clear.

Dick opened the door.

A short fae man stood outside. "Forgive the intrusion."

Dick's shoulders slumped. "No. I've told you I'm not interested."

"I've been requested to increase the offer. Nine million dollars."

"I don't have what you're asking for. I haven't a clue what you're talking about. Please leave, or I'll get a restraining order. This is harassment." Dick started to close the door, but the fae put his foot in the way.

The fae laughed. "Harassment? I'm trying to give you ten million dollars."

Scott didn't know what they were talking about. "I thought you said nine?"

"The offer has increased." The fae grinned, showing sharp teeth.

Dick showed no interest. "I don't have what you want. You should step back. I wouldn't want you to lose that foot."

The man looked at the floor. Dick and Scott followed his gaze to where Limpet was sitting behind them in the hallway, disguised as a cat. The thinner demon added to the illusion by licking his butt, one of his back legs extended delicately to point his little pink sheriff's star at the disgruntled fae.

"My employer wants that thinner. You might as well take the money because I'll be taking that thing with me sooner or later."

A light flashed, and Scott found himself suddenly unable to move. From the corner of his eye, he could see that Dick and Ruby were similarly impaired.

Dick struggled to speak. "What have you done?"

"Sooner it is." The fae stepped into Dick's house and over to Limpet. As he reached for the demon, Limpet disappeared through the floor.

"No!" The dark fae threw himself through the portal after the thinner demon.

Dick was still facing the empty doorway. "Scott, can you move? Did he get Limpet?"

Scott swiveled his eyes to where the portal had been. "I don't think he's going to catch him."

Seconds later, the spell wore off. Dick turned to a pair of shoes on the floor with the feet still inside them. "I did warn him about losing his feet, didn't I?"

Scott made the contraband visible again.

A whine drew their attention to Marcel sitting in the living room doorway, staring at the same spot and moping. He was licking his lips.

Dick opened a Gucci shoebox, tipped out the shoes, and dropped the fae feet into it. "Don't worry, chap. He'll be back."

When Scott left four hours later, the little demon still hadn't returned.

The mage went back to his condo. He stood at the doorway to Lexi's room, and his gaze lingered on her few possessions.

Lexi, if you can hear me, we're trying to find you. I'll never give up.

CHAPTER SEVEN

L exi awoke from a dream of Scott telling her he was trying
to find her, and he'd never give up. It was difficult to shake
off, not that she wanted to. The dream had been comforting. She
stashed her couch in her dimensional pocket, then followed the
sound of voices to the ground.

The tree was about fifty feet from the edge of a cliff. They left
Jonathan and Akeem at the tree, and Lexi followed as Philippe led
her down a hidden path cut into the cliff. It culminated in an
overhang where roots from the tree covered a hollow, forming
two huge wooden cages. The creatures inside were giant crab
monsters, the same ones she had encountered when she'd first
crossed over.

Philippe made the introductions, "I give you Mark Twain and
Napoleon Bonaparte."

Their pincers were held closed by twigs linked together. Lexi
studied the flimsy restraints. "How do they not break out of
them?"

"It's the oak. Anything made from that tree has magical
benefits."

She spotted a sack thrown across the shell of one of them. "And you ride these creatures?"

Philippe nodded. "Yes, it's perfectly safe, providing you don't forget they are capable of splitting your body in two with those pincers."

She was incredulous. "That's okay. I need to get my steps in."

Philippe chuckled. "They're quite fast. Walking to the fissure is going to take us three times longer."

Lexi sighed. She did want to get there quickly. "Fine. If you can talk the others into it, I'm game."

"Absolutely not." Akeem stood ten feet behind the others. "I'm not riding on that monster."

"No offense, but if anyone should be complaining, it's Mark Twain." Lexi patted the docile giant crab. "He's going to need a Wide Load bumper sticker."

Akeem folded his massive arms. "Offense taken."

"How about I climb aboard first?" Lexi was more concerned than she let on, but she'd be damned if she was going to show it in front of these men.

Akeem gawped at her. "You would ride this infernal beast?"

Lexi shrugged. "To shave two days off our journey, I'd marry it."

Philippe grinned. "Are you going to let this little girl shame you, Akeem?"

Lexi gave the Frenchman her best "I will cut you" stare.

He cleared his throat. "I meant to say, this young woman."

"Fine. Move out of the way." Akeem shooed Lexi and the other two shadow mages out of his way. His face was a picture of suspicion as he stepped to the creature's side.

Mark Twain tried to scuttle away, but Philippe gripped the

reins while the giant man wriggled his way onto the burlap cushion.

A mournful, high-pitched squeal came from the beast as Akeem settled into place.

Lexi hopped onto the cushion in front of the big man. "There, see? Not much different from a horse."

Philippe passed Lexi a long stick with a small cage on the end of it. Inside was the same kind of dog-sized spider Philippe had been roasting the previous evening. This one was alive.

Lexi grimaced. "What am I supposed to do with this?"

"The beast will go where you point the cage. They are motivated by food."

Lexi shoved the stick into Akeem's hands. "I'm taking the reins."

Akeem leaned forward and muttered, "Just like a horse."

Jonathan and Philippe climbed onto the second crab creature.

Philippe patted the monster. "Come along, Napoleon Bonaparte. Start walking."

Jonathan looked around. "What happened to George Washington?"

Philippe shrugged. "I was careless. Mark Twain tore him to pieces."

Akeem groaned behind Lexi.

Lexi was surprised by the smooth ride. She'd imagined they'd be holding on for dear life. However, beyond a little rocking, the crabs kept themselves level as they sped along in their futile efforts to catch the caged spiders.

The only problem was Akeem, who complained nonstop.

Lexi looked over her shoulder. "If you don't shut up, I'll shrink you and put you in the cage on the end of this stick. Don't think I won't."

Akeem called, "Jonathan. She has your manner." He leaned forward. "I'd be delighted to hear more about your shrinking idea. I could stand to lose a few pounds."

They stopped halfway through the day to let the crabs rest. Philippe took a precooked spider leg out of his bag and offered it around. Lexi politely declined, then turned so she wouldn't have to watch him eat it. That didn't stop her from hearing the loud crunching, which turned her stomach.

As she prepared to climb back onto Mark Twain, she saw the air stretch and warp slightly in her peripheral vision. She turned to face the anomaly, but it had gone. "What was that?"

Jonathan joined her. "What was what?"

Lexi searched, but everything seemed normal. "I thought... Nothing, I guess." She rubbed her eyes, and they continued the journey.

They reached the base of a rocky hill as the sun was setting. Philippe studied the terrain. "Let's camp for the night, then start in the morning. I don't want to be climbing this in the dark."

Jonathan and Akeem put up the tent, and Lexi helped Philippe to drive oak stakes into the ground around it. They linked them with oak-fiber twine.

As she entered Jonathan's tent, she noticed the wooden framed panels. "So this is why the critters never come into your tent. This wood is from the oak tree."

Jonathan nodded. "Yes. Philippe provides us with the wood and twine. Otherwise, we'd all be driving each other crazy in that tree, and we're crazy enough."

Akeem called them outside, having built the fire. They sat around it as night closed in.

"Anyone hungry?" Philippe asked.

"No!" everyone answered in unison.

Philippe laughed. "I've missed the company of friends."

The other men gazed into the fire and nodded.

Lexi asked a question she'd been pondering for a while. "Why didn't you all just live in that tree together?"

Philippe held his hands out to the warmth of the fire. "When we are together for any length of time, it draws the others. We tried to stay together at first, but the Darkness was relentless and insidious. We became suspicious of each other. In the end, it was safer to stay apart. Now, we only come together every fifty years to communicate with the people on Earth who haven't forgotten about us."

Lexi nodded. "The Order."

Philippe asked, "Have you felt them yet? I feel a light touch on my mind. It will be any day now."

The others nodded. Lexi hadn't felt anything.

Jonathan poked the fire. "Have you seen Yosef?"

The other men shook their heads.

Jonathan continued, "Do you think…"

Akeem shook his head decisively. "Yosef is the strongest of us. He has not turned to the Darkness."

Lexi moved her boots away from the fire as her feet became too warm. "Aren't there nine of them running around this realm? Where are they all? And why haven't they all escaped the way Mortimer did?"

Philippe shook his head. "Only two of them found the fissure, Mortimer and Crispin. Crispin helped Mortimer to escape. I covered the fissure with rocks after that."

This was the first Lexi had heard about another potential escapee. "So, this Crispin also escaped?"

Jonathan sighed. "He must have. I haven't seen him since then."

Philippe cleared his throat. "Actually, Crispin is still here." The Frenchman avoided everyone's eyes. "But I don't believe anyone but me knows the location of the fissure."

Jonathan frowned. "Philippe, what have you done?"

Philippe shrugged. "I know where he is. We can go to see him tomorrow. I'm going to turn in." He dusted off his pants as he stood, then went into the tent.

Jonathan watched him go with narrowed eyes.

Lexi sat back, mulling over what she'd learned as sparks from the fire drifted up into the night sky. "So, Azatoth got out. Why hasn't she communicated the location of the fissure back to the other possessed mages?"

Akeem shrugged.

Lexi sat back up. "Okay, so you've got this big cloud of Bad, and some of it seeped inside Mortimer. Can't it communicate with the rest of itself? Shouldn't the Darkness everywhere have known how to get out?"

Jonathan shook his head. "I see. You think the Darkness is one entity."

Lexi nodded. "I know it is. That's what Azatoth told me before I closed the portal. She was raving about how she was going to infect the world."

Akeem shook his head. "In a way, that is correct. It is made up of many thousands of beings, which over the eons have coalesced to become one awareness. To borrow from the Bible, the Darkness is Legion. But when it joins with an individual who accepts it, it creates its own identity."

Lexi nodded her understanding. "Which explains why Mortimer started calling himself Azatoth."

Jonathan flashed a lopsided grin. "We're kind of experts. We've watched them fight each other as much as they fight us."

"Then why is Azatoth now trying to free them?"

"I believe that when Mortimer—or Azatoth, as he became—found the fissure, he knew there would be a fight to get out. If he shared that information, nothing would escape. They would tear each other to pieces over that hole for millennia."

"Then why did Crispin help him?"

"Something of our character remains. As a human, Mortimer was always reckless and selfish. That's probably why he was the first of us to join with the Darkness. It was easier to not fight it. Crispin was cautious. Perhaps he wanted proof that Mortimer would survive. Then, of course, he'd need someone he could trust to help him escape."

Lexi squinted into the darkness, trying to penetrate the world beyond the light of the fire, but it was blackness, even with the enhanced vision that came naturally with her shadow mage abilities. "So, where are the others?"

"They appear occasionally and attack us, forcing us to use our magic. But their primary desire is to leave this place. They gave up on the demon gate long ago. I believe they travel endlessly, searching for a way out."

A thought struck Lexi. "If the Darkness is incorporeal, why couldn't it just drift out through the fissure?"

Jonathan shook his head. "We've formed theories over the years, but we don't know. Something about this place doesn't allow it to leave. The only way it has ever found to leave was when bound to a corporeal body, which it was never able to do before we arrived. No other creature has been strong enough to bond with it."

Lexi nodded. "So, if you hadn't been turned into shadow mages and abandoned here, it would have remained here?"

Akeem shrugged his massive shoulders. "Hindsight is a glorious thing. But while it couldn't have physically left here, it was still strong enough to manipulate people on Earth."

Clicking sounds from the dark made Lexi uncomfortable. She shuffled closer to the fire.

Jonathan glanced into the shadows. "Let's turn in."

They filed inside the tent, and Lexi pulled her couch from her dimensional pocket and laid down, much to Philippe's amusement.

Just before she drifted off, she sat bolt upright. "That's it! *That's* why I can't enter my dimensional pocket corporeally. It's the same as the Darkness being unable to leave."

"Yes, of course." Jonathan sounded surprised she hadn't figured it out sooner.

Lexi flopped back against her couch. "That's been annoying the hell out of me."

The piece of paper in Lexi's hand held the name of the casino where she had met the Order of the Shadow. She handed it to Millicent. "Pass this to the team. I want everyone in first thing in the morning. We're going to be crashing a party."

Eric stopped Millicent with a hand on the shoulder. "And come straight back. We're going to need you for the next part."

Millicent stepped into the elevator at Kindred Headquarters, and Lexi continued along the hallway in the opposite direction from the archives. She stopped by the wall at the end of the hall and swept her hand across it, revealing a portal with burned, fractured edges. She stepped through.

A glass cylinder fifteen feet high and four feet in diameter towered in front of her. It had been angled diagonally end-to-end inside a brass frame like a space telescope, filled with a thick, clear, pale purple liquid. The bottom of the cylinder narrowed to a point with a tiny brass wheel to the side of it. She turned the wheel, and a drop of liquid plopped onto her finger. She rubbed the glossy liquid between her finger and thumb.

A short man stared down at her from the gallery above. His ears were pointed and the tops curved forward, indicating his dark elf heritage. His face was set in a mean snarl, but she could see the fear in his eyes even from this distance. Beside him crouched a gray-faced, black-eyed, vaguely human-looking demon. The elf moved, and the demon flinched as though anticipating a beating.

"What is this? Where are we?" Lexi didn't seem to have been heard. She wanted to leave but found herself climbing the stairs and approaching the demon and the elf. She stopped beside the top of the glass cylinder. The demon shuffled away, and the elf took a step back. Lexi pulled a handle and opened the top of the cylinder. As she looked down into it, the liquid appeared to be a deeper purple.

Lexi grabbed the demon by its hair and forced it to lean over the railing above the cylinder. She glanced at the elf. "We're ready to make the next generation of legacies." Her fingers curled around a knife, and she cut the demon's throat. Black blood jetted from the cut, pouring into the cylinder in spurts that turned the pretty liquid ink-black.

Lexi's eyes flew open, and she screamed.

CHAPTER EIGHT

Azatoth dropped the slack demon to the floor and headed down the stairs. "Where's Millicent? She was supposed to come right back."

Eric frowned. "I'll message her."

Azatoth narrowed her eyes. "She probably thinks we were planning to test it on her."

Eric flashed a vicious grin. "The thought never entered my mind."

"Never mind. Get a mage from the archive." She waited impatiently with her arms folded until Eric returned with a mage she didn't recognize.

Azatoth put her arm around the man, feigning friendship. "Sorry to pull you away from your work. We just need some help with a little project."

"Sure. I'm, um, happy to assist?" The mage's gaze darted around the room.

Azatoth released him. "Eric, get the man a chair."

Eric translocated a wheeled leather chair from three feet away to the back of the man's legs. "Make yourself comfortable."

The mage sat, looking anything but comfortable.

Azatoth grabbed a teacup from one of the desks and walked to the glass cylinder. She turned the little tap at the bottom, and thick black liquid oozed into the cup.

"What's that?" The mage's voice was shaky.

"We're looking into giving the mages an upgrade." Eric watched with interest as she poked a finger into the pool of black gunk and drew a sigil on the mage's forehead. She stepped back. "How do you feel?"

The mage shrugged. "Fine, I guess. How should I feel?"

"You should feel great." She stood behind him and clapped him on the shoulder, wiping the gunk from her hand on his jacket, then continued around to the front. "And you should feel powerful. Do you feel powerful?"

No answer.

The mage's eyes widened and rolled back in his head. A string of drool dripped from his slack lips. Azatoth waved a hand in front of his face. "Anyone in there?"

Eric stood beside the chair. "How will you know if it works?"

"There are certain glamours a demon can perform that a shadow mage can see right through." She snapped her fingers in front of the dazed man's face. "But I think his brain might have just melted."

Eric stepped back and folded his arms as he assessed the mage. "Any other clues?"

Azatoth shrugged. "If it worked, he would be immortal."

"Well, that's easy." Eric sneered. A knife appeared in his hand, and he drove it into the mage's heart. The mage died instantly and toppled to the floor.

"Well, shit!" Azatoth turned to the elf. "Clean this up."

The two of them watched as the elf dragged the body across the floor and through a doorway at the back of the room.

Eric shrugged. "Do you want to try again?"

Azatoth considered her options before answering. "Let's try a legacy. This elixir was made for them, so perhaps we'll get better results. I wouldn't mind being a shadow legacy."

Eric disappeared again.

Azatoth waited for the elf to come back from disposing of the body. When he did, he walked past her, heading for the corner of the room.

She raised an eyebrow. "Where do you think you're going?"

He turned. She was pointing at a bloodstain beside the chair.

The elf looked around for something to wipe it up.

The demon rolled her eyes and rolled the chair forward to hide it.

Eric re-entered with a young legacy.

Azatoth recognized this one. He worked in the Overseers office with Scott. She recalled that he was a bootlicker but couldn't remember his name. "Excellent choice, Eric. Well done." She turned to the legacy. "Sit yourself down, erm…I'm trying to remember your name. Is it Beav—"

He frowned, interrupting quickly, "Bevan. Mark Bevan."

Azatoth grinned. Now she remembered. Lexi had called him Beavis, and he'd hated it. "How are things going in Overseers these days?"

"A bit chaotic with Vegas and everything." He froze as though he'd spoken out of turn.

"Don't you worry about that. We're sorting it out." Azatoth went over to the tap. "How's it working out with Scott?"

Mark's face soured. "He's not exactly management material."

"We can see that. He's not going to be with us for long." She turned the tap off and returned to Mark. "Before you know it, that office door is going to have your name on it."

The legacy beamed. "So, what's happening here? How can I help?"

Eric smiled, managing to look even more menacing than he

usually did. "We're going to give you an upgrade. Legacy superpowers."

"Cool. I'm down for that." He sat in the chair as indicated.

Azatoth drew the sigil on his forehead and stepped back to get a look at him. "Still with us?"

Mark frowned. "Yes. I'm okay. I think." He sniffed and looked around, then sniffed again. "I…I don't know."

Azatoth exchanged glances with Eric, then returned her attention to the legacy. "Would you like to clarify?"

Mark sniffed the air again and pushed the chair backward with his foot, revealing the puddle of blood.

"Ah, that," Eric stuttered. "We had a little mishap. Nothing to concern yourself—"

Mark dropped to the floor and licked up the blood.

"What in the…" Millicent had re-entered the room and was gazing in disgust at the legacy on his knees.

Eric didn't look up, just held up his palm to silence her. Her face set in a mask of calm.

Mark hadn't appreciated the interruption. He stared up at her with demonic black eyes and coughed. Blood sprayed from his mouth, along with several teeth.

"Ugh!" Millicent exclaimed as one bounced off her Manolo Blahnik, leaving a bloody smear on the toe.

Mark covered his mouth and whined. When he removed his hand, more of his teeth were in his palm. He spat the rest out, then smiled at Azatoth as pointed teeth grew from his gums. He ran an unusually long tongue over them. "I feel great."

Eric looked hopeful. "Immortality test?"

Azatoth rolled her eyes. "Good grief, you're bloodthirsty. Just poke him. He should start healing immediately."

Eric stepped up and stabbed him in the shoulder.

Mark squealed, then snarled at Eric.

They watched as the blood trickled down his shirt.

"It's not stopping." Eric didn't sound disappointed.

"We can't have everything. Stop him from bleeding on my floor." Azatoth clapped her hands. "I'm going to call this one a success. It's not going to work as a vessel for me, but an army of them will be very useful. Let's start production."

CHAPTER NINE

J onathan stood over Lexi, shaking her shoulder. "Are you all right? You were screaming."

She wiped beads of sweat from her face. "I had a freaky dream about killing a demon. I didn't want to, but my hands did it anyway."

Philippe's head peeked out from his blanket. "What would concern you about killing a demon? Have things changed so much at Kindred?"

"I wasn't fighting the demon. It was more like a sacrifice." Lexi shuddered and swung her feet to the floor. "It was gross. I shoved its head over a big cylinder of purple liquid—"

"The elixir?" Philippe sat up.

Lexi felt the atmosphere change. "That was the elixir?"

Akeem stood. His frame filled the tent. "May I sit on your couch?"

Lexi shuffled to make space for him.

Akeem sighed as he relaxed into the padded comfort and stroked the fabric. "It has been a long time since I experienced the comforts of civilization." He smiled at her. "Tell me everything you remember about the elixir."

Lexi recounted what she could recall about the cylinder. When she had finished, she added, "I knew the other way of making a legacy is by imbuing a normal child with the abilities of the supernatural races, but I didn't know how it was done." Lexi flexed her hands with frustration. "This must be Azatoth. She should be gone by now. I don't understand."

Philippe raised an eyebrow. "The demon has possessed a female?"

"Yes. But when I left, Scott had everything he needed to get the demon out of...the vessel." Lexi shivered, and nausea rose in the pit of her stomach.

Jonathan scratched his chin. "What could the beast be planning?"

Akeem patted the arm of the couch, then stood. "Could he be trying to increase the speed of turning the mage he's inhabiting into a demon?"

Lexi thought about that. "The vessel is a legacy."

Jonathan shook his head in disbelief. "How could anything other than a shadow mage contain him for so long?"

"Azatoth has taken control of an unusually strong legacy." Lexi was wide-eyed. "What if something happened to Scott and he couldn't stop her? Or if she's gone? What if I lost both of them, and coming here was for nothing?"

The three men exchanged glances and raised eyebrows.

Jonathan put a hand on her arm. "You're not making sense."

Lexi hung her head. "I have a sister. A twin sister."

Jonathan dropped his hand in shock. "I have another daughter? Why didn't you tell me?"

"For a start, you didn't take the news of one daughter very well." She closed her eyes and calmed her panicked mind. "Before anyone realized I was a shadow mage, Alicia developed twice the level of legacy powers. Caleb, the mage being used by Azatoth, recognized that she would be an ideal potential vessel and kidnapped her, then used a forbidden ritual to allow Azatoth to possess her. Her consciousness is still there, but the demon is trapped inside her." She finished by telling them about the seeing ball.

Jonathan stood abruptly and left the tent. Lexi followed him out. "I'm sorry I didn't tell you before. I was worried about dropping bad news on you when there's nothing you can do about it. It's frustrating enough for me."

He gazed at the predawn light creeping over the dry, scrappy landscape. "I didn't understand why you chose to strand yourself here rather than kill the demon along with its host. It makes sense now." He turned to her. "But you should have ended them both."

Lexi looked at her feet. "That was what Alicia wanted. I couldn't bring myself to do it. We have to get back there and warn them."

Akeem came outside. "Your connection to the seeing ball tells us we will soon be in contact with the earthly realm."

Lexi felt a ray of hope. "How do you contact them? Is there any way to do it now?"

"At first, the connection was simple. We had legacies on Earth who would anchor the connection. Since we lost them, we've relied on the closest proximity of the worlds and the Order of the Shadows."

Lexi's eyes widened as the memory of the dream was jolted from her mind at the mention of the Order. "We've got a problem. A huge problem." She recounted the first part of her dream to them. "Azatoth has discovered where the Order has gathered. It'll be a slaughter. If Scott's still alive, I need to contact him."

"It might be possible." Philippe stepped out of the tent.

Lexi turned to him. "What are you thinking?"

"We've been able to get away with using very small amounts of magic when combining our efforts. I suggest we put you into a waking dream and try to keep you there long enough to contact your mage." Philippe paused. "Or to find out it's not possible."

Lexi nodded her agreement. "Let's give it a try." She closed her eyes. The shadow mages stood around her. Akeem and Philippe each placed a hand on her shoulders, and Jonathan took her hand.

After a few moments, Philippe spoke, startled. "Where are we?"

Lexi opened her eyes. "Oh, we're in my dimensional pocket."

The three men looked around the cavernous room at the screens.

"It's so large. How did you do this?" Philippe picked up a stuffed chihuahua toy.

The toy chirped, "How cool is this?"

Lexi grinned. "That belongs to Scott. We have sort of a pet demon that likes to snuggle with it."

Philippe narrowed his eyes at her.

"Don't worry. Limpet's a sweetheart, unless you're a pixie." Lexi shrugged. "Mages are taught as children how to make their dimensional pockets and one for their legacy. It can be as large as you want. Most of us just don't think big enough."

"All I can fit in mine is my hammer," Akeem grumbled.

"What is all this?" Jonathan indicated the wall of screens.

"I keep my memories on here to preserve them so I don't lose anything if I'm counseled."

Jonathan frowned. "But counseling is for your own good."

Lexi grimaced. "You'd think so. I'll explain it later. We need to get me to sleep."

Jonathan smiled. "You *are* asleep. We are inside your dream."

"What should I do next?"

Philippe handed her the toy chihuahua. "Speak to Scott."

"I guess I'll call him." Lexi reached into her back pocket and pulled out her cell phone. In the dreamscape, it was fully charged and had signal. She speed-dialed Scott, then put it on speakerphone.

The mages all gazed at the little device with wide eyes.

Lexi bit her lip, worried for Scott. "This isn't working. He's not picking up. Can we amp it up a little?"

Akeem shook his head. "I don't think that's a good idea."

Jonathan squeezed her hand. "I will try."

"My friend, you are opening yourself to—"

Jonathan chuckled. "If I am infiltrated by the Darkness, Lexi can prod me with the sword."

"I've never heard anyone sound so amused at the thought of being stabbed." Lexi pulled a magically charged aventurine from her pocket. "I'll try to use Scott's magic, too.

The cell phone was still ringing in her hand. She felt the flood of energy from the mages and the little gem.

"Hello?" Scott's voice brought a lump to her throat.

"Scott?" Lexi's eyes stung.

"Hi, Lexi. What are you up to? I'm writing reports. I've got three to do, then I'm finished for the day. Can I call you back?"

Lexi's jaw dropped in shock. She was speaking to Scott for the first time in months, and he sounded like it was the most normal thing in the world.

Jonathan whispered, "He's dreaming. Be careful."

Lexi nodded. The connection was fragile. If she shocked Scott, he'd wake up, which might break the connection. She had to get her message across without disturbing him. "I'm just hanging with Jonathan, Akeem, and Philippe."

"I don't think I know them."

"Friends of Dolores'. You should ask her about them."

"I will. So anyway. I was just thinking your hair's really pretty."

Lexi raised an eyebrow at the phone.

He continued, "And I like how defined your back muscles are when you're working out."

Lexi felt her face go hot as the three men grinned at her. "Thanks. Hey, listen, I'm hoping you can help me with a little problem. I'm still connected to the seeing eye in Alicia's dimensional pocket."

Akeem grimaced and howled. He was fading.

Lexi shouted at the cell phone, "I'm in the demon realm. Azatoth knows where the Order is, and she's going to strike tomorrow morning. She's tainted the elixir." She awoke and was met with chaos.

A huge red-skinned creature with giant horns was gouging Akeem's chest while Jonathan and Philippe fought to restrain it.

Lexi pulled Harpe out of her pocket. "Move!"

Philippe jumped back, and Lexi ran the creature through.

It screamed, thrashing its head around, and continued tearing at Akeem until they were able to pull the possessed shadow mage off him.

It fell to the ground and turned pale as the life ebbed out of it.

Jonathan and Philippe tried to ease Akeem carefully to the ground, but the big man was too big and hit heavily.

Lexi stood over the creature in case it revived and attacked them again, but within minutes, it was a dry, powdery husk. "I don't understand. I thought we couldn't die?"

Philippe squatted down to study the creature. "He's not dead, but I've never seen one of us so far gone brought back. I imagine it will take him some time to return fully. Perhaps years."

Jonathan put a hand on Philippe's shoulder. "Well, I think it's safe to say we've drawn the attention of the Darkness. I'm afraid things might become a little difficult for a while."

CHAPTER TEN

Azatoth wiped her mouth, then dropped the paper in the toilet and flushed it away with the vomit.

Why is this vessel becoming so weak?

She heard someone outside the cubicle and regretted having been so far from her private executive bathroom when the nausea had hit her. She stepped out of the cubicle and met Millicent's gaze in the mirror as the woman applied her trademark deep-red lipstick.

The demon hated that someone had witnessed her weak state. She eyed the woman speculatively, wondering if it might not be better to blast the mage into pulp right now rather than let rumors spread.

Millicent turned to face her. "That was me yesterday. Honestly, I question the sanity of whoever awarded the contract for running the staff restaurant to goblins."

The demon smiled and washed her hands. "I feel sick every time I eat the tacos, but they taste so good."

"The downside to human bodies. We're slaves to our stomachs. At least you know your body is working correctly when it rejects what's bad for it." Millicent turned toward the door.

Azatoth raised an eyebrow. She doubted a single carb had passed the woman's lips in twenty years. "Oh, Millicent."

The mage froze and slowly turned. The deep-red smile plastered across her face did nothing to hide the fear in her eyes. "Yes?"

"Would you be a dear and ask Eric to pop by my office?"

"Just Eric?"

Azatoth wanted to bark a laugh. Millicent was terrified of the demon but couldn't stand to be left out of a conversation. "Just Eric."

"Of course." Millicent made a quarter-turn to the mirror, smoothed her already perfect hair, and left.

Azatoth stared after her. It was good the woman had thought it was the food. She turned to the mirror. She wondered if the body was beginning to crack under the weight of her demonic presence. The stomach constantly roiled. She splashed water on her face, grabbed a paper towel, and pressed it to her face. When she pulled it away and regarded herself in the mirror for a fraction of a second, it was like someone else was looking at her through her eyes.

She blinked and reasserted herself. Her eyes became yellow with a black streak down the middle. "Nonsense. This is my vessel, my body." She threw the paper towel in the trash and headed for the door.

But I think I'll get a second opinion.

When she returned to her office, Eric was waiting outside, staring at Nora with distaste.

Azatoth breezed past him into her office, and he followed.

Eric spoke in a matter-of-fact tone. "She has maggots."

"I noticed." She went to the window and looked out at Manhattan. "It's the circle of life."

Eric shuddered. "It's nauseating."

Azatoth spun. She narrowed her eyes but didn't detect a jibe. He was just making an observation. She shrugged. Who knew?

Perhaps Nora's decomposition was causing her sickness. "You might be right. I think I'll get rid of her." She walked over to her chair and sat. "How are our little projects going?"

"Almost all of the council is on board."

"Almost? Still having problems with Millicent?"

Eric scowled. "She'll be with us when the time comes."

Azatoth snorted. "*If* the time comes. I have to say, I'm disappointed by your progress. I need those spells."

"We're working around the clock. I won't fail you."

"What about Scott?"

Eric's lip curled. "He's making barely any contact with his friends, but he's taken to frequenting seedy bars and drinking heavily in the last few months."

"Really? Scotty might be more fun than he looks after all." Azatoth smirked. "Keep working on Millicent. If the council can become shadow mages, they can join with the Darkness when I finally breach the portal. Once Millicent has access to our powers, you will have them, too."

"I'm still talking her around. Don't worry, I can be very persuasive. And if she doesn't agree—"

Azatoth shrugged. "She will become one of you whether she likes it or not. She can just disappear like Alicia did. It won't be any loss."

Eric left the office, and Azatoth steepled her fingers in thought. Her gaze landed on a fly on the edge of her World's Greatest CEO mug. Her stomach turned, and she swept the mug aside. It flew across the room and hit the wall before landing quietly on the thick carpet.

"Nora."

The rancid secretary shuffled to the door and stared at Azatoth through milky yellow eyes.

"Drop yourself down the elevator shaft with the others."

The zombie shuffled off.

CHAPTER ELEVEN

Scott towel-dried his freshly washed hair and dragged it into a ponytail. He smelled better than he had in a long time. Since Lexi had disappeared into the demon realm, he hadn't seen the point in hygiene, opting instead to empty a can of Axe bodyspray over his body and clothes. He hadn't seen the point in anything beyond trying to get her back. He used the corner of the towel to wipe the steam from the mirror in the bathroom and scratched his beard, considering that he might shave tonight.

Lost in his memory of the dream, he had been unable to shake off the feeling of it being real. He hadn't been able to return to sleep. He was certain this was it.

It had been her this time.

He wasn't due in the office for another hour. He pulled on clothes and checked for Azatoth's bugs, then translocated to the conference room in time to see the coffee urns being placed on the table at the back of the room, which was already half-full. Some of the people looked exhausted. They had been working through the night, trying to contact the demon realm. He wanted to be there with them every day, but they were safer if he stayed away. Even so, this was the second time he'd joined them this week. He headed over and grabbed a cup.

Sebastian approached him. "Exactly when the coffee comes out…again. How do you do that?"

"It's one of my many talents." Scott bounced on his toes.

Sebastian scanned him. "I hope you haven't got your hopes up again."

Scott poured his coffee, then turned to face the room. Dolores wandered around as new arrivals walked or popped in every few moments and took their seats, setting the tables up with herbs and crystals, bones and entrails—whatever their specialty was. He felt a flicker of doubt. "Has no one made contact here yet?"

Sebastian shook his head. "But it's going to be any day now." He frowned at Scott. "Are you okay? You certainly smell better."

"I had a weird dream about Lexi. It sort of left me feeling…I don't know. I think it was real."

Sebastian turned and whistled. Dolores looked up to see Sebastian giving her the "come here" signal. He turned back to Scott. "Are you sure it wasn't just a dream? Like the one where she was being eaten by a monster, or the one where the demon burst in here and killed everyone?"

Dolores made her way through the tables and gave Sebastian a withering look. "We've talked about the fact I'm not a dog, haven't we? Don't whistle at me."

Sebastian grinned and grabbed a coffee mug. "He had another dream about her."

Dolores gave Scott's arm a squeeze. "Tell me."

"I was back in the house with my Kindred unit. The phone rang; it was Lexi. We chatted a little. We got cut off…" Scott's voice trailed off, anticipation mixed with anxiety unsettling him.

Dolores smiled kindly. "What did you talk about?"

"She said she was in the demon realm, and she could still see through the seeing ball in Alicia's room. She said Az knows where we are, and she's coming after us this morning." The room looked the same as it always did. He shrugged. "But you're all fine. It's just the timing, you know?"

Dolores frowned. "What do you mean?"

"With the wards going back up today. Are you sure you should still be here?"

Dolores nodded. "It's risky, but the portal is here. We're hoping it might help us to connect faster. That's an interesting point about the seeing ball, but it could easily have come from your own mind. Is that everything that happened in the dream?"

Scott shook his head. "It got stranger. The signal became distorted, but it sounded like she said Az had painted the Luxor. Then we got cut off. Oh, and before all that, she said she was hanging with some friends of yours. Jonathan…that's her father's name, right? She also mentioned Akeem and Philippe. Do those names mean—"

Dolores put her fingers into her mouth and whistled so loud the whole room paused. "Out! Now!"

Chairs screeched across the floor, candles were extinguished, and paraphernalia of all kinds was scooped up in tablecloths by the owners. Four fae doors appeared, and the room cleared.

"I'll see if there's any sign of them outside." Scott pulled his hair out of the ponytail and let it fall on his face. He pulled up his hood and translocated to one of the slot machines on the casino floor. He fed five dollars into the machine while discreetly checking out people around him. He recognized several faces. Yep! Kindred was there. It looked like they were getting into position.

He froze as Eric stopped beside him, mercifully with his back to him. The white-eyed legacy faced a squat-looking dark elf. "Try to control yourself. We don't want to spend the rest of the day counseling people and scraping guts off the ceiling."

The nasty elf smirked. "Tell that to your boss."

Eric leaned into him. "Stay here and keep your eyes open, or you'll be talking to the boss yourself." He marched off.

The elf's face went as white as Eric's scarred eye.

The elf stared at the slot machine in front of Scott. "Are you going to play that or just stare at it?" His gaze moved to Scott's face. "Hey, you look fam—"

He slumped at Scott's hastily-muttered spell, unconscious.

Scott grabbed the elf by the scruff of the neck and slid off the seat while sliding the elf onto it. He made sure no one was watching, then put a hand on his head. "You were distracted by the pretty lights on the slot machine and fell asleep."

He left the elf leaning against the machine, snoring.

Scott muttered a spell to make himself unobtrusive. Not a glamour, which would have been picked up easily by some more powerful creatures. He was just...not interesting. He moved through the slot machines until he saw Eric approaching Azatoth and Millicent, who were waiting near the sign outside the conference room. Scott walked behind Eric to get closer.

Azatoth read the sign out loud. "Entrance to the prison realm? Why does it say that?" She stepped back and narrowed her eyes at the row of huge doors to the conference room. Suddenly, she didn't look like she wanted to go in there. Scott had never seen her look so uncomfortable.

Millicent was listening to her cell phone but stared at the sign and glanced at Azatoth with her brows drawn together in puzzlement. When the demon looked at her, she covered the cell to speak. "Any second now."

Scott veered off and stepped behind a slot machine, then translocated back into the conference room. "They're outside the room."

There were a dozen or so people remaining, but the fae doors flickered and disappeared.

Someone shouted, "The wards are back up!"

The remaining fae and witches gathered in the center of the room, where Sebastian, who had Kindred authority to translocate in Vegas, took them away.

Scott gripped Dolores's shoulder and pulled her into his dimensional pocket. He spun on his heel and ensured no one had been left behind.

The door opened, and Millicent's face appeared. She locked eyes with Scott as she stood in the doorway.

"Well?" Azatoth's voice came from several feet behind the mage.

Millicent looked back. "It's just an empty conference room. Put people on the exits. If they are in here, they shouldn't be able to—"

"Get out of my way." Azatoth's voice came from behind Millicent.

Scott translocated to the diner in Boulder City and found that his friends from the Order had all arrived safely. He pulled Dolores out of his dimensional pocket.

She nodded at everyone, relieved they had arrived safely, then turned to Scott. "She saw you and delayed Azatoth. I saw it on the screen."

Scott scratched his beard. "I still don't trust her. Millicent does what's best for Millicent. If she regrets what she just did..."

Dolores put up a hand. "Let's not invite trouble. She just lied to the demon. There's no coming back from that, and she knows it."

Sebastian joined them. "I don't understand what Lexi said about painting the Luxor. Did it make any sense to you?"

Scott shrugged. "Maybe that was just me sliding into another dream."

Dolores nodded her agreement. "Let's send the girls to the Luxor. Have them look around. Maybe it's best they do something productive and keep their minds off petty larceny."

Sebastian put a hand on Dolores' arm. "I think it's time Scott and I headed to the office. I'd like to be there before the demon if we can manage it."

Dolores gazed around the diner, which was bulging with

magical patrons. "Okay, folks, there's no coffee at the next location, so fill up. We're moving on."

Scott stood in line at the coffee shop and grabbed his ringing cell phone. He checked the screen. It was Azatoth. He pressed the answer button. "Yep?"

"Where are you?" The demon sounded pissed.

Scott smirked. "I'm at the coffee shop. Did you want something different than your usual?"

"Never mind that. I want you in my office *now*."

Scott tried to keep the satisfaction out of his voice. "Okay. I'll be along in a second."

"I don't see you."

"Oh, you mean *now*-now."

Scott stepped out of the coffee shop without his coffee and translocated to Azatoth's office. "You called?" His voice halted when he saw that Millicent and Eric were also in the room. He altered his tone to something more somber and tried not to look at Millicent. "What's happening?"

Azatoth looked furious. "Apparently nothing. Never mind. It has come to my attention that we are perilously low on legacies and mages around here."

Scott was at a loss for words, thinking, *That's because you sliced and diced nearly half of them.*

He recovered his wits. "How can I help?"

"I want you three to organize a census of how many legacies and mages we have, any strong contenders for moving to head office, and where they can be backfilled from. Identify any gaps. See if there are any units with members who want to head their own units."

Millicent stuttered, "A-are you expecting trouble?"

"I *am* trouble." The demon flashed her yellow and black eyes.

"I'll get right on it." Scott tried to leave the room without looking at Millicent but managed to walk into her as he was staring at the floor. "Sorry," he mumbled.

The demon's voice piped up behind him as he tried to leave the room. "What's wrong with you?"

Scott turned back. "I haven't had my coffee yet."

"For God's sake, just get one from the kitchen." She turned to Millicent. "Is there a list of potential legacies anywhere?"

Millicent's eyes locked on Scott before she turned back to Azatoth. "There should be one in the archive. If I can get my hands on it."

The demon grinned. "Make sure you do. Have it sent up to me."

Scott left the office.

What was she playing at? How would more legacies benefit her?

Try as he might, he couldn't see what her plan was. But there was no way she could be interested in boosting the ranks of Kindred, the only organization with a hope of stopping her.

CHAPTER TWELVE

Dawn found Lexi feeling more optimistic than she had been since entering the demon realm. Making contact with Scott had made her eager to move on to the fissure and get out of this place.

She and her three companions stood around the fragile powdery corpse of the shadow mage who had attacked the night before.

Akeem turned his head this way and that. "It *could* be Yosef."

Jonathan squinted at the husk. "It could be you. It could be any of us."

Lexi pulled on her boots. "What are we going to do with him? Will he be safe in here while we're away?"

Philippe shrugged. "What do you think might happen to him?"

She glanced around the barren landscape. "I don't know. What if something comes along and eats him?"

They carefully moved the chalky body onto a blanket and dragged it into the tent.

Jonathan folded the blanket over it. "That will do for now. In the long run, I might be able to build a coffin of sorts. We can sweep him up and take him somewhere safe, so he can…"

He didn't seem to know how to finish the sentence.

Lexi tried, "Reconstitute?"

Jonathan nodded. "Let's see what the situation is when we return." He pulled his shoes on. "It's time to head out. We'll need a full day of light." He tied up the tent flap, and Philippe added some extra lengths of twine from his tree to keep anything harmful from entering.

After a five-hour hike, Philippe informed the group that they were near the fissure. Lexi moved more quickly, energized by the news. A few minutes later, Jonathan put a hand on Lexi's shoulder to stop her. She opened her mouth to ask why but froze when she heard thuds coming from the trail ahead.

Philippe groaned. "Oh, no." He looked at the rocks scattered on the ground. "Oh, dear."

When they rounded the corner, Lexi's first instinct was to throw up. Blood was everywhere. A demonic-looking creature, or what was left of it, was hacking at itself and poking bits of its body through a gap no more than two inches wide and ten inches long.

"Oh, Yosef." Philippe shook his head in dismay.

The creature looked up, having not noticed them until Philippe spoke. It waved the sword with its remaining arm.

Lexi spun and marched back around the corner, and Jonathan followed.

She leaned against a pile of rocks with her head in her hands before wiping her face vigorously and scraping back her hair. "This is it? This was how Mortimer got out? By feeding parts of his own body through a tiny hole?" She paced, her eyes stinging.

"I can't do that. I can't. That was why it took two hundred years, wasn't it? Waiting for the body to reform itself on the other side. That's disgusting."

Lexi marched around the back of the large group of rocks beside the fissure. The pathetic creature had its back to her and was waving the sword at Akeem, who stood just out of range with a pitying look on his face. She crept up behind the bloody, pathetic mess and plunged Harpe into his back. He screamed, and the demon left him. What remained was the shell of a man, already turning white. "I don't get it. How would his head have gotten through?"

Akeem raised an eyebrow. "We've talked about that. We think one of the others assisted Mortimer. I don't know how Yosef would have managed. He seems to be on his own up here."

"Why didn't you just tell me? Wait, don't bother. I wouldn't have understood without seeing the fissure. I guess I received a more visual lesson than any of us expected." She thought for a moment. "How did you find the fissure? Could there be others? Bigger ones?"

Akeem looked sadly at her. "We've never found another."

Jonathan crouched beside Yosef and picked up a white sliver of leg. "Look at this. It's no longer connected to him, but it's turning white like the rest of him." He pressed it between his fingers, and the remains crumbled.

Akeem turned away from Yosef as their old friend continued to turn to ash. "Philippe, do you have the world glass?"

Philippe took the bag off his back and set it on the ground.

Lexi blinked. "The what now?"

Jonathan explained, "We're not just here to show you the fissure. It's a thin place that does just as well as the demon gate to aid in our communication with home. That's probably how Yosef found it. Your connection with your seeing eye and Scott has shown us it's time."

Philippe pulled out something covered in animal hide from the bag and unwrapped a circular piece of stained glass. It was stained green and blue and looked like the Earth. "My wife gave this to me when we parted. When we're synchronized with Earth, we're able to see through its companion glass. Before she died, she had the other one placed in a church in Boston so we could see our home city, but the last time we tried to look through it, there was nothing. It was black. It still helped us communicate with the Order, but we saw nothing." He steadied the glass on a rock, and the four of them stood around it.

Lexi's companions each held out a hand to the glass.

Philippe warned, "The lightest touch."

Jonathan grinned. "You say that every time, my friend. We know."

Lexi stayed out of the magic, watching the others as they each released a tiny touch of magical energy toward the glass. Just looking at its vaguely Earth-like design made her ache for home.

The glass blurred and a picture emerged, but it wasn't the streets of Boston.

Philippe frowned. "What is this?"

A large, brightly lit room with wood-paneled walls and parquet flooring had appeared. Desks and chairs were spread throughout, and the walls were lined with bookcases. Above them were stained glass windows.

Dotted around the room were young men and women with their faces buried in books or scribbling in notepads.

Lexi's heart skipped a beat. She shouted, "Hello?" but no one responded.

Philippe turned to her, his mouth a sad, thin line. "The glass only gives us sight."

"Can they see us? If they look up, are they going to see us staring at them?"

"The spell has to be cast at both ends, but it strengthens our connection with the Order. They will hear us."

"And Scott? Will he hear us, too?" Lexi grabbed Jonathan's arm and pushed her will toward the little glass conduit.

She opened her mouth to call Scott when she heard a disembodied voice.

"Lexi definitely said that Azatoth was painting the Luxor. I'd stake my life on it."

CHAPTER THIRTEEN

The server's brow drew down. "Painted? I don't think so." He turned and walked away.

Dick pinched the bridge of his nose. "Could you just stop asking everyone? You've done the helicopter thing, haven't you? I should hate for people to overhear us."

Scott shrugged. "Of course I have, but asking is the only way we're going to find out." He swiveled his head, searching for someone he hadn't already spoken to.

Dick smoothed an eyebrow. "You've asked a dozen employees the same question, and none of them has a single clue what you're talking about. Surely that means no, the hotel has not recently been painted."

"Maybe we're just asking the wrong people. It could be the bedrooms. Maybe some rooms have been painted by a demon somewhere."

"You know how insane that sounds, don't you?"

Ruby dropped into a chair at the table. "I'm not asking anyone that stupid question again."

Rosa sat beside her. "Same here. People are looking at us like we're idiots."

"Who have you spoken to?" Scott asked.

Rosa counted off on her fingers. "The bellboys, the maids, the clerk at the desk."

"The desk clerk thought we were looking for work." Ruby snorted.

Scott pursed his lips. "Lexi definitely said Azatoth was painting the Luxor. I'd stake my life on it."

Well, you'd be an idiot, then. Lexi's voice was as clear as a bell in Scott's mind.

Scott jerked his head up and spun. "Lexi? *Lexi!*"

Lexi's voice replied, *Rein it in. I'm in a different realm; I'm not deaf.*

Scott grinned at his friends, then realized from their puzzled faces that they couldn't hear her. "It's her! It's Lexi. I can hear her."

Dick raised an eyebrow. "Are you sure you're not imagining it?"

Scott shook his head. "She said I'm an idiot."

Dick's face brightened as he looked around. "Lexi, darling, how are you?"

Scott asked, "Can you hear Dick?"

No, just you.

Scott reached out, and the others put a hand on his arm. He drew them into his dimensional pocket. "We're at the Luxor."

Lexi's voice came from all around them. "I gathered as much."

Dick grinned. "Lexi, I hear you."

"Hey, Dick. How are Albin and the girls?"

"The wards have just gone back up, so Albin's much happier, although it complicates our efforts to get you back. Not that there's been any progress in that department. The girls are here, but we feel your absence and miss you terribly."

Rosa shouted, "Hi."

Ruby muttered, "No one knows anything about the Luxor being painted."

After a moment's pause, Lexi continued, "That must have been where we lost the signal."

A deep African voice sounded. "Lost the signal? The hole in my chest hasn't fully healed."

"Who's that?" Scott found being unable to see Lexi frustrating.

"Akeem Kofi. I am pleased to make your acquaintance."

A French voice piped up. "*Bonjour*, people of Earth, I am Philippe Mayeur."

Dick's face was a mask of joy. "*Bonjour*, Philippe. *Je m'appelle* Dick."

Lexi groaned. "What I said was, Azatoth has tainted the elixir."

Scott frowned. "Tainted the elixir? I don't know what that means."

Lexi explained what she'd learned from the other shadow mages and seen in her vision through the seeing ball.

Scott's eyes bulged. "I knew about the process, but I've never heard it called the elixir. I saw an Unseelie hanging around down there the other day. I'll check out the portal you saw, and I'll speak to Sebastian about it. He might know more."

Lexi paused, then asked, "An Unseelie at HQ?"

"They're all over the building these days. Az has struck a deal with a few unfavorable elements."

"What happened at the casino?" Lexi's voice held concern. "Did she turn up? Is Dolores okay?"

"Yes. Thanks to your warning, everyone got out before she arrived." Scott thought for a moment. "It's good to hear your voice. The demon has me working flat out to find a way to get you back or open the portal."

"I've missed you too. It's boring here, and pretty much everything wants to kill me."

Ruby snorted. "So, it's like Australia, then?"

Lexi laughed.

Scott curled his fingers around the edge of the desk, desperate to ask his next question but fearful of the answer.

"Have you found out how Azatoth escaped? Can you get out the same way?"

There was silence for a few moments. Finally, Lexi spoke. "Yeah, I won't be leaving that way. But I need your help with something."

Lexi told them about the stained glass they were using to communicate. "The other piece has been moved, but we don't know where it is." She described the room they were seeing, and Philippe shared his wife's name and what he knew of her from their communications through the glass after they had been separated.

Scott became animated. "The two pieces of glass could be used to make a portal."

Philippe interjected, "We tried it in the twenties. It didn't work."

Lexi seemed determined. "Scott's the best mage I've ever seen. If anyone could make it happen, it's him."

A lump rose in Scott's throat.

"Which reminds me. Scott, why is the demon still in Alicia? It's been months."

"I'm trying to find something that will hold the demon's essence. I'm working on it. Don't worry, Lexi. We'll find that glass."

A new man's voice interrupted. Scott assumed it was Jonathan. "Lexi, we need to get back to the tent before dark."

Lexi's voice returned. "I'll speak to you tomorrow."

"Looking forward to it." Scott didn't want to break the connection. "It's good to hear your voice."

"Yours too." Then she was gone.

Scott felt the sharp sting of tears in his eyes and blinked. "I guess we need to find Clara Mayeur and the other piece of stained glass." His cell phone chirped. "It's Az. Dammit."

The demon sounded annoyed. "Where are you?"

"I'm talking to some contacts in Vegas. I'm hoping they'll be more helpful now that the wards are back up."

Azatoth's reply dripped sarcasm. "Really? Because I hear you're sitting in a bar with your buddies."

Scott's head shot up and he gazed around the room. His eyes found a familiar face—one of the team that sat outside his office. But the man looked different. His eyes were darker.

Scott continued to speak into the cell phone as he looked at the man. "They're helping me. Unlike you, I can't be everywhere at once."

"If you needed help, you should have told me. Here, take one of mine."

The man pushed away from the wall he was leaning against and walked toward them.

Scott disconnected the call and turned back. "You need to get out of…" He blinked when he saw that Dick had disappeared. He turned to the girls. "Can you leave the table, please? Slowly and casually. I'll see you later."

As the girls walked away, Scott swiveled back to the approaching man. Dick was behind him.

Dick raised an eyebrow. Scott read his expression as, *"Shall I snap his neck?"*

The mage gave the slightest of headshakes, but the man picked up on it and turned. There was no one behind him.

When Scott turned back to the table, Dick was in his seat.

The vampire threw back his drink. "We'll track her down. You get back to work, and be careful." Then he was gone.

The man sat at the table. "Friend not staying?"

Scott pursed his lips. "No need. I've got you."

"What is he? He moved pretty fast. I'd have guessed vampire if it wasn't the middle of the day."

"Didn't you recognize him? That was Usain Bolt." Scott had assumed he was speaking to Azatoth, but it seemed not. The demon knew what Dick was. Still, she could be messing with him. Besides, even if she wasn't speaking through him, she could still be watching. "You seem to have something in your eyes."

"I've had an upgrade." The man grinned. His teeth were pointed. "Let's get to work."

"Sure. What should I call you?" Scott stood and grabbed his glass to finish his soda.

A long tongue shot from the man's mouth and the glass smashed. "I've been sitting outside your office for months, and you don't know my name?"

"Of course I do. It's Beavis, isn't it?" Scott smiled.

He snarled. "It's Bevan. Mark Bevan."

Scott reached over and straightened the man's jacket. "Of course it is. That's what I meant." He walked out ahead of his new partner.

I think I know what the tainted elixir does.

CHAPTER FOURTEEN

Philippe rolled his shoulders. "Ready to contact the Order?"

Lexi felt heat in her face. "Sorry. I didn't mean to take over."

"It's all right. But you should probably stay out of this one, or we'll be back speaking to Scott."

Lexi nodded and stepped away. She walked around the rocks to the fissure and crouched to examine it. It looked like a tear in nothing. The air rippled above it. The ground around it had been dug out, probably by someone trying to extend the fissure. It had remained the same dimensions, but now it hovered a few inches above the ground.

Lexi felt a breeze on her face. At first, she thought it was coming through the fissure, then she realized she was feeling it on the side of her face. The significance didn't immediately hit her. Then little pieces of white dust rolled across the ground beside her. "Oh, no. Jonathan?"

Jonathan stepped up beside her. "What's wrong?"

"How bad would it be if Yosef blew away in the wind?"

He looked at the darkening skies. "It looks like the storm is coming back around."

The formerly possessed shadow mage lay at Lexi's feet, looking like a broken statue. It was a much less gory sight. "We can't just leave him there. He'll be scattered across the landscape."

Jonathan gazed at her. "I don't see how we're going to avoid it."

Lexi rolled her eyes. She stood and pulled a baseball bat from her dimensional pocket, then approached the white husk. Jonathan jumped out of her way as she brought the bat down on the statue formerly known as Yosef. It cracked. After three more strikes, she realized Jonathan was watching her in horror. "Get the others. We need to push the bits through the fissure. If he's not possessed anymore, it's safe to let him out of here."

The man leaped into action.

Although the job looked to be complete, Jonathan gazed around. "What if there are specks of him in the sand?"

Lexi shrugged. "Scoop the surrounding sand through. Let God sort him out."

Five minutes later, they were ready to leave. Akeem glanced into the fissure. "I wonder where it goes?"

Lexi glanced at what had been her best and possibly only chance of getting out of the demon realm. "If I ever get hold of Azatoth, I'll be sure to ask."

Back in the tent, Lexi puzzled over something as the wind battered it. She chewed her lip as she thought.

Jonathan raised an eyebrow. "Problem?"

"I know you said Crispin was cautious, but one hundred and fifty years cautious? He knew the location of the fissure. Surely it would have occurred to him to go through it."

Jonathan shrugged. "When we meet him tomorrow, you can ask." He turned to his French friend. "Philippe, are you sure he'll be where you think?"

"I don't think he's traveled anywhere for a while. I'm quite certain he'll still be in the last place I saw him."

Lexi didn't like the feeling of trepidation she was getting from

Philippe's vague answers, but she was too tired to delve any deeper. She turned over and went to sleep.

The morning was bright, with no sign of the storm. The four of them set out riding the crab creatures across the barren landscape and stopped near the edge of a ravine.

"Let's stop here. There's a trail down the cliff over there. We need to get down to the bottom." Philippe tied vines around the feet of Mark Twain and Napoleon Bonaparte.

They descended the rough trail and crept along a narrow ledge toward the next slanting path downward. A slide of pebbles broke the quiet as Akeem lost his footing. Lexi and Jonathan grabbed him and pulled him back against the cliff face.

Akeem craned his neck to look down. "I think I should have stayed at the top. I'm not built for these kinds of adventures."

They moved on until Philippe held up a hand, then brought a finger to his lips.

Quiet.

As they approached the edge, they looked at a giant, brightly colored flower. It was around thirty feet high, and it lay against the rock like it couldn't support its own weight. Its disgusting smell permeated the air, and it flopped around like there was a breeze. There was no breeze.

Philippe whispered, "Don't get too close."

Lexi wondered why Philippe was whispering but did the same, "Is it poisonous?"

The Frenchman shook his head. "No, it's carnivorous."

As he spoke, the petals fluttered again. Philippe pulled Lexi away from the edge as a long stem unfurled from inside the circle of petals. It whipped the air where Lexi had been standing, then curled lazily back down.

Lexi risked another glance over the edge and saw that the inside was coated in red sludge.

Jonathan was looking, too. "I've never seen one so huge. How did it get this big?"

Philippe gazed warily at the flower as he answered, "I dropped Crispin into it."

"You did *what?*" Akeem forgot to whisper.

The petals opened, and as one, the four shadow mages bolted as the stalk flew up and whipped through the air again.

They continued their descent. "I couldn't let him tell the others how Mortimer had escaped."

"But that was…" Jonathan swallowed. "He's been inside the plant all these years?"

Philippe shrugged. "I guess so. The plant turned him into pulp, and because he's immortal, the plant can feed off him forever."

Lexi glanced back at the huge triffid-like creature. "Is he sentient? Do you think he knows what's going on?"

Philippe shrugged again. "I hope not."

They made their way down a trail that took them to the base of the cliff, then walked toward the plant.

As Lexi moved closer, the creature seemed to sense her. The flower at the top flopped and wobbled, drawing her attention. She didn't notice the vines creeping toward her until they gripped her foot and yanked her onto her back.

"Lexi!" Jonathan ran toward her.

"Stay where you are. I'm fine. I was going this way anyway." She didn't struggle as the vine drew her closer to the plant's thick stalk, but she pulled out Harpe when it began wrapping itself up her leg. She waited until her arm was in danger of being tangled, then sat up and slashed the huge stalk.

Lexi whipped her blade at the vines securing her and rolled out of the way to avoid the clear, sticky liquid that spilled out, turning white as it gushed across the ground.

A screech came from deep within the flower as it thrashed about. The flower fell away from its severed stalk and dropped to the ground beside Lexi, landing with a heavy thud.

She got to her feet and hacked at the thick red petals. They curled back, revealing fist-sized white lumps that looked alarmingly like teeth on the inside of the petals. She pulled her shirt over her nose and mouth in an effort to stop the pungent smell from making her vomit.

Lexi took one look at the sea of red sludge inside the flower, then stabbed it with her blade, speeding up the process of turning it white. She lifted the corner of a blanket-sized petal and wiped her blade on it, then sat on a nearby rock. "This could work out okay."

Jonathan stared at her in disbelief. "Okay? I was at Crispin's wedding. We grew up together. Now I learn this was his fate all these years."

"I mean, that's three down. If they keep coming at us, we can dispossess the Darkness of its vessels one at a time."

Philippe hung his head, red-faced. "I am truly sorry, Jonathan. I knew you would be unhappy about this. It's why I never told you."

Jonathan sighed. "Let's get back to your tree."

Philippe pulled a wooden stake out of his bag and dug it into the stalk at ground level. He stepped on the stake, driving it into the root. "That will kill it. It won't grow back."

They followed the trail up the cliff to start their journey back to the tree. As Lexi reached the top, she assessed the sword in her hand. She was musing over whether Crispin would return to normality if she had a piece of the unfortunate shadow mage left on her blade when a length of twine on the ground caught her attention. She bent to retrieve it.

As she straightened up, she was jerked backward by Akeem as a black pincer swept out from the top of the cliff.

Akeem called back to Philippe, who was still rounding the last bend. "Philippe, your pets have escaped."

"They never escape. I tie them up in oak twine."

"You mean, this stuff?" Lexi dangled the twine in the air. She returned Harpe to her pocket and pulled out the katana.

The crab came at them pincers-first again.

Akeem met the attack with a giant hammer he produced from his dimensional pocket. The hammer smashed into the pincers, which disappeared when the crab backed off.

As they gathered at the top of the cliff, Philippe called, "Try not to kill them, or we'll be walking back."

Lexi could only see one creature, which was facing off against Philippe and Akeem. Akeem danced out of the way. Lexi was surprised at how nimble he was. "Where's the other one?"

Jonathan pulled out an ax and went to join them. "Behind you."

Lexi spun to find Napoleon Bonaparte had been broken into pieces and scattered across the ground. Another length of twine lay on the ground beside one of the pincers. She snagged it and rubbed her thumb over the end of it. "Someone deliberately did this."

A giggle came from beside her. The air shimmered, and a man with an ugly caricature of a face frozen into a rictus appeared. "Hello, pretty. You're new."

She slashed at him, belatedly realizing that she was holding the wrong blade. He jabbed a knife into her side and disappeared before she was able to make a second attempt with Harpe.

"Lexi!" Jonathan called as he ran over. She spun around with her hand over her left side, expecting the man to appear again. She swapped the katana to the hand over her wound, and Harpe appeared in her right hand.

Dizziness overcame her, and she staggered.

"Fuck this 'no magic' bullshit." She waved a hand, releasing more magic than she'd used for weeks. "Reveal."

No one was hidden in the vicinity. He had gone.

Jonathan grabbed Lexi as she slid to the ground. "I've got you." Dizziness overcame her.

Lexi came to and shook her head. Her hand darted to her side, but the pain had gone, and so had the scar.

As they readied themselves to move on, she poked a finger through the hole in her shirt and touched the clean, unblemished skin beneath it. "That's wild."

Philippe went to get the cage ready. Mercifully, the spider hadn't escaped. He muttered as he passed her, "You should see what happens when we lose a limb."

Lexi pulled her finger out of the hole in her shirt. "Why? What happens?"

He didn't turn as he called over his shoulder, "You don't want to know."

She scrambled to her feet and followed him. "I do. I want to know."

With only Mark Twain remaining, they drew straws to see who would ride back to the tree with Philippe and who would walk. Lexi raised a hand to the others as she and Philippe rode out ahead of them. As the distance grew, she could still hear Akeem swearing almost until they were no longer visible.

CHAPTER FIFTEEN

Scott polished the leaves on the plant he'd given Lexi when she started working at head office. This was his office now, much to the dismay of the pencil-pushers in the main room outside. But he was going to get Lexi back soon; he was sure of it. He smiled.

"You look happy. Have you been speaking to anyone we know?"

His smile disappeared as he turned to face Azatoth. "Looking after Lexi's plant relaxes me."

Azatoth scowled. "I don't *want* you relaxed. I want you to work on getting that portal open or bringing her back."

"I am working on that. It's pretty much all I'm doing." Scott dropped the cloth and returned to his desk.

Azatoth put her hands on her hips. "Really? Because according to Mark, all you did yesterday was drag him around Las Vegas asking for a fae called Droggy, who no one had heard of."

"He's a contact who knows a lot about realm travel. Droggy might not be his real name. It's just a matter of finding someone who knows him by that name." Scott repressed a snicker. It would have been a miracle if anyone had seen Droggy since he'd made him up.

Azatoth raised an eyebrow. "It sounds like a colossal waste of time to me. Speaking of fae that no one can find, we need to have a little conversation about a chap with no feet."

Scott felt uncomfortable under the demon's scrutiny. He turned his attention to the desk, which was piled high with large leather-bound tan tomes. "I've still got to go through six volumes of *The Compendium of Realms*. They have several realms we haven't tried. I've listed them. I'm waiting for someone to take the first six volumes back to the archives. Millicent's already been through them to check my work for you."

Azatoth snapped her fingers. "Show me the list."

Scott grabbed a sheet of paper with a list of fourteen fae realms and handed it to the demon.

She scanned them and put the sheet back in his hand. "They're no good. Keep looking."

Scott's jaw dropped. "If you've already checked these, why am I going through them?"

Azatoth stepped up to Scott. Her eyes turned yellow and black. "Problem?"

Scott wanted to wring the demon's neck, but it wasn't worth it. Lexi might never get home without his help, so there was no point in getting himself killed. "No. I just thought you were in a hurry to get this done."

The demon glanced at the plant. "Maybe you do need to relax, Scotty." She turned on her heel and walked out.

He hated it when she called him Scotty. He took a few deep breaths, muttering, "Breathe in the good shit, breathe out the bullshit." He reminded himself he'd spoken to Lexi. She was okay, and he was going to get her back. He turned back to the plant and found the leaves were withered and brown. Closing his eyes, he took a few more breaths.

He checked for bugs, then, satisfied the demon hadn't planted anything on him, he grabbed several of the books he'd finished with and stepped out of the office.

Mark stood from his workstation. "Where are we going?"

Scott held out the books. "I wondered if you could take these down to the archive for me? No sense in both of us going, and I've got three more on my desk to go through."

"I'm not your lackey." Mark gave him a smug grin and headed into Scott's office. He picked up the remaining three. "I'll check these. You do your own dirty work."

"Okay, Beavis, calm down." Scott left the office and made his way to the archives. When he stepped out of the elevator, instead of turning left to the archives, he turned right. The hall ended with a solid wall, but not in Lexi's dream. She'd seen a glamour hiding a portal to the elixir. He wondered if he would sense the glamour if he went closer.

"What's wrong with you?"

He jerked his head around to face Millicent. Her brow was wrinkled in puzzlement as she looked down the hall at him.

He blinked. "The light flickered. It was...creepy."

She scowled. "Do you need someone to hold your hand?"

Scott was annoyed with himself. *I must really be off my game. That's twice I've had someone creep up on me in as many minutes.* "Actually, I wanted to speak to you."

"Not here." She waved her ID at the wall for the elevator.

"Then where?"

Millicent turned away from him. "Nowhere. I don't want to know. Keep me out of it."

"So, you're not going to say anything about what happened in Vegas?"

"I don't know what you're talking about." The elevator doors opened, and Millicent stepped in and pressed a button.

They maintained eye contact until the doors closed.

Scott raised his eyebrows and walked toward the archive. He

guessed that was the best he was going to get from her, and it was more than he had expected. He'd call it a win.

After dropping the books at the desk, he headed to the historical archive. Employee files were usually held in HR, but when they were this old, they were moved down here. He opened drawers and flicked through files until he came to the name he sought: Clara Mayeur. There wasn't much. She was a legacy. Her husband Philippe Mayeur was her Kindred match. Scott found a note in the margin beside the husband's name: missing, presumed dead.

That was a joke. Kindred had known exactly where he was, just like they knew he wasn't dead. He read that she'd had two children, but unusually, no names were listed. No links to other files. Neither was there mention of a spelled glass for contacting demon realms.

She had died in the 1940s and was buried in a cemetery in Boston. He made a mental note of the details and returned the file. He desperately wanted to meet with the Order and initiate contact with Lexi again, but he told himself to wait until she contacted him. In the meantime, he needed to speak to Dick.

He left the archive and translocated home. Dick was out with Albin, so he grabbed a sandwich and went to bed.

The next morning, he knocked on Dick's door.

"Scott?"

He spotted Rosa waving to him from beside the pool and walked over to join her and Ruby. "How's college?" He sat on the lounger next to hers.

Rosa picked up a bottle of lotion from the table between the loungers. "Okay. Ruby's bored, but I'm enjoying my classes. I just need to ace my finals and I'm done."

A splash of water hit Scott in the face. "I *am* bored!" Ruby called from the water. "Come in! The water's great."

"I can't. Things are happening." Scott turned back to Rosa, but before he could say another word, Ruby dropped into his lap.

"What things?"

Scott checked their surroundings. "You need to not move like that out in public. And you've soaked my jeans."

Ruby frowned but got up.

"Why are you bored at college?" Scott asked.

Ruby sighed. "It's not a challenge. I remember most of what I read. I understand it faster than I ever did before. It's...well, it's *boring*."

Scott chuckled. "I think you'll find the application of those skills more interesting once you graduate."

Ruby ignored his platitude. "So, what things are happening?"

"I have to speak to Dick. I need help."

Rosa dropped the lotion on the table. "He'll be right back. He's walking Marcel. That poor little dog doesn't know what to do with himself since Limpet disappeared. I hope that weird little dude is okay."

"I can't imagine that creep got him. Not after leaving his feet behind." Ruby shuddered.

"The demon knows about that, so be careful." Scott walked toward the condo and met Dick and Marcel on the way back. He walked with them to the back of the building, where Dick dropped a little bag into the dumpster.

Scott picked Marcel up, and the dog licked his face. He waited until they were back in the condo before talking. As they entered, he noticed that Ruby and Rosa had also moved indoors.

Scott spun his helicopter sigil. "Would you mind visiting a grave for me?"

Dick's eyes widened. "You found Clara?"

"She's buried in Boston." Scott took the details from his pocket and dropped them on the counter. "It's a long shot, but maybe we'll find some record of other family names. They were removed from the files, or maybe they weren't recorded in the first place. Either way, I'm hoping we can find something that could help in a records search."

"I'll go right now if you can watch Marcel later."

Rosa rolled her eyes. "Albin again? I'm surprised you can still walk."

"Mind out of the gutter, please. We're just going to dinner. Why aren't you studying?"

"We don't need to." Ruby stuck her tongue out.

Dick pursed his lips. "Do it anyway. It's a good habit to get into."

"Fine!" Ruby followed Rosa out of the condo.

Scott smiled. "They seem to be doing well in college and with other things."

"Their parents would be proud. I know I am." Dick turned to Scott. "Don't you dare tell them I said that."

Scott picked Marcel up. "Do you want a lift to Boston?"

"Dolores is taking me to Phil's. I'll see if she can meet me earlier." He tapped his cell phone. Seconds later, he confirmed. "I'm going to meet her at the diner. She'll take me to Boston, then drop me at Phil's."

CHAPTER SIXTEEN

The Boston sky was overcast and threatening rain as Dick wandered through the cemetery with a bunch of lilies in his hand. He walked up and down the rows, glancing left and right. He paused now and again to read a headstone.

After forty minutes, he stopped in front of a headstone. It was old and covered in moss. Tilting forward in the ground, it looked like no one had visited in a hundred years. The name was indecipherable. He crouched and spent some time pulling the weeds from around it. He made sure no one was nearby, then pushed the stone to set it into its proper position. Finally, he laid the flowers in front of the stone, stood, and wiped off the knees of his charcoal suit pants.

A funeral was taking place at the other end of the cemetery. People gathered around the grave with their heads low as the priest droned on. Despite the distance, Dick heard every word of the service. He pondered that these services never seemed to be about the person in the box. He wondered what his memorial service had been like. He liked to think it had been outrageous and dramatic, but in truth, it would have been a sad affair like this one. He would have to ask Betsy since she'd been there.

Dolores appeared beside him. "Maudlin thoughts?"

Dick shrugged. "Appropriately dour for the location."

Dolores squinted at the faded inscription. "Are you sure this is the right one? I can't even read the stone."

Dick nodded. "Positive. Shall we go?"

They walked toward the back entrance of the chapel and through the door into her apartment.

The fae closed the door. "I assume it wasn't that one?"

"I found it a few rows from there. I didn't stop. I feel like we're being watched." He picked up Dolores' little notepad from the table and wrote.

Clara Mayeur. 1861-1941. She served well. Truth is within ourselves. One—when a beggar, he prepares to plunge, One—when, a prince, he rises with his pearl. I go to prove my soul.

Dolores read it. "Does this mean anything to you?"

Dick shook his head. "I have no idea what it means."

She looked doubtful. "Do you think it could be a clue?"

Dick stroked an eyebrow. "I think it had damn well better be because that's all that was written on the stone, and there were no records in the chapel." He checked his watch. "Mind dropping me at Phil's?"

"Of course." She pointed at the door they'd just entered through. "It's straight through that door. I'll update Scott."

Dick walked out and found himself at the front desk of the restaurant. He straightened his cuffs and walked through the spell that caused his fangs to descend and revealed his vampire nature. He approached the maître d' but turned at a squeak behind him. Two fae had entered. Short fellows, and from the way they gawped at the lush surroundings, it was clear they'd never been here before. One of them looked everywhere but at Dick, and the other stared intently at the vampire and nowhere else.

He wondered if they had a problem with the undead. It was no skin off his nose if so. He smiled broadly at the fae who was gazing at him. The other elbowed his friend, making him lose eye contact. When they took a step, he heard the squeak again.

They stepped through the spell, which revealed their black eyes and pointed teeth. That confirmed they were Unseelie, although he'd surmised as much. When they moved behind him, the squeak sounded again. Dick looked down at the starer's shoes. "Perhaps you should oil them." He turned back to face the maître d'.

A light touch grazed his shoulder, and he turned back.

One of the fae was behind him. "Might one enquire where a dapper gentleman such as you acquired such beautiful and silent footwear?"

Dick beamed. "Gucci."

The fae inclined his head.

"Monsieur Erwin, your table is ready." The maître d' checked off Dick's name with a flourish and led him through the restaurant. They stopped at a booth in the corner. "Would you like me to send Magda along with your usual drinks?"

"Yes, please." Dick nodded and slid into the booth.

He glanced around absently, recognizing a few of the usual faces—patrons talking quietly over a good meal. The two fae remained at the other end of the restaurant and were shown to a high table with tall stools near the bar. It took them a few tries to get onto the stools. Squeaky gazed around the room, briefly met Dick's gaze, then looked away.

When the bourbon and the martini arrived, the hand holding them was significantly larger than Magda's.

Phil's giant horned head loomed above the vampire. His expression was concerned. "Has there been any sign of little Limpet?"

Dick shook his head. "None. I've been wondering if they could have anticipated where he would drop out of our realm and waited for him there."

"That occurred to me too." The minotaur sighed. "I've left a couple of pixie brains out where he came through that first time." He blinked. "I didn't mean to bring you down. That's not very good for business, is it?"

Dick smiled. "It's comforting to know you care about Limpet. Even after he caused such disruption here."

Phil chuckled. "There's something about him. His connection to Lexi is quite endearing. I've never seen a thinner like that. In truth, I've only seen a few in all my years. Well, here comes your date. Have a lovely evening."

Dick heard the minotaur greet Albin as they passed.

The incubus slid into the booth opposite Dick. He took a sip of his martini and popped the olive into his mouth while giving Dick a wink. "Any further contact with Lexi?"

"Not that I've heard. Let's…" Dick whirled his finger like a helicopter, the way Scott did when he wanted to magically secure a conversation.

"I'll get it." Albin took an incense cone from the middle of the table and held it to the candle. He lit it, and they watched as a puff of smoke surrounded them, then disappeared. "There, we're in privacy mode. How did it go at the cemetery?"

"I found her. There was no mention of anyone else on the stone and no records in the chapel that went back so far. There was, however, an odd little poem on the headstone." He recounted the words.

Albin raised an eyebrow. "Browning. Any idea of its significance?"

Dick raised his glass to his partner. "I had no idea it was Browning."

"Didn't you google it?"

"Why would I do that when I have you?" Dick grinned.

A movement drew Dick's gaze. One of the fae had dropped to his feet. He had his cell phone out and walked quickly away from the table. Dick grimaced.

Albin narrowed his eyes when his partner's demeanor changed. "What?"

Dick shook his head, and Albin stopped speaking.

"Anyway, that's not the biggest news. You're never going to believe what I learned today."

"Podwr!" The second fae called to his friend and waved a hand, encouraging him to return to the table. A few people looked over to locate the noise but then returned to their conversations. The fae disconnected his cell phone and returned to the table.

Dick quickly removed his jacket and found a shell a quarter the size of his fingernail stuck to the back near the shoulder.

Albin leaned forward, frowning when he saw the tiny fae listening device.

The vampire put the jacket back on. "I'll tell you in a moment. I'm going to grab us a couple of drinks from the bar. What do you want?"

"They'll come to the—"

"It's fine. I can't wait. You're going to need a stiff drink when I tell you this." Dick took a napkin and scribbled on it as he spoke.

Albin caught on. "Well, let me think. I could have another martini or a whiskey, I suppose. No, wait. I'll have a margarita."

Dick stopped writing and raised his gaze to Albin, who shrugged and mouthed, "I panicked."

"A margarita it is." Dick folded up the napkin in his hand and headed to the bar. He drew the attention of a server and slipped the napkin to him as he ordered the margarita.

The server glanced at it, then looked again. "Certainly, sir." He passed the napkin to a colleague, who walked away with it.

A minute later, the server put the drink on the bar. "Anything else, sir?"

Dick felt like seeing if he could get under the skin of the listening fae spies. "I fancy something dark and spicy." That was a polite way of requesting dark fae blood.

The drink came in a metal flask with a red napkin. He turned around, holding the flask, and casually surveyed the room. He caught the eye of the fae who liked to stare. He gave him a dazzling smile and lifted his drink, receiving a withering glare. Dick turned back to the bar.

A moment later, Phil appeared at his side. Dick shifted his position to allow the minotaur to see the tiny shell on the back of his jacket.

The minotaur plucked the shell from the jacket and turned to watch the room while he crushed it between his massive fingers. As he did so, one of the fae squealed, and his hand went to his ear.

The two dark fae tried to scramble down from their high stools, but they weren't fast enough. Phil grabbed them both. Two audible clicks sounded, and the spies put their hands to the iron rings he'd clapped around their necks. They squealed as the huge minotaur hauled them into the air.

Squeaky Shoes pedaled his feet in the air to no effect. "What have you done? Take this off. It burns! You have no right to do this. I'm a paying customer! Take it off!" He waved his arms as he attempted to cast magic to no avail, thanks to the iron.

His friend, who still held his glass, threw beer into Phil's face.

Dick winced at the little fellow's poor judgment, then winced again as Phil smacked their heads together. The glass-thrower slumped.

Squeaky Shoes' legs dangled, but he was conscious. Dick wandered over and smirked at him. He narrowed his eyes at the squeaky shoes. "You know, now that I think about it, I've got some fae shoes like that at home. Unfortunately, they're currently occupied. Have a great day."

He watched as Phil hauled them past the mural on the wall, which read, No spying on customers. Anyone found spying on customers will be ejected into a dumpster realm. How you get home from there is your problem.

The vampire grinned smugly as he returned to the table and put a margarita in front of Albin, who stared at it suspiciously.

"How's your drink?" Dick grinned.

Albin took a sip. "Salty but nice. Should we—"

Dick put up a finger to silence Albin. Moments later, a scream was cut off by the sound of a door slamming. "I'm afraid we're going to have to postpone dinner. Phil's ironed them, so it's probably going to take them a while to get out of the dumpster realm. After that, Azatoth is going to be on the warpath."

Albin gulped down his drink. "That's okay. I got a message from Dolores. They have news."

CHAPTER SEVENTEEN

S cott, Dick, Rosa, and Ruby filed out of Dolores' fae door. She lived in the Armstrong-Browne building at Baylor University. Waco spread in front of them.

Rosa did a three-sixty. "This is a nice campus."

Dick's eyebrows rose. "Are you thinking of doing post-graduate studies? Should I get the forms?"

Ruby elbowed her. "Slow down. You haven't got your college degree yet."

Dolores stepped through, and the door disappeared. "Come along, then. Let's hope we're still ahead of the demon."

They walked down the short path to the entrance of the building. When they arrived at the door, Dick attempted to enter, but the air blocked him. "Well, that's just rude. I can't get in."

Neither of the girls could enter. Scott tried, and finally, Dolores. "How are we supposed to get in there?"

A woman approached them from the road. "Problem?"

Dick smiled. "We were going to visit, but we seem to have run out of time."

"Such a shame. Have a nice day." She walked past them to the door.

"Excuse me," Scott called to her. "Is there a guide to the collection of stained glass?"

The woman stepped inside and grabbed a leaflet. She stood next to the door and held it out, but she was too far within the building's invisible boundary. Her lip twitched when none of them moved. It was clear she knew what the problem was, but Scott couldn't identify what she was since she was hiding her nature.

Scott stepped up beside Dick. "We have a problem. I think you know what it is."

"I know." She folded her arms.

"Do you know Philippe?" Scott asked.

Her eyebrow twitched. "I can't say that I do."

"I have a friend who has gone to visit him." Scott nodded when the woman's eyes widened in disbelief. "So, you know where that is."

She shrugged, then glanced at Ruby, who was poking the air in front of her shield, testing the resistance. "You won't get through."

Ruby continued. "I've never felt anything like this. It's weird."

Dolores took Ruby's hand and moved her arm back down by her side. "Stop poking the shield, dear."

The woman looked at the little fae in her skirt suit. "What are you?"

Scott narrowed his eyes. While Dolores hid her true face and shape most of the time, her nature was visible. If the woman was supernatural, she should have been able to discern that Dolores was fae. Dick and the girls were another matter. Their natures were hidden to protect them while they were out in the daylight. "I'm a mage. Dolores over there is fae, and these three are shifters. What are you?"

She looked at the group with suspicion. "I'm human, which is why I can enter this building and you can't."

Scott frowned. "I've never heard of a shield to keep out all supernaturals. Who created it?"

"I'm not at liberty to say, but only humans can enter this place."

"I have a friend who's a shadow mage. She's stuck in the same place as Philippe. I want to get my friend back. They have one stained glass, but we need the other to complete the connection."

The woman scoffed. "That won't be leaving this building."

Dick tried to rescue the situation. "We're in somewhat of a race to get this thing. A demon has escaped the realm and is currently causing havoc. She's trying to open the demon gate again to bring an army across. She's not going to be far behind us, so we're a little stretched for time."

"She's got as much chance getting in here as you have."

Dick took out a card and flicked it at the woman. It spun and landed at the woman's feet. "I assume you intend to leave at some time. You really aren't safe. If you need us, call."

They walked away from the building. Dolores's door appeared, and they entered the diner.

"Well, that was a bust." Ruby slumped into a chair. "That woman's not going to know what hit her when Azatoth arrives."

Dick shrugged. "It might not happen. When Albin and I were spied upon, I just mentioned a few lines from a poem. The demon might not know what we're after. A university with a building that specializes in Browning-themed stained-glass windows might not be obvious."

"Do you really think the subject of the glass didn't come up when Az was over there with Philippe?" Scott pointed out.

Dick pressed his lips together. "I didn't think of that."

"I don't understand who would have created the shield around that building. A shield to stop virtually all supernaturals from entering. Surely the Order should have been aware of that glass." Scott thought for a moment. "We need a human. Does anyone know a human?"

"I could—" Dick stopped speaking when his cell phone rang.

"Help! That monster with the awful eyes is going to kill me!" the woman's voice screamed from the phone.

Dick tried to calm her. "We'll be there in a moment. Is she still there?"

"No, she's gone. She said she's coming back with an army."

"We're on our way." Dick disconnected the call. "We are not ready for a faceoff with Azatoth."

Dolores stood. "If we can get there before she returns, we might be able to get the woman and the glass out of there."

She called the door, and they stepped through.

The front door to the building was mostly closed, with the woman's face poking out from inside. She stepped out when she saw them. "Thank goodness you're here."

Scott stood on the other side of the shield. "You can come with us, but it would be helpful if you could bring the glass. We don't want her to get hold of it."

The woman narrowed her eyes. "The glass is safe. It's me that's not. She could bring the hosts of hell and they still couldn't get in here."

Dick tapped Scott on the shoulder. "What about a host of mind-controlled students?"

They all turned around to see a large crowd of blank-faced students streaming out of the residence halls across the street with bike chains, knives, and baseball bats.

The woman stepped out and threw a bag on the ground at her feet. It burst open in a cloud of powder and dried herbs, and the shield disappeared. "Get inside."

Dick followed the girls through the door, but Scott hung back to let Dolores enter ahead of him. A movement in the corner of his eye made him turn in time to see a second bag hit the ground.

Scott realized that the shield was back up. "How are we going to get out?"

"I'm not abandoning my responsibilities." The woman didn't

take her eyes off him for a moment. "I'm here because of the world glass, but I'm responsible for all the art in this building. You're going to help me defend it."

Scott's jaw dropped. He marched inside to Dolores. "Did you hear that? We're stuck in here."

The fae woman straightened her jacket. "Let's see if we can get Lexi back. Dick, keep an eye on the horde." She turned to the woman. "My name's Dolores. Can you show us to the glass?"

The woman paused. Indecision crossed her face.

Dolores added, "I promise we have no intention of damaging it."

The woman nodded. "Maria Catterall Breen, Head of Antiquities." She led the way through the building.

Scott frowned. The sign said the window had been incorporated into the building when it was built in 1950.

Maria explained, "The world glass was included in this window when it was built in 1950, but it was previously part of a window in Boston."

Scott waved a hand at the glass and muttered the words, then waited for a few moments. "Lexi?"

The glass wavered and turned dark.

Scott! Wow, you're clear as a bell. I've been trying to contact you. Is everything okay?

Scott was flooded with relief when Lexi's voice sounded in his mind. "We're not bored. What's happening with you?"

The remaining possessed shadow mages have surrounded us. Azatoth has been in touch with the Darkness. She threatened you and Dick, then Betsy and Edward. News of my sword is out. They're keeping their distance but throwing a lot of magic at us. We're hiding in a magic tree. Don't ask.

"We found the other glass, but I can't make the connection from this side."

Lexi called, *Philippe, where's the glass?*

The glass in the window wavered, and Lexi's face appeared. "Hey, Scott. You're a sight for sore eyes."

Maria drew a sharp breath when she saw Lexi. At the same time, Lexi, Scott, and Dolores said, "Not the demon."

Dick walked into the room. "Apparently, Maria has five minutes to come out with the glass, or she's sending them in. I heard your warning, Lexi. I'll head to Palm Springs as soon as we've gotten Maria and ourselves out safely."

A crash sounded. Lexi frowned. "What's going on over there?"

Scott winced. "Az took over a horde of students and sent them after us. It's not good numbers. I want to try to pull you through."

Another face appeared in the glass. "It won't work. We tried it."

"Well, I'll give it a go now, then we'll try to get the glass out of here somehow."

Scott waved his hands and muttered his spell. At first, he felt like it was working, but then his magic hit a wall.

He sagged. "It's not working."

Lexi nodded. She wasn't surprised. "That's okay. Get out of there. Is Kindred coming to help?"

"The head of Kindred is the one trying to break in."

"So what? Call them anyway. Report a full-scale attack. Gotta go."

Maria wheeled a ladder over to the window. "Give the glass a quarter-turn counter-clockwise. It will come out."

Rosa shouted down the hallway, "They're coming."

Dick disappeared.

Scott climbed the ladder and did as Maria suggested. The glass came out, and he placed it in his bag.

"Will it be safe in there?" Maria spun at the sound of hammering on the front door, then turned back to him.

Scott nodded. "It's safer than we are right now."

Dick reappeared with Rosa and Ruby. "Rosa called Kindred and reported a zombie horde. Kindred started popping up almost immediately. Is there a back door?"

"We're not stuck. My fae door will get us out of here. Scott, can you stall them? I'm sure they're going to start breaking the windows."

Maria gasped and ran into the hallway just as the front door flew open. She tottered on her stiletto heels to the first hammer-wielding maniac and punched him in the face. He went down like a sack of bricks.

Ruby zoomed out and started punching students.

Scott stared in horror as the students were knocked into the crowd behind them. He opened his mouth to call her off, but she grabbed Maria and was back at his side before he could form a word.

Ruby grinned. "Lady, you're a firecracker!"

Scott pointed at the floor. It wavered, and the students began sinking as though into deep mud. Those behind were unable to enter because the ones in the entrance were stuck.

Dick checked a window at the front. "Kindred is dealing with it. They're starting to turn back. There's no sign of Azatoth."

Scott's cell phone rang. The screen showed it was Azatoth. "Speak of the devil."

"Where are you?" The demon sounded snippy.

"I'm at the office." He grimaced and shrugged.

Dolores called her fae door and mouthed, "Go."

They looked through and saw the street outside Kindred HQ.

"I'm standing in your office. You're not here."

Scott stepped onto the street. "I'm in the foyer..." He walked through the door and smiled at one of the women from the Castings department. "Chatting with Angie from Castings. I'll come up."

"Never mind. I've got a meeting. Meet me in the archives in half an hour."

Scott headed to the elevator and went to the archives. When the elevator door opened, he burst out of it and ran...straight into Millicent, who was leaving with a pile of books in her arms.

She frowned at him and held the books away so he couldn't see the titles, then tried to cover the move with a bluster of annoyance. "What's your rush?"

Scott eyed the books, aware of the glass in his dimensional pocket. He shuffled his bag out of sight. Her beady eyes registered the movement. They were at a standoff.

Scott muttered, "She's meeting me down here."

Millicent's eyes went wide. She was up to something, too. "Right." She stared at the wall as though Azatoth would appear in the elevator any second, then headed back into the archives and disappeared into the stacks.

Scott quickly moved through the stacks in the opposite direction. He stepped up the ladder to the thesaurus and went into the dimensional pocket, then wrenched open his bag. The mage pulled out the glass and placed it carefully against the wall at the back of the desk. He touched the thesaurus on the desk and appeared back in the archives.

He grabbed a book on fae realms from the shelf and walked around the corner. Once again, he bumped into Millicent.

CHAPTER EIGHTEEN

Scott was unsurprised to see Millicent carrying a pile of books in one hand. Curiously, her shoes were in the other. She was attempting to move silently through the archives.

Scott opened his mouth to speak, but Millicent shook her head.

"Ah, Eric. There you are. How did it go?" Azatoth's voice made both of them jump.

Footsteps approached.

"It was semi-successful. We put the demon into the vessel, but after a few seconds, it exploded. They're cleaning the conference room now. Interestingly, the essence of the demon wasn't killed along with the body it was bound to. We divided the essence and placed it in six other vessels, using a slightly different version of the spell to bind each one. Two mages, two legacies, and two of your upgraded legacies. They didn't explode, but all six immediately went catatonic."

As Eric spoke, Millicent looked perplexed. Scott surmised she knew nothing of these experiments.

"Have you been able to release the essence?" Azatoth demanded.

"We can try that now if you prefer," Eric answered. "We were going to leave them for a few days to see if they come round."

"The mage experiments have been a disaster." Azatoth hissed in annoyance. "But if what you say is right, I might not be trapped inside this vessel as we first thought. If I need to get out, I can just kill it."

Scott clenched his jaw.

Azatoth continued, "I don't want you attempting any of these experiments on our lucky lady yet. She's the only mage on the council who isn't an escaped lunatic. I don't want to use her until I have to."

Millicent's eyes went wide, then her lips curled into a snarl at the realization that they were planning to put Azatoth into her. She took a step toward the voices, looking like she was going to confront them. Scott put a hand on her shoulder and pulled her into his dimensional pocket.

Eric's voice dropped. "Did you feel that magic?"

Scott silently berated himself. The magic he had used to translocate Millicent had been felt by Eric. If he used magic to hide, they'd definitely feel it. As he weighed his options, several books flew overhead and swooped into the aisle around Azatoth and Eric.

Azatoth growled. "It's the spirits again. Good grief. It's getting worse in here without a curator."

They continued to talk, and Scott silently sighed.

Saved by the archive…again.

He ensured that Millicent could also hear the conversation.

Azatoth asked, "How's the other project going?"

Eric was silent for a few seconds. "We have a vacancy on the council."

Azatoth groaned. "What happened this time?"

"Marko jumped the gun on the time portal experiment. He was sucked into a vacuum."

Scott's heart hammered. They were experimenting with time portals. This was bad.

"I said no experiments until I've checked the research. Was that somehow unclear?" Azatoth sounded like she was speaking through gritted teeth.

"They did it while Millicent and I were out of the room," Eric explained. "It's getting difficult to contain the council."

Azatoth snorted. "Luckily for us, the Hollows is full of insane mages who will try anything. Just find another one. I'm expecting Scott down here any minute. I'll redirect him to my office. It sounds like I need to check on the crazies. I mean, the council."

"I'll see if I can track Millicent down." Eric sighed. "She keeps vanishing just when I need her. Silly woman."

Scott winced, knowing Millicent was listening. He waited for the footsteps to recede, then entered his dimensional pocket and found Millicent studying the whiteboard.

She turned to face him. "What is all this?"

"It's my dimensional pocket."

She moved along the row of boards. "I can see that. All these years, I've only known of two other mages who were able to expand their dimensional pockets. You're one of them. It's shocking when you consider how many mages have visited Phil's Cornerdown Kitchen hundreds of times and not given it a thought."

Scott was glad she wasn't facing him to see the shock on his face. Of course, Phil's was a pocket dimension. How had he not seen that? But now he had another problem. He couldn't believe that instead of sending her to his decoy room, he'd let her be inside here unsupervised. "It's where I record our efforts to get to the demon dimension."

She gave him "a don't bullshit me" stare. "These aren't *our* efforts. These are *your* efforts. I think you're a little ahead of where we are. Although, if I'm honest, I have the feeling that Azatoth is way ahead of both of us."

Scott shrugged. "I work on it when I can't sleep, and I don't sleep much anymore. But we've all got our secrets. Speaking of which, what can you tell me about the council's projects?"

She folded her arms. "If you mean the project to turn me into the next vessel for that psychopath, I suspected they were up to something like that."

"I meant the time portal," Scott clarified.

"Oh, that. It's a ridiculous scheme. She's got it into her head to go back a few months and stop Lexi from jumping through the portal." Millicent pinched the bridge of her nose. "Time travel, for the love of God. The mage council is made up of me and twelve unhinged magic-damaged mages. They don't fully understand what they're supposed to be doing, and I don't think it could be done even with a real council."

The relief Scott felt must have made its way to his face because Millicent narrowed her eyes. She rounded on him. "What do you know?"

"I only know of one mage who spent decades studying the concept of time portals." He opened his mouth to say, "*and Azatoth has already murdered Devon.*"

Behind Millicent, the air shifted. Scott found himself observing his own face as it appeared through a portal. Blood dripped from deep slashes in the skin, and an eye was missing. The horrific vision shook its head and mouthed, "*No.*" Before the ghastly version of himself could pull itself out of the portal, it closed, and his head tumbled but vanished before it hit the floor.

"What's wrong?" Millicent looked behind herself, then at him. "You look like you've seen a ghost."

"Sorry, that was a startling vision…erm, memory. I was just remembering." He pulled himself together. "I never knew the name. It was a story my brother Warren used to tell me to frighten me at night. It had a horrible ending. He probably made it up."

Millicent looked disappointed. "Naturally. Your brother gave me the creeps." She collected her pile of books from a desk.

Scott nodded. "I hear that more often than you'd imagine. Well, they've gone." He pulled her out of the dimensional pocket.

"Thank you." Millicent gave him a curt nod and headed for the exit.

Scott's cell beeped.

Big Bad: Meet me in my office instead.

He sent back: **I just got to the archive. Be right there.**

Millicent stepped into the elevator as he left the archive, so he jogged to catch up and strode in.

She frowned. "I don't think it's a good idea if we're seen together."

Scott rolled his eyes. *I guess our little moment is over.*

The doors started to close, and Scott heard footsteps running from the dead end on the right of the elevator. He held the door, then wished he hadn't when he realized it was Azatoth.

Oh, shit!

She entered the elevator. Scott frowned and glanced at the empty hallway. "Sorry, I didn't see you."

The demon ignored him and nodded at Millicent. "Eric's been looking for you."

The mage gave Azatoth a tight smile but said nothing.

Scott held his breath. Please keep your shit together, Millicent.

The demon raised her eyebrows. "Okay, then." She turned her attention to Scott. "What are you up to, Scotty?" She took the book from Scott's hands, flicked through it, and handed it back. "Well, that was about as interesting as I expected."

Scott found his voice. "I'm going over some records. Trying to find…" He paused as the elevator stopped and the doors opened.

"Excuse me." Millicent stepped past them out of the elevator with her books in one hand, smoothing her hair with the other.

Azatoth held the doors open and watched Millicent in her tight skirt suit and five-inch stilettos march across the hallway and into an office. As the elevator doors closed, Azatoth pressed the button for the archives again. She smirked. "Thank goodness she's gone. You could cut the sexual tension in here with a knife."

Scott furrowed his brow. "Why are we going back to—"

She spoke over him. "Don't give me that look. I don't blame you. She's a handsome woman. Maybe a little mature for you, but who am I to judge?"

Scott was horrified. "I can assure you—"

Azatoth pressed on. "You sneaky dog! You and Millicent. I'd never have guessed it."

Scott opened his mouth to protest but realized the demon was redirecting his attention. He lowered his eyes and felt his face flush with heat from his neck to his scalp.

He followed the demon back into the archives, wondering what she was up to. She walked slowly past the stacks, stopping briefly at the end of each one before moving on. Finally, she stopped at the one where the thesaurus was stored. The steps leading to the dimensional pocket were still in position.

I should have moved them.

Azatoth stopped beside the steps and put a hand on the rail.

Scott's heart hammered in his chest.

The demon stepped onto the ladder and went up the few steps to the top. She trailed her fingers across the books. Scott almost winced when her finger touched the thesaurus.

Nothing happened.

Not sighing out loud took some effort.

The demon's trailed her finger past the thesaurus to the end of the row of books. Azatoth sniffed. "No, I don't think she was up this far." She climbed back down and sniffed the air. "She was definitely in this aisle recently. That perfume she wears; it clings to everything. Did you see her in here?"

"Millicent?"

"Of course."

"You think she's up to something? Why are you telling me?" Scott had just discovered he might have an ally in all this, but if he wasn't careful, he could lose that ally just as fast.

Azatoth shrugged.

If the demon suspected Millicent was acting against her, he didn't want to think what would happen. He chanced it. "Are you trying to find out if I know she's been spying on me? Because I *do*. I know because I was right here earlier." He held up the book in his hand and slid it into the space he'd taken it from on the opposite side of the aisle from the dimensional pocket.

Azatoth raised an eyebrow. "Don't you need that?"

"I'm sure Millicent's read it and already knows it's useless."

"Don't be like that, Scotty. Let's go up to my office and have a little chat."

They were silent in the elevator until they reached the executive level. When the elevator doors opened, Eric was walking through the hall.

"Eric. Excellent timing. Would you mind bringing a couple of coffees into my office? Actually, strike that. I'll have a ginger tea. I'm trying to cut down on caffeine. Coffee all right for you, Scott?"

"That's fine, thanks." Scott thought Eric did a great job of hiding his outrage. He was tempted to ask for a cookie just to tip him over the edge.

Azatoth directed Scott to an armchair beside a little table.

What now? I just want to get out of this place.

"I know you miss Lexi. I know what it's like to miss people and places so much it hurts."

Scott blinked. "The demon realm?"

The demon clicked her tongue. "No. That place isn't so much realm as a prison."

Scott didn't understand, but he thought he might be about to learn something useful. He stayed silent.

Eric entered, placed two mugs on the desk, and left without a word.

Azatoth lifted her mug and went to stand beside the window. Looking out across the city, she absently dunked her teabag into the cup by its string. "That realm was specifically made to hold us."

Us? Scott had been under the impression that the Darkness was one entity. She'd said as much previously. Were there other entities there? "Made by who?"

The demon laughed bitterly. "By us. We did it to ourselves."

Scott froze, not wanting to shake the demon out of her reverie before he learned something that might be important.

"We were a beautiful, shining people. In the infancy of our abilities, but millennia ahead of any other race. We had magic and science that propelled us far beyond any other society. But our home was plagued by disasters, one after the other. Storms, earthquakes, floods; you name it, we suffered it."

Azatoth took a sip of her ginger tea. "The augurs warned us of an earthquake that would split the island. They told us the gods were angry at us for not being pure enough. We prayed to them, promising we would be better if only we were spared their anger. They told us we would be saved if we cast away the evil within us —every negative emotion, bad intention, and cruel thought. Any tendency toward unkindness, jealousy, pride, or anger. I knew nothing of the magic they used for the spell. I learned after, when it was too late, that many had doubts, but they'd gone ahead with it regardless. We didn't know we were letting them tear us asunder. We cast ourselves out without form or substance into a realm created to bind us for all time. We might have survived if we hadn't gone so far. There are other races that are naturally divided, such as the fae with their seelie and unseelie."

Scott was blown away. He couldn't think of a thing to say.

She bounced the teabag around in the mug by the tag on its string. "So, the place you call the demon realm is our self-made prison. I was there for thousands of years." She sipped the tea. "We saturated the land with our outrage and despair. We infiltrated the low creatures so we could physically touch something, but they didn't last. It warped them, and they became monsters." She turned to face him. "Seriously, you should see the size of the crabs and spiders over there."

She walked over to the trashcan and dropped the teabag into it. "The first time we touched the minds of others through the veil, it was a thrill. It would have been joyous if we had been capable of joy. But we drove them mad. It is our nature. Then the shadow mages came. They were resilient, and they had form. They drew us into them with their magic, not realizing they were doing it. Then one day, I found the fissure. It might have been there all along. I don't think I would have seen it without Mortimer's eyes. So, I escaped. It took a long time. It was... painful. As my body reformed, my consciousness reached out to the others in that realm, but they were gone. The worlds had moved too far apart. When I finally became whole, I set out to explore my new world, but it was barren. I was alone there. I occasionally touched the minds of mortal men, but they slipped away. Then one day, I heard Caleb. He reached out with spells and forbidden magic, searching for power. I promised him everything, *anything*. I showed him magic and told him there would be more if he could bring me back to this world."

She sat in the chair opposite Scott. "Which is where you and your friends entered the story in Palm Springs. I was *so* close."

CHAPTER NINETEEN

S cott tensed. He didn't like where this was going. "But you're here now. You have form. Why aren't you off living your best life, or finding the realm you came from? Couldn't you connect with the other half of your people and become whole again?"

Azatoth shook her head. "My people are gone now, and there's no one to blame but ourselves. When I joined with Mortimer, he accepted me willingly and we joined completely. The betrayal he felt when Kindred abandoned him in my realm became mine. My millennias-long rage became his rage. His desire for vengeance became my own."

Scott was confused. "But you left his body behind."

"His body, yes. But he was with me for two hundred years. In a way, he always will be."

Scott hesitantly asked, "Is Caleb with you?"

"I was only connected to his mind. We were not joined, but I have some of his memories."

Scott didn't want to ask this question, but he had to. "What about Alicia? Is there anything left of her?"

Azatoth's expression showed uncertainty. "When I awoke within this vessel, it was empty but for me. Or so I thought."

Scott turned in his seat at a knock on the door.

Eric entered with a well-dressed middle-aged man.

Azatoth put her cup onto the table and stood. "At last we meet, Miles. Eric has told me so much about you. Thank you, Eric. I'll speak to you shortly."

The legacy gave Scott a cold, smug smile, then left.

The man was taken aback when he faced the demon and she made no attempt to hide what she was.

The demon smiled and patted Scott's arm. "Don't worry. You can still get out of this alive."

It took Scott a few seconds to work out where he knew the guy from. Though he'd never met the man, he had seen a recording of him in Lexi's dimensional pocket. It was the counselor Lexi had met in Peoria when she'd inadvertently hopped into the body of her shifter friend Mike. He had to admit, Azatoth had played a good game, getting him in an emotionally empathetic mood to make the extraction easier, but he was already battening down the hatches. As he sat sipping his coffee between polite smiles, he was racing through his dimensional pocket, closing down everything he didn't want them to see. As far as they would know, his dimensional pocket was a five-by-four closet filled with innocuous stuff: Marvel comics, books on magic, and a sack full of plushie chihuahuas.

He made one last change to the little room, then stood. "Should I leave?"

"Not at all." The man smiled, but his relaxation game was way off after meeting the demon.

"Are you sure? I could grab you a coffee from the kitchen. I mean, it's not great. You know what they say; you'd probably get better from a Peoria jail cell."

The man furrowed his brow. "True. But no, thank you."

If Azatoth had been able to see his face, it would have given the game away.

"If you're sure." Scott sat back down and tried to look like he wasn't expecting it.

The man walked behind him. "You stay where you are, young man." He put a hand on Scott's shoulder, then one on his head.

"I've got a problem, Scotty."

"A problem?" Scott blinked, then looked around. They were in the archives. He didn't know how he'd gotten there. He pushed down his panic, but his first thought was the glass. Had the counselor somehow found out about the glass in Devon's dimensional pocket?

Azatoth continued, "A few problems, actually. I know you're working with the fae woman and your friend Dick."

Scott opened his mouth to respond.

"Don't waste your time denying it."

Scott shrugged wearily. "I wasn't going to."

Azatoth raised an eyebrow. "You weren't?"

Scott snorted. "Of course not. What would be the point? You know we won't stop trying. In fact, I'd be surprised if you believed I wasn't trying night and day, on and off the clock, to get her back."

"Even though I told you to stay away from them?" Azatoth asked pointedly.

Scott shrugged. "Honestly, I assumed you knew I wouldn't listen."

Azatoth sighed. "I'd rather hoped you would. You know, that vampire has been a real nuisance. He keeps getting in my way. Caleb did *not* like him. I've decided I'm going to have to teach him a lesson."

A chill ran down Scott's spine.

Azatoth grinned. "Of course, I never did find the old lady. I might send some friends out to look for her. If I get my hands on her, I could do all the things I told Caleb I'd do." She grimaced. "Goddamn it." She popped another antacid and rubbed her solar plexus with a hand.

Scott narrowed his eyes. "Why are you telling me this?"

"I'm a good sport. Let's call it a head start." Azatoth indicated the exit with a sweep of her arm.

Scott was torn by the dilemma. He didn't want to leave the building without the glass, but he had to warn Dick. He raced for the door.

The hallway outside the archives wasn't empty. Four legacies stood in the hallway with the gnarly elf he'd seen down here before. The legacies muttered to one another, shifting nervously.

The elf snarled, "What are you staring at?"

Scott called the elevator, which appeared immediately. Azatoth was standing in the hall behind him when he stepped in. She stared at him with her head tilted and a speculative expression. He maintained eye contact until the doors closed. His hand went immediately to his jacket pocket. He pulled out his cell phone and tried calling Dick.

The vampire didn't pick up, so he messaged Dolores.

I need to see you now. I'm coming to the coffee shop.

He stepped out of the elevator on the first floor. Groups of employees were standing around chatting. Scott wanted to scream at them to get the hell out of the building and keep running. As he walked through the security barrier, he became aware they'd stopped talking. They were all staring at him. One of the young women smiled at him. Her eyes flashed black and her teeth were pointed, then she looked normal. He knew it wasn't an accident. Azatoth wanted him to know they were everywhere.

As he walked, he opened the memories in his dimensional pocket, unlocking everything up to the moment the counselor had put a hand on his shoulder. Halfway down the street, he glanced back to see that a couple of black-eyed legacies were following him. He'd never get into the apartment with them nearby. Instead, he stepped straight into the coffee shop. He paid for a coffee and discreetly gave himself a magical scan for bugs while he waited. He found two in his hair and one in his pocket.

He looked back through the glass door. The legacies were outside, watching him through the window. He walked back to the door and opened it. With them on the outside, they couldn't move fast enough to follow him through. He walked straight into the apartment and closed the door immediately behind him.

Dolores was sitting with a glass of bourbon in her hand. Her foot was bouncing. She jumped to her feet when Scott appeared. "What's happened?"

"She's altering the legacies a lot faster than I realized." Scott took her glass and knocked it back, coughing as the bourbon burned his throat. "That's really horrible."

"Well, it was mine." Dolores eased the glass from his hand. "Tell me what has you in such a state."

He stared at his shaking hand. "The coffee shop's burned. We can't use it again."

Dolores nodded. "I'm surprised it worked as long as it did."

"She's threatened Dick and anyone he knows. Betsy, you, Edward, Albin. She said she's giving him a head start by warning me."

Dolores frowned. "Obviously, that's not what she's doing. She wants us distracted. Why?" She looked at him, her face a mask of concern. "I don't think it's safe for you to go back."

Scott's eyes widened. "I have to. I had to leave the glass in the archive."

Dolores pressed her lips together. "Perhaps that's what she's after. If she thinks Dick has the glass, she could be trying to get him out of the way so she can find it."

"I'm not sure. She's usually more direct than that." Scott sighed. "She might know about the dimensional pocket in the archive, but she was definitely after something. She had me extracted by a counselor."

Dolores didn't look surprised. "What's that, the third time?"

"This time, it wasn't someone from the office. I think they were relying on me being unprepared. Luckily I recognized the guy, so I saw it coming. They didn't get anything I didn't want them to. She knows we've been trying to find Lexi. I left proof of that in my decoy dimensional pocket." Scott scratched his cheek. "She told me a story about her past, where the Darkness came from."

Dolores scoffed. "Probably all lies."

"I don't think it was. She had him make me forget everything in the last half hour. I think the fact that she didn't want me to remember means it was true, and she said something she didn't even realize she'd said."

Dolores' brow furrowed. "What was that?"

"When she was talking about Earth, she spoke about getting *back* to this realm."

"She's suggesting she came from this realm?" Dolores laughed. "I highly doubt it."

Scott repeated the story Azatoth had told him. He narrowed his eyes at the shock on her face. "What are you thinking?"

"It's not possible, although..." Dolores took out her cell phone and made a call. "Hello, dear. Could I borrow that pretty globe you keep beside the window? Thank you. I'm out front."

A minute later, the front door of the apartment opened, and a lady entered. She was dressed for a ball in a long lilac dress. Scott would have guessed she was in her fifties. She swept back her salt and pepper hair as she put the globe on the table.

Scott thought the woman looked familiar, then the penny dropped. "Betsy!" He jumped up, delighted to see her.

"Scott, dear. If I'd known it was you, I'd have brought cookies." Betsy offered him a solemn smile. "I'm so sorry about Lexi. I'm sure you'll get her back." Betsy hugged him, finishing with a tap on the butt.

"You look incredibly well. How's Todd?" Scott looked through the door and saw a very large armed fae behind her.

"He's doing very well. We're planning a wedding. He's marrying a lovely young fairy when we're no longer under house arrest." She gave Dolores a stern glare.

"You'll be glad of the security measures. Azatoth has threatened Dick and anyone who knows him, including you."

The huge, square-jawed fae entered the apartment, ready to defend Betsy.

Dolores asked him, "Have you seen anything unusual?"

He shook his head and stood next to Dolores.

"Fine. I'm going back to my cell." Betsy kissed Scott on the cheek and headed back into what looked to Scott like a very opulent room.

"Nice cell." He closed the door. "I don't think that's my necklace making her look like that."

Dolores grinned. "The king is very fond of her."

Scott raised an eyebrow. "She's moving up in the world."

"Did you really need to borrow this from Betsy?" he asked as Dolores positioned the globe on the table and twirled it.

"No, Google Maps would have worked as well. I just needed to see that she was safe." She pointed a finger at the Atlantic between Europe and Africa.

Scott squinted. "Am I supposed to be seeing something?"

Dolores chuckled. "Not anymore. But a very long time ago, you would have been looking at Atlantis."

Scott's jaw dropped. "Atlantis? *The* Atlantis? As in, 'the lost city of?'"

Dolores waved off his excitement. "Calm down. Yes. It was destroyed when an earthquake caused the whole island to be swallowed by the sea. It was a huge loss for the human realm. They were the most brilliant among you and the only humans with real magic at the time. Although, they were somewhat arrogant because of that."

Scott nodded. "She said as much. It's impossible to think she went from that to this."

"There were several fae living on the island. As the legend goes, they woke up one morning, and every Atlantean had mentally reverted to infancy and couldn't be brought out of it. The best my people could do when the earthquake hit a few days later was to take as many through to Faerie as they could. I believe they rescued a few hundred, mostly children. After the quake, the island disappeared. The adults and older children never recovered, but the babies grew up to be quite normal and still magical. It was assumed to be an attack. They never imagined the Atlanteans could have done such a thing to themselves. So sad that their obsessive desire to be perfect imprisoned them in that realm."

Scott pushed his hair back from his eyes. "What are we going to do about Dick? I've messaged him, and there's still no answer. What if she'd already gotten to him? She could have been trying to get me to lead them to you. Have I put you in danger? Or to get me out of the way so she could get the glass. Shit! I need to get back!"

Dolores put a hand on his arm. "Breathe. Have you tried calling the girls or Albin?"

Scott groaned. "I didn't think of that."

Dolores smiled. "I'll do it. You be careful."

Scott nodded and went to the apartment door. "They'll be waiting for me to come out."

Dolores chuckled. "They'll be disappointed."

Scott opened the door. For a moment, he was disoriented. He was on the opposite side of the street.

The two demonic legacies were still in front of the other building. One was inside and one outside the coffee house.

Scott made his way to the crosswalk and re-entered the Kindred building. He didn't stop to look at any of the people in the lobby. He marched straight over to the elevator, ignoring the hairs rising on the back of his neck.

The elevator doors opened, and there was Azatoth. He wasn't surprised. He had to admit he'd half-expected to see her there.

"Scotty boy." She stepped out and smirked. "What, no coffees? Let's go for a walk."

CHAPTER TWENTY

S cott just wanted to grab the glass and get the hell out of that building. "I'm not sure I, um—"

Azatoth's eyes glittered with malice. "I suppose I could just get straight to finding Betsy."

Scott sighed. "Sure. A walk sounds great."

Azatoth put a hand on his arm.

He found himself standing outside, looking at water. "Where are we?"

"Pier Forty-Six." Azatoth kept her eyes ahead and pointed. "Over there is New Jersey. Sometimes I stand here for hours."

He didn't answer. He felt outmatched in this game of cat and mouse. Instead, he stood in silence, taking in the view.

Azatoth started walking, and he followed her toward the barriers. At that moment, if he'd had Harpe, he would have plunged it into her back.

She put her hands on the barrier, then leaned back on her heels and swayed from side to side.

Scott remained still but followed her with his gaze. She turned around and leaned against the barrier.

She cast a look in the direction of the water taxis to the side of them and sighed. "Scotty, I'm bored."

Scott intended to blink but left his eyes closed for a long moment as he took in her statement. He opened them. "Bored?"

Azatoth nodded. "I didn't take the best part of two hundred years, shredding my body and waiting second after agonizing second for it to reassemble, to come here and spend my days reading executive summaries and cost-benefit analysis reports. I'm *bored*."

Scott was hit with the momentary horror of imagining Lexi doing what the demon had described to leave that place. He swallowed. "Then why *did* you come here?"

She wandered a little way down the barrier, then leaned against it again and folded her arms. "I came to watch it all burn. To *make* it all burn."

Scott swallowed. He didn't want to ask this question, but he didn't seem able to stop himself. "Then why haven't you?"

Azatoth looked across the water at New Jersey. "I like waffles and coffee and ice cream sundaes. I like the water. If I lay waste to this realm, all those things will be gone."

"It sounds to me like you need a vacation," Scott suggested.

"A vacation?" She raised an amused eyebrow.

Scott shrugged. "Sure. You could learn to waterski or go diving."

Azatoth turned to face him. "I've been toying with a novel idea. Lately, it just won't leave me." She took the packet of antacids from her pocket and rolled it between her fingers. "I thought there might be a possibility…"

Scott held his breath. That you're insane? Definitely!

"That Alicia is somehow still alive in here," Azatoth finished.

Scott froze. "What makes you think that?"

"It's not that I don't want to burn the whole stinking race of you to the ground, but every time I think about it, I feel nauseous." She sighed again. "That would explain why Lexi didn't kill me when she had the opportunity."

Scott snorted. "I'm pretty sure if Lexi believed her sister was still alive, it's because you *told* her that her sister was still in there."

Azatoth giggled. "Oh. Yes, I did do that, didn't I? I miss Lexi. She was...fun." The demon sighed. "Well, it doesn't matter. I now know that I'm alone in here. Although I'll be honest, that's not as comforting as I thought it would be."

Scott felt like a deer in bright headlights. All he wanted was a way out of the conversation and to get back to the room for the glass. He leaned on the barrier and swept the view with his gaze. Inside, he was checking his dimensional pocket. He couldn't understand why he had come around in the archives.

His decoy pocket had been searched. He found a sheet of paper with the picture of a business card on it. The counselor from Peoria. Someone had scribbled on the paper.

I'll do what I can.

I'll do what I can? What did that mean?

He entered his operations room and found his seeing ball, then connected his mind to it, needing to find out what had happened while he was being counseled.

They were back in the office. The counselor stood beside him. "I found notes on his activities with a fae and a vampire. They've been searching for someone called Lexi."

Azatoth grimaced. "I knew it! Has he found a way to reach her?"

The counselor shook his head. "It seems not, although his memories suggest he's a lot farther ahead in his search than he would have you believe."

"Anything else?" Azatoth asked.

The counselor lifted his hands. "He seems obsessed with stuffed dog toys."

Azatoth sighed. "That's disappointing. I was sure he was hiding something else."

"If that's all?"

"Actually, no." Azatoth tapped the side of her head. "I'd like you to take a look in here."

The counselor frowned. "You wish to be counseled?"

Azatoth waved a hand. "No, no. Just have a look around. Let me know if you find anything...*unexpected*."

"As you wish. What about this one?" He indicated Scott.

"Remove the last half hour and leave him in a trance for now," Azatoth ordered.

The man walked around the table to where Azatoth sat opposite Scott, leaving him gazing into nothing.

The demon leaned forward and waved a hand in front of Scott's face.

"He's unconscious," the counselor assured her. "Would you prefer me to close his eyes?"

Azatoth sat back in her chair. "No. Just get on with it."

The counselor put a hand on Azatoth's head. The man winced as he worked. He jerked and closed his eyes as tears escaped them. His breathing became faster until finally he cried out and wrenched his hand away. "Dear God." He staggered and sat down between Scott and Azatoth.

"Well?"

"Well, what? Do I know what you are? Yes. Where you came from? Yes. What you did to escape that place?" He put the back of his hand across his mouth and nodded.

"Am I alone in this vessel?" Azatoth enunciated.

The counselor looked at her in alarm. "What? Yes, of course. I sensed no other being in there."

Azatoth looked relieved.

He continued, "But the vessel isn't strong enough to contain you. It's dying."

The look of relief left the demon's face, replaced by a snarl. "When will he come out of the trance?"

"I can do it now," he offered.

She eyed Scott speculatively. "Will he stay like that if you don't release him?"

"No, he'll come out of it by himself in ten minutes or so."

"Good." Azatoth whipped a hand through the air and a red line appeared across the counselor's throat, followed by a fountain of blood that gushed down the front of his shirt and onto the table.

The demon got to her feet and opened the door. "Eric."

"Yes?" The legacy entered the office and blinked at the dead counselor.

"Get someone to clean this up. We're moving the plans up."

The demon lifted Scott with no difficulty and carried him to the elevator. She took him down to the archives and dropped him into Devon's chair.

"Right, ghosties and spirits. This is Scott. You know Scott, don't you? He's the mage of your beloved archivist, Lexi. Now, I know you saw what I did to the last archivist. If you don't stop getting in the way of our searches for documents, I'm going to tear this one to pieces too, but I'll do it more slowly. You remember how slowly I did it last time, don't you?"

The lights dimmed, and the room became chilly.

Azatoth continued, "I thought so."

She sat on the desk and tried to spin the puzzle until he came to.

"Well?" Azatoth poked him in the arm.

"Sorry?" Scott blinked. "I was miles away." He turned away from the river and faced Azatoth.

She rolled her eyes. "I asked if you want to go for waffles."

Scott couldn't stand to be in the demon's presence a moment longer. "No, thanks. I'd rather get back to work."

"Come on, then." She led the way back to the street, then abruptly stopped and turned to him. "I think you've done quite enough *work*. You've lost your archive privileges for now. You can go in there with Eric or Millicent, and that's it. Off you go, then. I'm bored with you."

Scott looked down the street. "Where are you going?"

"I'm going home to bed, which is just up there." She pointed at the building they stood in front of.

"You live here?" Scott didn't hide his surprise.

Azatoth nodded. "I've got to live somewhere. Where did you think I lived?"

"I suppose I've never thought about. It looks swanky."

"Well, it was Caleb's." She shrugged. "No sense letting it go to waste."

Scott went straight back to the condo. There wasn't any point in trying to get back into the archives. He went into his dimensional pocket and picked up a book on fae dimensions, then dropped it back on the desk. Instead, he went to a bookshelf and ran his finger across the books. He stopped at *The Legacy's Guide to Etiquette and Fine Manners*.

He smiled as he pulled it out of his dimensional pocket, then lay on his bed and opened it. He'd already flicked through it, looking for secret messages from Devon, but there was nothing. He closed the book and put it back in his lap. He found himself gazing at the cover, then blinked and sat up.

How did I miss this?

CHAPTER TWENTY-ONE

Azatoth entered the building and went to the desk. "Any mail?"

The desk clerk blinked, confused.

"No? Never mind." She translocated to Caleb's apartment, knowing the clerk would have no recollection she had been there.

She went to the kitchen and took a bottle of beer out of the refrigerator. After removing the top, she headed into the living room and went to the glass front wall, which gave her a stunning view of the river. She took a deep draw on the beer and leaned on the grand piano that neither she nor Caleb was able to play.

She didn't see the point of owning the thing. Her gaze took in the room. White rugs, white leather sofas. The apartment was a triplex with six bedrooms. She failed to see the point of any of it.

The demon went back to the refrigerator and considered her options for dinner. Everything she laid eyes on made her want to heave. She had to eat, but this body didn't seem to want food.

It was weak and tired and disgusting. She closed the fridge and went back into the living room, where she sat on the sofa and stared at the water until the darkness took the outside view away and left her with a reflection of herself. Once again, it was as though someone else was watching her through those eyes.

"I know you're there. I know you are. It's you. *You're* killing this body, not me." She threw the bottle against the glass. It was the bottle that smashed. The demon screamed and screamed until she was hoarse. Then all she could do was curl up and sob.

They're all going to pay for what they did to us. To Mortimer, and to me.

Eventually, she dragged herself from the floor and went to Caleb's crystal collection. She placed the stones in a circle on the floor and sat inside it.

"Where are you? It is time to speak in the waking world. You have touched my dreams but never my waking hours. I'm here. I'm reaching out to you, brothers and sisters. Where are you?"

We are here.

Azatoth threw back her head. "At last. It's been so long. I am here. Our home is gone. Beyond myths and legends, there are no records of our beautiful island. Our flesh is no longer even a memory. The gods abandoned us. Our sacrifice was for nothing."

The wailing in her head was deafening. *Have you abandoned us too?*

"I tried to free you, but a shadow mage closed the gate before I could summon you."

The one with the sword. She steals back that which we have fought so hard to gain.

"I will free you. We will take our revenge upon the gods who abandoned us. We will destroy the rest of their creation."

We will destroy.

Azatoth watched her reflection as her lips spread into a tight, thin smile. "I can help with the mage. Find her. Let's have a little chat."

CHAPTER TWENTY-TWO

Lexi climbed out of the tree and sat beside Philippe in the shade. "Good morning. What are you going to do about losing Napoleon?"

Philippe shrugged. "I'll catch another one. It isn't difficult."

Lexi remembered how many of the crab creatures had attacked her when she first crossed over. "Will you have to go back to the portal?"

He shook his head. "No. There are nests of them dotted all over the place."

Lexi grinned. "I've got nothing better to do if you want to do that today. I guess we're not going to see the others for at least another day."

Philippe nodded. "As you wish." He climbed into the tree and threw down several lengths of rope made from the oak twine. He dropped out of the tree and picked up two ropes. He put one in his dimensional pocket and one over his shoulder. Lexi did the same. They took Mark Twain from his cage and two spiders in cages, then set out in the direction of the rising sun.

After a couple of hours, Philippe raised the spider cages above Mark Twain's head, and the creature stopped. He passed the cages to Lexi and slid off the creature's back. Lexi held the cages high. The creature's attention was solidly on the spiders. It didn't even notice Philippe winding the twine around its feet.

He straightened when he was done. "Okay, you can get off now."

Lexi slid off and passed a cage to Philippe, who put it on the ground about ten feet behind Mark Twain. The crab was docile at this point.

The Frenchman laid two ropes in a rough circle around the cage. He took Lexi's ropes and did the same around Mark Twain, then took the stick from the cage and drove it suddenly and viciously into Mark Twain's shell.

The creature screamed in pain, and Lexi jumped back. "Holy shit! Are you hoping to make them mad? What if fifty of them come running?"

"They won't. They push the weakest out first. If it doesn't come back, the next weakest will come."

Lexi recalled fighting the creatures. They had come at her one at a time, and they had gotten successively stronger and larger. She hadn't thought about it at the time, but she had grown in proficiency as she fought them—learning their weaknesses, studying how they moved. She curled up her lip in disgust. "That's a terrible strategy."

"It is. But in this case, the creature will only be expecting to find one of its own kind dying."

"Will it try to pull it back to the nest?" Lexi eyed the struggling crab.

Philippe stared at her. "No. It will dismember the weaker crab like Mark Twain did to Napoleon Bonaparte."

Lexi blinked. "Mark Twain did that? I thought the guy who stabbed me did it."

Philippe shook his head. "It's coming. Let's get back behind the crab."

A crab creature appeared over a pile of rocks and crept

toward Mark Twain. It stopped a few feet away, its head moving back and forth.

Lexi whispered, "What's it doing?"

"It sees Mark Twain is bigger. I think it's trying to assess the best way to beat him."

The spider in the cage seemed to sense another predator and made an effort to get out. That got the crab's attention. It changed direction and headed for the cage, clicking its massive pincers. The moment it entered the circle of oak, it slumped. Philippe ran over and put twine around the pincers. "Welcome, George Washington."

"No new name?" Lexi teased.

Philippe chuckled. "I find it easier to rotate around a few names, but you may name this one if you wish."

Lexi tapped her lips with a finger. "Is it definitely a male?"

"I have no idea. I've never been able to assess their gender, nor wanted to."

Lexi thought about it for a moment. "I'm going to represent the ladies. Natasha Romanov."

"What has this Natasha Romanov achieved?" Philippe asked.

Lexi grinned. "She kicks ass."

Philippe nodded. "Let's get back to the tree before they send the next one. I only have space for two of them." He handed a spider cage on a stick to Lexi, and she climbed onto the beast.

The next day, Lexi sat in the shade of the tree with a mirror in her hand. She had her top lip curled up and was picking at her teeth with a spider fang she'd fished out of Philippe's cooking fire.

"I'm sure you'll make some young man a fine wife one day."

Lexi looked up to see the man with the rictus grin standing

about thirty feet away. "Dude, let's not be judgy. Have you seen your own face lately?"

The grin didn't change. She hadn't expected it to. That thing looked like it was glued on.

"So which one are you? Or, who were you?" She waited a moment, then started to walk toward him. "Why don't you meet me halfway."

The first flicker of annoyance appeared on his face.

She stopped and put her hand in her pocket, curling her fingers around Harpe's hilt. "I could help you. Do you want to be helped? I could get the Darkness out of you."

His gaze darted to her hand. "You have the sword."

She was surprised he knew about it. "Have you evil sons of bitches been gossiping about me?"

"Did you think you were the only one to make contact? I bring Azatoth's regards. I have a message for you."

Lexi tried not to let the shock show on her face. If Azatoth is in contact with the others, she can tell them how to get out. They could be chopping each other up right now and stuffing bits through the fissure. She ignored the flip of her stomach at that thought.

He giggled. The sound was so creepy the hairs stood up on the back of her neck. "You're to pick names. One to live, one to die. Scott or Dick, you decide."

Lexi snarled. "If anything happens to either of them, I'll do what I should have done with this sword months ago."

"One of Dick's friends, then? The old lady, the shifter, the incubus. Plenty to choose from."

Lexi realized she was communicating directly with Azatoth. "Hey Az, you're running out of friends over here." She remembered the spell Scott did that she could never master. She liked her chances this time.

She left a shadow of herself standing there and smiling at the possessed mage, then translocated behind him with Harpe in her hand. She thrust forward but staggered forward when she met no resistance. He had been an illusion.

A second too late, she knew exactly where he was. She felt the sting of his blade, this time in her back. As she fell to her knees, his hand came around and wrestled for Harpe. She gripped harder.

He dug his knee into her back and her arm went numb. She watched helplessly as he wrenched Harpe from her hand...only to see it drop to the ground as a scream bellowed out behind her. She threw out a hand and retrieved the sword.

She blinked in confusion when she looked up at Rictus. His head was three inches to the left of where it should have been on his shoulders, having been knocked out of place by the weight of Akeem's hammer.

The horrific apparition disappeared and reappeared twenty feet away a moment later. "You have a day to give us a name or the sword," he warned. Then he disappeared.

Jonathan lifted her to her feet and pulled her back to the safety of the tree. "What was Kenneth talking about?"

Lexi rubbed her wrenched shoulder. "Oh, that's his name? He didn't introduce himself. It seems Azatoth has been in touch with Team Darkness. They know about the sword. I'd guess they probably all know about the fissure, too."

Jonathan grimaced. "What of the names?"

"I'm supposed to choose which of my friends is going to die." Lexi leaned against the tree. The air warped beside her, and she stepped back. "He's back." She stood ready with the sword.

Jonathan grew a ball of energy in his hand and flung it at the anomaly. He grinned when the shimmer disappeared. "By the gods, that felt great."

Akeem turned in a circle, his hammer at the ready. "How could he get into the roots of the tree?"

Lexi shrugged. "Perhaps that's why he didn't fully appear?"

"What is happening?" Philippe appeared with two spiders in cages.

"We had another visit from Kenneth," Jonathan informed him.

Still in pain from the dagger in her back, she didn't relish climbing into the tree. "Is there any point in not using magic right now because I don't want to climb up?"

Philippe rolled his eyes and shooed Lexi toward the tree. "I have no problem with that, as long as I can stick you with the sword. I owe you one."

She grinned. "It's not just me. Jonathan just threw an energy ball." She translocated into the tree.

"It's fine. We're safe near the tree, and Philippe knows it." Jonathan appeared beside her. "Turncoat."

She chuckled.

When Philippe joined them, Lexi asked. "Can we contact Scott? My friends are in danger."

Jonathan looked into the distance. "I'm afraid that's going to have to wait. They're coming."

CHAPTER TWENTY-THREE

Azatoth was sitting in her office with Eric when Millicent entered.

Eric's face soured. "Fashionably late as usual."

She checked her watch. "I'm precisely on time. Speaking of which, I have something for you."

The legacy eyed her suspiciously. "You have?"

Millicent sat down in the remaining empty chair and took a deep breath. She glanced at Azatoth. "Perhaps now isn't the right time."

Azatoth's eyes gleamed. She sat back and twirled a pencil around her fingers. "Oh, no, you don't. I'm curious now. Out with it."

Millicent turned to Eric. "All those years ago. I was so angry when you left, I cut up the clothes you left at my place."

Eric scowled. "You also threw out my class ring and my father's watch. I remember."

Her cheeks pinked. "I even poured your aftershave down the toilet."

"I assumed as much." Eric returned his gaze to his tablet's screen.

Millicent pushed on. "Well, here's a bottle of aftershave to replace the one I poured out. And, well, I lied about the ring and watch."

He turned back to her.

"I didn't throw them away." She pushed two boxes toward him. "Since we've been working together, I've been feeling guilt and shame over the way I reacted. I feel it's long past time to put things right."

He opened the larger of the two boxes and took out the gold watch. He gazed at it for a few moments and turned it over in his hand. "I still remember my father wearing it, and when he told me that one day it would be mine. I cursed the day I made the mistake of leaving it at your apartment."

"I reacted poorly the night I found out about you and Lilith. Of course, it's clear in retrospect that the two of you were meant for each other. I couldn't see that at the time. I couldn't see past my own bruised heart."

Silently, Eric fastened the watch around his right wrist.

Millicent's cheeks turned a deeper pink. "I had to get it repaired. It was in a box in my basement for all those years."

Eric opened the ring box and took out his old class ring. "Good heavens, it seems a little gaudy now. He tried to push it onto the same finger he had previously worn it on, but it was too small. It snuggly fit the little finger on his left hand.

"It still sort of fits." He moved to take it off. But Millicent put a hand over his.

"I do hope you'll find a way to forgive me."

Eric pulled his hand away. "Well, there's still the matter of clothes."

"I'm sure we can come to some arrangement." Millicent stood abruptly and grabbed her cell phone, which hadn't rung. "Just one moment, I have to take this." She walked quickly out of the office.

Eric looked up to find the demon staring at him. "What?"

"We're suppos—" She cut off abruptly when the sound of Millicent blowing her nose made it clear she was just outside. Azatoth lowered her voice. "We're going to need her to commit to the ritual any day now. Wear the watch, wear the ring, and wear the fucking aftershave. Tell her you forgive her and make sure she believes you mean it. Am I clear?"

"Absolutely." Eric opened the aftershave and sniffed it, then screwed up his face.

Azatoth could smell it from across the table. It was like something from a dollar store. She cleared her throat so Eric would see she was still staring at him.

Eric sighed, splashed the stuff into his hand, and put it on his face.

Azatoth smirked. She could see he was trying to hold his breath.

A minute later, Millicent came back into the room. Her face was solemn, but two steps into the room, she beamed. "You're wearing the aftershave. Do you like it? It was terribly expensive."

Eric smiled. "It's very nice, thank you." He held out a hand, showing her he was wearing the ring.

To Azatoth's absolute delight, she misinterpreted his action and took Eric's hand in hers. The legacy's smile remained on his face, but his eyes went to the demon.

Azatoth would have pitied him if she had the capacity for such things. She leaned across and put her own hands around theirs. "Am I sensing forgiveness in the air?"

Millicent looked at Eric with wide, hopeful eyes.

Eric forced a smile. "Of course I forgive you, Millicent. It was all so long ago. And I don't even know how to express the gratitude I feel at seeing my father's watch again."

The smile on Millicent's face broadened. "So, what are we discussing today?"

CHAPTER TWENTY-FOUR

Everything was quiet. Clouds hid the sun, making the view from the top of the tree gray and muted. Lexi sat silently, making sure not to raise her head above the outer leaves. She didn't want to give them a reason to start the barrage of fire again.

"Lexi." The whisper came from lower in the tree.

She made to start down but frowned at a curled brown leaf. She plucked it and descended.

When she entered the house in the tree, Jonathan greeted her with a nod. Akeem was snoring softly on her couch. She put the leaf on the table in front of Philippe. "Is the tree okay?"

Philippe nodded. "It gets like this during a sustained attack. It'll grow back when they've exhausted themselves."

Jonathan looked out. "They're not happy about your sword."

Lexi snorted. "Speaking of the sword. Why are we hiding in the tree? Let's go out there and blast them all to shit. If any of you start giving me the side-eye, I'll poke you with Harpe."

"And what do we do if you are affected?" Jonathan pointed out.

"Surely, it can't affect me that quickly? It took you two

hundred years to get a little paranoid, and it doesn't seem to have affected Philippe at all."

Jonathan shrugged.

Lexi continued, "Next time they come, you three do the blasting, and I'll creep around with the sword."

Jonathan settled into a blanket on the floor, "I'm going to get a little rest while it's quiet."

Lexi didn't have the heart to disturb Akeem. She left the big man on her couch and settled down on a bed of leaves.

The explosions started again too soon. Lexi's eyes were tired and gritty. Brown leaves were scattered around her. The tree was not faring well.

Jonathan nodded at her from his blanket. He took out a whetstone and set about sharpening his knives.

Philippe looked like he hadn't slept. He sat at the table, rolling mud and twigs into tennis- ball-sized spheres. The table was covered with them.

Lexi raised an eyebrow. "You're going to throw mud at them?"

Philippe's mouth stretched in a grim smile. "No, you are. I'm going to weaponize these projectiles, and you are going to throw them while we fight back with magic."

Akeem sat up. He was the only one who looked refreshed. "An excellent plan, my friend. Would you like me to do that while you concentrate on your other job?"

"Thank you, yes." Philippe walked to a wall at the center of the tree. His eyes fell on the glass, then he looked at Lexi. "Keep that safe."

Lexi put the glass into her dimensional pocket, then put a hand on her couch. It disappeared into her pocket as well. She grinned when Akeem sighed loudly. "Don't worry, big man. You'll see it again."

Jonathan got to his feet as loud screams filled the air. "They have crabs with them. If they've been riled up by the demons, they won't be coming in one at a time."

Lexi rubbed her hands together and nodded at the balls of mud. "Magic up my balls. I'm going to war."

Akeem held out his arms. As he muttered, a nimbus glow settled around the balls and sank into them. Lexi scooped one up. It crackled in her palm. She grinned and stuffed them several at a time into her dimensional pocket.

The leaves of the tree began to rustle loudly, and Lexi turned to see Philippe raising his arm into the thick branches. When he pulled it back, he held an acorn. "And so it begins again."

"What does that mean?"

"The tree isn't healing itself. I have to grow a new one." He popped the acorn into the pocket of his shirt and nodded. "Let's get started."

The air outside the tree was thick with dust. Lexi pulled a bandana from her pocket and wrapped it around her neck, then pulled it up over her mouth and nose. "I can't see through this. How am I supposed to throw my balls?"

Jonathan raised his arms and pushed the dust outward, but it came back. Akeem and Philippe joined him. It seemed to Lexi that the shadow mages were focused more on the dust than what was causing it. She didn't like it, wondering what was happening behind the dust. She turned back to the tree and climbed back into it. She climbed through the first level and continued upward. When she reached the top, she saw the wall of dust around them and the six monstrous shapes of what had previously been shadow mages. Around them were hundreds of the crab creatures. They didn't seem to be snapping at each other or the mages. They were facing the tree, waiting. The dust cloud was moving out slowly toward them. When it reached them, there would be nothing between the tree and those monsters. And Philippe had taken the magical heart from the tree. This was bad.

She translocated down to the ground.

When Philippe turned to her, his face was strained and sweat ran down his temples with the exertion of pushing back against the dust. "I don't hear explosions."

Lexi shook her head. "Stop what you're doing. Don't push the sand wall back. All six of them are out there, and at least a hundred Mark Twains. They're waiting for you to exhaust yourself. If I blow up the mages, the crabs might lose their shit and come in faster."

They disconnected their energy immediately, and the wall came closer. The roots of the tree were losing their magic at the ends.

"How long will it take for the magic to leave the tree?" Lexi asked.

Philippe pressed his lips together. "A few hours, maybe."

Lexi's brow furrowed. "Can you open the roots to create a passage through the ground to the crab cages?"

Philippe nodded enthusiastically. "Genius."

"I'll head back up and try to thin the herd. I'll concentrate on one area. Over there." She pointed. "I'll make it look like we're trying to clear a path. We might be able to get out long before they realize we're gone."

Jonathan grabbed her shoulder. "You'll be a target up there. Stay safe."

Lexi nodded. "Sure thing, Dad. You too." She dropped a dozen balls on the ground at the base of the tree. "Just in case I get knocked off my perch. Don't step on those."

She turned back to the tree to climb up.

Jonathan shouted. "Look out!"

The air expanded and rippled beside her.

Everything happened at once. The three mages turned their magic onto the new threat. In the same moment, Lexi jumped toward the anomaly, screaming, "*No!*"

She was hit by three bolts of energy. The force of the blasts blew a hole in her side, sending up a spray of blood as she flew off the ground and directly into the strange bubble of air. She floated half in-half out of it for a few seconds. The pain was like nothing she'd ever experienced. She held one hand over the hole in her side and summoned Harpe.

The sword appeared in her other hand, and she threw it. Harpe spun through the air and impaled itself in the ground at Jonathan's feet.

She tried to say something to the mages as they stared at her in horror, but the bubble overtook her and the demon realm melted.

Lexi opened her eyes, dizzy and confused. The acrid air stung her throat. A creature crawled onto her chest. It crawled up her body, hissing as it jerked this way and that. It was red like Azatoth had been when she first encountered her. Pus-filled lumps covered its skin. One ear was ripped almost in half and hung uselessly at the side of its head. It lifted its swollen and distorted face to gaze at her. One of its huge amber eyes was puffy and half-shut, but it had the widest smile.

Tears sprang to Lexi's eyes. "Hey, little guy."

Limpet flopped onto her.

Her face stung, and every inch of her felt the combined blast she'd received, but her new surroundings felt unsafe. Wherever they were, it stank. She couldn't wait until she had healed. She sat up. A glance down at her stomach told her moving wasn't an option. There were parts peeking out that she felt sure needed to be on the inside. She grimaced as she poked them back in before pulling the crab shells from her dimensional pocket. She crawled into one shell with Limpet in her arms and pulled the second over her.

Lexi reached across to Limpet and put a hand on his head. She had barely any energy to heal the wounds she could see. She did what she could and hoped it would be enough. The thinner had clearly been through hell to get to her. She thought about the times the bubble of air had appeared as she wandered through the demon realm, always appearing, she now realized, beside her. He must have been trying to break through for weeks.

She pulled a piece of sulfur from her pocket and placed it onto the thinner's chest, then rested her hand upon it. She hoped it would magnify what little strength she had and heal her friend.

CHAPTER TWENTY-FIVE

L exi had no idea how much time had passed, but when she awoke, still aching, she was instantly aware of the feeling of motion. Someone or something was dragging the shells with her inside. She rolled to the side, placing the still sleeping Limpet beside her. He groaned as she tried to gently separate herself from where his sores had dried and stuck to her. They did seem much better but weren't fully healed.

She pulled her katana from her dimensional pocket, missing the feel of her demon-killing sword. While Harpe was less easily wielded, its effectiveness against creatures in the demon dimension had been comforting. She hoped the others were making good use of it, then put them out of her mind.

It wasn't the time to be distracted.

She crouched and waited for the motion to cease. Not knowing what was going to be on the other side of the shell was a disadvantage. Either way, it was time to move.

Lexi gripped the edge of the shell and stood, spinning around as she looked for the direction of the threat. She was in a cave. The threat was everywhere.

Tiny flying bugs attacked her from every direction, stinging her face, neck, and hands. The Lexi-napper had its back to her, pulling the shell. It towered like a mountain above her, seemingly unbothered by the bugs.

She slashed the rope with her katana, and the creature was left with slack strands in its hand. It turned. The face was humanoid, but its size most certainly was not. It was a giant. She'd never seen an actual giant before. They stared at each other for a long moment. As Lexi contemplated the best way to strike the behemoth, the giant screamed and ran. She felt the vibrations of its feet through the shell beneath her.

Lexi blinked. The bugs were coming in for a second attempt. She scooped up the sleeping thinner, then whirled a hand around her head, and a blast of light burst from her hand. Smoking black raisins bounced on the ground. She high-tailed it in the direction the giant had taken.

Outside, the air was hotter but less acrid. A quick check behind her told her the bugs hadn't followed. She looked at the back of her hand where the welts from the stings were already starting to disappear.

Limpet put his arms around her neck.

"I missed you. I don't know how you got to me. But thank you."

Pictures flooded into her mind of hundreds of attempts to get into the demon realm. The thinner had a pretty clear idea of where she was but couldn't get through. First he had been working with Dick and Dolores, then he'd traveled farther and farther into a maze of worlds.

Lexi sighed with dismay. Even with Limpet's help, it was probably going to take at least a week to get home. Her last communication with Scott had told her she needed to be back straight away.

She pulled the glass from her dimensional pocket and leaned it against a rock. The inside of an empty room gave her no clues. "Scott?"

No answer.

"Damn. How am I supposed to make this work as a portal?" Lexi scratched her face absently. "I guess if I just think really hard about wanting a portal and push my energy into it…"

Limpet's face popped up between Lexi and the glass. *Tell me you're joking.*

The thinner touched the glass. Its surface wavered, and he stuck an arm into it. When he pulled it back out, he was holding a bottle of Mountain Dew.

Lexi grinned. "That's great, but is there any Coke?"

Limpet rolled his eyes.

Vibrations moved through Lexi's feet. It felt like there was an earthquake.

Limpet put a hand on the glass, holding it secure before it could slip off the rock.

A glance out from the rocks told her two things. The giant was coming back, and it wasn't an adult. It was joined by two more twice as big as it. "Oh dear, here comes Mom and Dad, and they look pissed."

Lexi touched the surface of the glass and translocated into the room at the other end. She recognized it as the dimensional pocket in the archives. So, Scott had escaped from their previous situation. That was a relief.

Limpet hopped out of the portal and pulled the glass through from the other side. He placed it beside its companion piece of stained glass.

Lexi dropped into the chair and returned the bottle to the desk. She was back in her world.

Limpet jumped into her lap.

"Let's go home." She touched the thesaurus on the desk and found herself in the archives. A hundred voices all whispered at once. Her hands flew to her ears. The sound was deafening. She realized Limpet wasn't reacting to it. Only she could hear it.

The lights flashed and hummed as the archives came to life. Limpet frowned and clung to her, looking around wildly.

He could see them.

"What the hell is going on down here?" Millicent's voice was very close by.

It was time to go. Lexi translocated out of the archive and appeared in the kitchen of the condo. "Scott?"

No answer.

The place looked much the same although it was untidy, with dishes in the sink and a lot of fast-food wrappers on the counter.

She headed upstairs and almost cried at the sight of the bathtub. She stripped off her clothes and turned on the shower. She was just about to step in when she laid eyes on the toothpaste.

Five minutes later, having clean teeth caused tears to well up. She spent twenty minutes washing her hair and scrubbing her skin raw.

She took one look at the bed and contemplated diving onto it. Instead, she opened a dresser drawer and took out a clean pair of panties.

She held them to her chest. "Clean panties. I'll never take you for granted again." She put them on, then pulled out a pair of leather pants and a linen blouse from the dresser and threw them on the bed. She paused. She'd been wearing leather pants for months and didn't feel compelled to throw on another pair. She felt cool and clean, and she smelled good. She brushed her hair and wandered into Scott's room. It looked like a bomb had hit it, with clothes and food wrappers everywhere.

Lexi picked up a pair of folded jeans from a chair and held them out. She pulled them on. They felt good. She rolled them up at the bottom, then opened a drawer. She pulled out a Star Wars t-shirt.

"May the fourth be with you." She chuckled, gave it a sniff, and pulled it on.

The front door opened. She went to call out but froze when she heard voices. One seemed familiar, but she couldn't place it.

"We can turn the place upside down to find it if we have to."

Scott sounded bored. "You're going to have to do that because I haven't a clue what you're talking about."

"You won't be saying that when we bend your little fae friend over backward and slice her down the middle."

Cold fury settled into Lexi's core. Her first instinct was to fly down there and tear them to pieces. Whoever they were, they were threatening Scott and Dolores. She stepped back from the railing and breathed a relaxing, cleansing breath. She rolled her shoulders, cracked her neck, and focused on a glamour. She thought about Azatoth's eyes, the hideous black and yellow.

Another deep breath to ensure she wasn't going to lose her shit, then she translocated to the bottom of the stairs.

There was a standoff in the living room. She could see the two Kindreds facing Scott, who was out of sight on the other side of the open living room door.

She realized one of them was Beavis from the office. She opened her mouth to order them out when the one she didn't recognize burst into flames. The heat was so fierce, she had to step back. His face melted in seconds. Beavis turned in horror to his companion and saw her. He pointed at Scott, then burst into flames and dropped to the floor.

Lexi suddenly doubted it was Scott in the room. She suspected it was Azatoth. She took a step into the room and leaped back as a firebolt flew from Scott's hand and incinerated part of the door.

Lexi removed the glamour and shouted out to her wild-eyed friend, "Stop! It's me."

Scott snarled. "I know it's you. I've had enough. If you want to kill me, come and try it."

She held up her hands. "Scott, it's me. *Lexi*."

"Bullshit." Another firebolt hit the already burning door.

Lexi translocated behind Scott, grabbed him, and translocated them both.

Scott pushed her off and positioned himself to blast her again.

She didn't move to defend herself.

He froze, then glanced around, taking in their surroundings. They were in the foyer of Phil's Cornerdown Kitchen.

The maître d' stared in horror at them.

Scott turned back to Lexi as the spell revealing their true nature covered them. He gulped, then pulled her into a hug.

He stepped back and put his hands at his sides, blushing. "I don't understand how—"

It wasn't a conscious decision to kiss him. She just found her lips pressed to his. Neither of them pulled away.

Finally, a loud crunch made them break apart. Limpet stared at them as he sat on the desk with a jar of pixie brains, shoveling them into his mouth like popcorn.

CHAPTER TWENTY-SIX

"L et's ask Phil if we can use a booth. You can catch me up, and I can eat my bodyweight in food."

Scott looked around wildly. "No, we need to get out of here. She has spies everywhere."

Lexi sighed. "But I haven't eaten for months."

Scott grabbed her hand. "I'll buy you a Mcdonald's Quarter-pounder."

"Fine." Lexi picked up Limpet in one arm, then translocated them. A moment later, they were standing outside a fast-food restaurant.

Scott swiveled his head. "We're in Palm Springs. This is where you kicked that little thief in the balls. Why here?"

Lexi nodded and headed toward the entrance. "It was the first place I thought of. Good memories."

They sat at a table while Lexi ripped into her third burger, then followed it with a fistful of fries. Her eyes rolled up, and she groaned loudly.

Scott returned the gazes of the couple on the next table. "When Harry Met Sally. Great movie."

They looked away, and he discreetly helicoptered his finger above them. He scanned the diner.

Lexi slurped her coffee. "I missed you *so* much."

Scott returned his attention to her. "I missed you, too."

"I was talking to the coffee. But yeah, I missed you, too." She grinned. "How did you not realize I was back? I sensed you straight away."

Scott sighed. "She's always messing with my head, pretending to be you with glamours. I thought it was just her doing stuff again."

Lexi sat back from the food. "Did you forget the spell to get the demon out of my sister?"

Scott shook his head. "No. Of course not."

Lexi raised an eyebrow. "But it's still in there. Why didn't you get it out?"

"I came across an unexpected problem. I didn't have a vessel I was certain would hold the demon's essence. Besides, I knew you'd get back. We can fix it together now."

Lexi knew there wasn't any point in taking this out on Scott. She'd had her chance to kill Azatoth, and she hadn't been able to risk it either. She grabbed his Coke and chugged half the cup. "I'm guessing those assholes at the condo were her demon legacies."

Scott nodded. "She's been pulling them in from units around the country and using the demon-tainted elixir on them."

Lexi's face fell. "Where's—"

"Your unit's fine. She's keeping them for leverage, I think." He stopped speaking and stared at her with confusion.

Lexi wondered if she was still a mess after her months in the demon realm. "What?"

"Is that my t-shirt?" he asked.

Lexi shrugged. "I've been wearing the same leathers for months, and I've been washing in sand like a fucking chinchilla."

Scott grinned. "I don't mind. It looks good on you."

Lexi returned her attention to her fries. "What do you think she's going to do when she finds you melted her monster Beavis?"

Scott sighed. "I should probably clean that up."

"Dick's not going to get his security deposit back on that place." She snorted, then grew serious. "I know she's had the cabal searching for the Order. What else has she been up to?"

Scott's face sobered, and an overwhelming feeling of sadness came through their bond.

"What is it?" Lexi pressed.

"She suspected Alicia was still in there. She didn't find anything, but the counselor told her the body is dying."

Lexi clenched a hand. "That's not happening. Not after all this. We need to get that monster out of there."

Scott sighed. "We will. I promise we will. She's still looking for the shadow mage spell, and she's had them trying to make a time portal."

Lexi's jaw dropped. "She told you that?"

He paused before answering. "Millicent told me."

Lexi narrowed her eyes. "Millicent was chatting to you about Azatoth's plans? What was Eric doing, making you a friendship bracelet?"

Scott chuckled. "No. He's still a douche, but she's on our side."

"You haven't…"

Scott grimaced. "No! Why do people keep asking that? She's, like, twenty years older than me."

Lexi blinked. "I was going to ask. You haven't told her anything, have you?"

"Oh." Scott blushed. "No, I haven't. But when I went to warn the Order about the raid, she saw me and let me get away. She lied to the demon's face. But she's got good reason to be on our side. Azatoth and Eric are planning to put the demon into Millicent."

"That's interesting." Lexi pondered the turn of events. Could

Millicent be trustworthy? She couldn't see it. "So, what *have* you done?"

"I've mostly been trying to slow down Azatoth's efforts to find another way to the demon dimension." He furrowed his brow. "There is something else. I think I found something, a clue last night. But I don't know what to make of it."

He pulled a book from his bag and placed it on the table.

Lexi smiled. "The Legacy Etiquette book." She picked it up and flicked through the pages, looking for a handwritten scribble. There was nothing.

"Look at the author's name."

She read. "Devon wrote this?"

Scott continued, "Look at the author's note in the back."

She flicked to the back and found the page. It was a poem. She read it. "I don't get it."

"Read the last line out loud."

As she read, she raised her eyebrows.

"The question she must understand. The answer lies in Leksea's hand. Lek-sea, Lexi? The answer's in my hand?" She clenched her right hand, then opened it. "I don't get it."

She read the poem again. "Where hearts are joined, the truth is banned. The answers lie in Lexi's hand." She screwed her fists into her eyes and yawned. "I got nothing. What does Dick make of it?"

Scott shrugged. "I only found it last night. We haven't discussed it. We've been trying to keep him out of the demon's way since she threatened him. He's been helping the Order, and I've stayed away to keep them safe."

Lexi frowned. "Where are they?"

"Chicago."

Lexi got to her feet. "Let's go, then."

They stepped out of the restaurant and translocated to the Windy City.

Scott took them one more jump to a jazz club.

Lexi grinned. "Ha! I remember this place. Tell him to meet you at the side door."

Scott sent a quick text.

A few minutes later, the door opened, and Dick looked out. He stood under the awning for a moment, then stepped out. "I prefer not to use this exit. What's—" He stopped speaking and looked up at Lexi, who was perched on the awning above the doorway with an eyebrow raised at him.

She grinned. "This is a familiar view—" Before she could finish the sentence, he was beside her, hugging her.

"We thought you were captured or dead."

"We did?" Scott frowned.

"The Order contacted the shadow mages today. Jonathan's beside himself. He went on a murderous rampage, believing you had been snatched by the enemy or somehow blipped out of existence." He glanced at Scott. "We drew straws to choose who should break it to you. Haven't you seen Sebastian? He lost."

Lexi translocated down to the ground. "It was Limpet. He got me out. Him and around ten million volts."

Dick dropped back down to the ground. "Is he okay? Where is he?"

"He's in my dimensional pocket." She looked inward at the demon curled up on the couch with an empty pixie brain jar beside him. "He's snoring. He's been through a lot."

Dick smoothed his jacket. "Marcel's been inconsolable. Limpet was missing for days."

Lexi nodded. "I missed Marcel, too. Scott, read the poem to Dick."

Scott went through the whole poem, then finished with the last two lines. "Where hearts are joined, the truth is banned. The answers lie in Lexi's hand."

Dick frowned. "Her name's just written there for anyone to see?"

Scott shook his head. "No, it's spelled wrong to hide it."

"Let me see. Devon wrote this?" Dick took the offered book and read over the poem. "I think you're right. This whole poem has been written to hide these two lines. If we assume that Lexi isn't the only word disguised, what does that leave us with? *Where* could be *wear* as in an item of clothing... Lexi's hand. Gloves? 'Were' as in shifter? 'Hearts, joined, truth.' I can't think what other words they could be. 'Banned' seems significant because it's linked to truth. It could be 'band,' like hair band, jazz band." Dick palmed his face. "Of course!"

Lexi stared at him. Trying to keep up with his thought process, but she couldn't.

Dick pointed at Lexi's hand. "You wear a band on your hand. A *wedding* band."

Scott caught up. "Engraved with two joined hearts."

Lexi looked at her mother's ring and thought about Devon's engraving equipment. "Do you think he might have engraved it? It has two dates, my birthday and my parents' wedding..." She paused, stunned that she hadn't thought of it before. "That can't be their wedding date. They were married in the 1800s."

Dick stroked his jawline. "So the answer to the puzzle is 05161980. But what does it mean? Perhaps each number stands for a letter and it spells a word. Otherwise, what? A safe? A lock? A telephone number? No, of course not. What has eight digits?"

Lexi and Scott grinned at each other.

Dick frowned. "What am I missing?"

Scott became animated. "The puzzle on his desk."

Dick's face was blank. "The what?"

"Devon had a puzzle on his desk in the archive. It has eight brass wheels."

Lexi groaned. "He said as much when I met him. He told me the puzzle could only be solved by someone with the combination to hand. The sneaky old bastard. Can we go now?"

Scott frowned. "I've lost my archive privileges."

Lexi pulled out her ID. "Where's your ID?"

He took it out.

Lexi tapped her ID to his. When Scott looked again at his ID, it read, "Assistant Archivist."

CHAPTER TWENTY-SEVEN

S cott walked into the office. All of his legacy colleagues now had black eyes. The mages looked worn out. He tried not to look at any of them and barely glanced at Beavis' empty desk.

One of them stood. "She wants you."

"Okay." Scott nodded and headed for his office door.

"Now." The voice came from so close behind him he felt the guy's breath on his neck.

Scott turned. He looked the black-eyed demon legacy in the face. "I said, okay."

The legacy heard the danger in Scott's voice and didn't seem so sure of himself. He backed away from Scott. The mage stepped into his office, picked up a couple of files, and headed for the hall.

He had the clearance to teleport up to the executive level but wanted the time to think. He called the elevator and pondered what Azatoth might want.

Does she know Lexi is back?

When the elevator arrived, he stepped in. He didn't want to go up. He wanted to go down to the archive and spend the day in Devon's dimensional pocket. He hit the executive level button.

A black-eyed young man sat at Nora's desk.

Scott walked into Azatoth's office. "I haven't seen Nora for a couple of days."

Azatoth smiled. "She took a personal day."

Scott blinked. He didn't know how to respond. He couldn't imagine what sort of personal day a rotting zombie would need to take.

Azatoth rolled her eyes. "I'm kidding. I killed her. The flies were too much."

Scott frowned.

"Don't look at me like that. Your girlfriend killed her first. My kill was sloppy seconds at best. And when I say sloppy." Azatoth made a vomiting gesture.

Scott maintained a stony expression. "You wanted me for something?"

Azatoth stared at him.

Scott felt the chill of whatever the demon was thinking of doing to him.

She smiled. "We have a disturbance in the force. Or to be more precise, in the archives. It seems to have perked up considerably." She walked from behind the desk and sat on the edge, facing him. "You wouldn't know any reason why the archives would suddenly become so chipper, would you?"

Scott narrowed his eyes. "No." He almost said, "You did threaten to butcher me," but stopped when he remembered he had been in a trance at that point.

"You're sure?"

He shrugged. "Positive."

Azatoth scrutinized him for a long moment. "Take a look for me, would you?"

Scott nodded. "I'll see if Eric's free."

Azatoth frowned. "Why?"

Scott wondered if she was messing with him again. "You said I lost my archive privileges and could only go down there with Eric or Millicent."

"Oh, right. Well, I lied."

"I'll get down there." Scott walked toward the door.

"Oh, Scott?"

He paused.

Azatoth smiled. "I sent Mark over to check on you because I was worried about you. But he and his friend seem to be missing."

Scott feigned surprise. "Oh, that was Mark? I thought they were there to rob the place."

"What did you do?"

"I burned them alive." Scott walked out the door.

After two seconds of silence, Azatoth howled with laughter. The sound of it reverberated in Scott's ears all the way to the archives level.

He entered the archives and something crunched underfoot. When he lifted his shoe, he found a pile of broken glass. There was another little pile on Devon's desk and another at the edge of the stacks. He smiled. They were Azatoth's spying devices.

"Any more?" he muttered and was rewarded with more shattering.

The archives stretched a mile in each direction, but he knew he was alone here, although he didn't know how he knew.

"You need to calm down," he murmured.

A book flew past his head and danced in the air.

Scott ducked. "I'm not kidding. This is causing problems."

He moved quickly to the desk and started moving the numbers around on the puzzle.

Zero, five, one, six, one, nine, eight, zero.

The lights in the room went crazy, and books levitated as the panels on the box whizzed forward and back then lined up. The puzzle became solid, then popped open.

So did the door.

Eric entered and stared at him. "What are you doing?"

Millicent entered behind him, looking at the flickering lights before turning her attention to Scott.

Scott shrugged. "She asked me to see if I could figure out what's going on in here."

They stood at the opposite side of the desk, but the row of books along the back edge hid the puzzle from their view.

Millicent asked, "Any luck?"

Scott felt as though keeping his gaze away from the box was a physical fight.

"If almost getting my head caved in by *The Third Council's Treatise on Magical Theory* is lucky, then yes. Otherwise, no." Scott could see a slight glint of metal coming from the box. *Don't notice it. Don't notice it. Don't notice it.*

"While you're here, put these away." Eric dumped an armful of books on the desk, and the lid wobbled slightly and started to lift up.

Millicent dumped a large hardback register on top of the pile so that the spine was upmost. It blocked Eric's view of the edge of the open box. She pointed at the writing on the spine. "See this? It says 1910, not 1990. It took me days to find it. Whoever wrote the dates on this needs to have their fingers broken."

"I'm sure if it was written in 1910, they're probably already quite dead." While he leaned forward and looked carefully at the scrawl, Scott slid his hand into the open box, and transferred the contents to his dimensional pocket, then closed it with a soft click. Turning one panel on the box returned it to its original, ethereal state. The lights in the archive flickered faster and brighter.

Scott took hold of the register and laid it with the others. "I'll make sure it goes back in the right place."

Eric scanned the desktop.

Millicent rolled her shoulders, then turned to Eric. "I'm going to need coffee before we start on all this again."

Eric stared at her for a beat. "Fine. You could have said that upstairs." He strode out the door ahead of her.

Millicent turned back, briefly glancing at Scott before they left. Her look said, "Do whatever you're doing and get out of my way."

Scott had an uneasy alliance with the other mage, but it seemed that as long as their activities didn't appear to be in direct conflict with each other, she was willing to let him go about his business. That was okay with him.

The door closed behind them, and Scott blew out a breath in relief. He called the items back into his hand and opened it to find three brass numbers with holes in them and a key. Door numbers. Two, two, two. He dropped them into his bag, pulled out his cell phone, and fired off a text to Dolores.

I'm coming now.

Scott reached the door and turned around. The lights flickered again. "You need to calm down. You're going to get us into trouble."

The lights dimmed, and he left.

He crossed the street and walked down it. A glance through the coffee shop window told him Eric and Millicent were already being served. He stepped up to the door of the insurance office and opened it.

CHAPTER TWENTY-EIGHT

L exi was passing an empty plate to Dolores when the door opened. She turned to see Scott entering.

The little fae woman smiled at Scott. "She's eaten me out of house and home."

Lexi delivered what she hoped was her most innocent face. "I haven't eaten since—"

"Since McDonald's?" Scott smirked.

Lexi sat up about to defend herself but admitted, "No. I've had a bag of chips since then."

Their eyes locked for a fraction of a second longer than usual. Something had changed with them, but now wasn't the time to explore it. Lexi sighed inwardly. They might never get the chance to explore it.

"Were you able to get into the puzzle?" Lexi followed Scott over to the table where Dick sat waiting.

Scott placed the brass numbers on the table one at a time, then the key.

Dick sat forward. "Hmm. Interesting." The vampire's eyebrow raised as he dangled the key between his fingers. "My old room key from the Chelsea Hotel, and these would be the missing door numbers from the back entrance. Another portal?"

Lexi brushed pastry crumbs from her shirt. "There's only one way to find out. Let's go."

Dolores threw up her hands. "Thank goodness. It'll give me time to replenish my food stocks."

Lexi rolled her eyes. "Can you drop us on West Twenty-second Street?"

Dolores pointed. "Straight through the door."

Scott picked up the numbers and the key. Before Lexi left, she turned to Dolores. "Tell Jonathan, Akeem, and Philippe to make their way to the gate and wait. We're going to get them out of there."

Dolores raised an eyebrow. "How?"

"I haven't figured that part out yet," Lexi admitted before following Scott and Dick to the back of the hotel.

Scott took the brass numbers from his bag. "I didn't bring any screws." He held one up to the wall over the worn outline. It jumped from his hand and stuck to the wall. "Okay."

He presented the other two, and they attached.

The door appeared.

"Here we go again." Lexi stepped up to the door and opened it.

Not much had changed. The lighting seemed less antiquated, and the fire extinguishers were new.

Music filled the upper floors.

Dick's shoulders dropped into an uncharacteristic slouch. "Oh, dear God, it's the eighties. You're on your own." He turned back to the door, but Lexi and Scott grabbed his arms.

Lexi pulled him along the hallway. "Come on, Dick. You survived it once."

Dick grimaced. "I survived the eighties by renting a house in the middle of nowhere and staying there for a decade."

Scott grinned. "I like eighties music."

Dick rolled his eyes. "*Quelle surprise!*"

Lexi glanced up the stairwell as they headed down the hall. "Did you still have your place here?"

"I still paid rent, but I sublet the room. My beautiful Chelsea had gone to the dogs by then. I couldn't even get a decent meal. Everyone was drugged up to the eyeballs and it made me nauseous."

Lexi scoffed. "Are you telling me no one was taking drugs in the sixties?"

Dick shrugged. "Different drugs."

They stood at the bottom of the stairs. "Archive, or my room?"

Scott looked up. "The clues are leading us to your room. I say we go there first."

Dick frowned as they reached the lobby. He was right. Rather than the bohemian vibe the place had exuded in the sixties, this was seedy. The check-in desk now had a screen of bulletproof glass, and drug deals were taking place in the open where previously groups of musicians had huddled together, playing music and discussing their craft.

Dick turned away and led the way up to his room.

He paused at the door. "I don't know what we're going to find in here. Remember, it wasn't my room anymore." He turned the key and opened the door.

Dick's art was gone. It had been replaced by posters of Cher and Madonna.

Though the room had been even more cluttered with paintings and furniture when Dick had inhabited it, it now seemed somehow smaller.

A man stood at the window looking out onto 23rd Street. He turned away from the window, and Lexi saw it was Devon. He was quite old but hadn't gained the years of the Devon she had first met. She narrowed her eyes, trying to work out his age.

Devon smiled. "I'm not the Devon of this time. He's downstairs in the archive. He's got quite a busy day ahead of him."

The three entered the room.

Scott asked, "When did you create this portal?"

"Today. I've had a busy day, too." He sat in the armchair. "So far, I've created the portal you used to find me in 1968. I've been to 1989, found your mother stumbling confused through Las Vegas, raving about demons, and extracted her memories to ensure her and your safety. I also gave her the ring I engraved with the clue that brought you here to 1984."

Lexi blinked. "That does sound like a busy day."

Scott asked, "So, why are you here now?"

"I had a delivery on this day. A collection of documents from Salem. Among them, I found a very old scroll with my own seal. I suspected the spell you had been seeking might be there, but I never got to read them." Devon glanced at his watch and then at Lexi. "And you're due down in the archives shortly."

Lexi crossed her arms and leaned against the wall. "While I've got you here, I have a question. How can we get into the room with the elixir?"

Devon tilted his head. "Why do you need to get into there? Wait, can you be vague so I can help but not know too much about the future?"

Lexi opened her mouth but paused, trying to figure out the best way to approach the problem without messing up Devon's timeline.

Dick put out a hand. "I've got this. How would one fix the elixir if, hypothetically speaking, someone emptied a gallon of demon blood into it? Hypothetically."

Everyone stared at Dick.

He shrugged. "What? I said hypothetically. Twice."

Devon pinched the bridge of his nose.

Scott gazed around the room. "We haven't popped out of existence." He narrowed his eyes at Devon. "What does happen when you alter the timeline?"

"I don't know. I've been careful not to do anything stupid." He gave Dick a withering look, but the vampire was plucking at an invisible dust mote on his sleeve and the effect was wasted.

Scott asked. "How do we fix the elixir?"

Dick crossed his arms. "Why would you want to? Kidnapping children and using them to create an army of legacies seems somewhat repugnant."

Devon's face creased in disgust. "Where do you think the first legacies came from? Humans were part of the first accords, and what's more, most of the first legacies were the children of the witch-hunters."

Lexi's jaw dropped. She didn't even know how to process that news.

Dick looked unimpressed. "What were the first mages? Vampire hunters?"

Devon shrugged. "No one knows where we came from. The best guess is that it was an evolutionary leap. As best as anyone can tell, we spontaneously appeared all over the Earth at roughly the same time."

Dick's attention returned to his sleeve. "It was a rhetorical question."

"Very well, I'm not going to give you a history lesson right now. But you need the elixir to cure anyone who has been altered." Devon narrowed his eyes as he watched Scott wandering around the room. "Actually, this makes sense now." He pointed at Lexi and Dick. "You two go down to the archive. I directed this portal to this moment in time because we've just had the delivery of scrolls from the Salem office. Hopefully, you'll find it quite useful. Don't mention to me that I'm up here. I don't want to give myself a headache. You've got until Scott comes down to find what you need."

Lexi and Dick headed out.

Scott didn't look happy to be separated. "What are we going to do?"

Devon smiled. "We're going on a little adventure."

CHAPTER TWENTY-NINE

Scott and Devon spoke for a half-hour before the older man stood and put out his arms, weaving them around in a complicated fashion while Scott watched intently. The air rippled and spun before revealing a dimly-lit library. Devon picked up a bag from the floor and pulled out two black robes. He passed one to Scott and put one on himself. He stepped through the portal, and Scott followed him.

They stood in the dark recesses of an upper-level while movement and conversation went on below.

Scott peeked out to see twenty-six mages. Thirteen were sitting in a circle facing inward. They lay back on the floor, and the thirteen remaining mages each placed a finger on their foreheads and sent them to sleep. They then placed pieces of yellow stone onto their chests and stepped back.

Another mage walked into the center of the circle with a scroll and read from it as the standing mages held their hands above the yellow stones and flooded them and the mages with light.

The mage in the center finished reading from the scroll and stepped out of the circle.

Scott watched the man as he put the scroll on a table at the side of the room. He noticed that Devon was watching him, and they both nodded. They needed that spell.

Devon turned around and looked through the scrolls on the shelves beside them. He lifted up scrolls and kept looking back down at the one on the table. Finally, he selected one and hid it within his robes.

The mages opened their arms, causing light to flow from their fingers and pulse around the circle. The light became too bright to look at. The mages stepped back as the light enveloped those who were lying on the floor. Slowly, the light pulsed until it dimmed and disappeared completely. The yellow stones had gone.

One by one, the mages sat up.

One of them looked around, alarmed. "I can't feel my legacy."

A tall mage clapped him on the back. "Don't fear, Mortimer. We will reverse the spell when you return. How do you feel?"

Mortimer put a hand to his chest. "Powerful."

"You are. That will increase a thousandfold when you enter the demon realm. You will obliterate the foul beast that has plagued us, and you will return heroes." The tall mage picked up the scroll and took the staircase.

Scott panicked, thinking they were going to be caught.

Devon touched his arm and directed him to go into the next aisle.

Scott moved quickly out of sight.

"What are you doing up here?" the mage demanded.

Scott's heart leaped in his chest.

The mage's suspicion faded. "Oh, it's you, David."

Scott frowned, wondering who else was up there that he hadn't seen.

Devon answered, "Yes. Just me. Can I help you?"

The man thrust the scroll at Devon. "I have a scroll to be destroyed. Make sure it happens."

Devon accepted the scroll with a nod. "As you wish."

Scott's heartbeat slowed as the man's footsteps retreated. He was about to step out when Devon shoved the scroll into his hand. Smoothly, the other scroll appeared in Devon's hand as the footsteps grew louder again.

"If you don't mind, I'd like to watch you destroy it."

"Of course." Devon placed the scroll onto the desk, sprinkled green powder on it, and whispered, "Burn without flame."

The scroll turned to ash.

From his hiding place, Scott tried to figure out what the green powder was, but he couldn't identify it.

The mage was also curious. "What is in the bottle?"

Devon explained, "It burns without fire and does not allow the action to be reversed. The scroll is gone forever."

The man muttered some words at the ash, but nothing happened. "Excellent." He walked away.

Scott noticed the shelf beside him had many such bottles. He snatched one and slipped it into his dimensional pocket.

When the mage had gone, Scott stepped out. "So, we just take the scroll with us?"

"Not quite." Devon took a wax stick from his pocket, pressed it against the string holding the scroll closed, and whispered. The wax melted, and he pressed his signet ring onto it. "This is my seal. Now the scroll cannot be opened without it." He pushed the ring into Scott's hand, then pushed the scroll into the middle of another scroll and ran a finger along the edge, turning it green.

Scott was confused. "Why don't we just take it with us?"

Devon shook his head. "Because I recognized my seal on this scroll two hundred years later but had no idea how it got there. I had been moments from investigating it when I was disturbed. As I said, I try not to interfere with the timeline. The scroll is waiting for you in the archive, as are your friends. We must leave."

Devon opened the portal, and they stepped back through it.

Scott had a question. "Why did that guy call you David?"

"What would you do if you had the ability to visit any moment in time?" Devon asked.

Scott shrugged. "I don't know. Kill Hitler, maybe?"

Devon sighed. "And now we're back to disturbing the timeline. I don't just drop myself into important moments in time. I visit many times, anything up to a year before. I make sure that people are familiar with my face. I give myself a name. I'm a visitor from another town, a transfer from another office. If I go to a Kindred office, whatever time I'm in, the archives accept me. If the archives accept me, everyone accepts me."

CHAPTER THIRTY

L exi grabbed the door handle of the broom closet and muttered the words that Scott had told her to use. When she opened the door, she found very little had changed in the archive since they'd last entered in the late nineteen sixties.

A buzz came from deep within the stacks. They followed the sound until they found Devon crouching over his engraving equipment. He was making numbered brass plates for the shelves. They stood silently, waiting for him to finish the intricate scrollwork around the numbers.

When he looked up, he jumped in surprise, then frowned. "Oh, no. Not again." He removed his glasses.

Lexi opened her mouth to speak, but a nearby shuffling sound made him put a finger to his lips.

Devon walked to the end of the aisle and looked out. A sour expression crossed his face. He indicated they should stay there and remain quiet before marching toward the interloper.

His voice rose in indignation a moment later. "What do you think you're doing? You're not allowed in that section and you know it. Get out before I revoke your archive privileges."

"You wouldn't dare, old man. My father would have your job, and if he doesn't, I'll be your boss one day. Don't you forget it."

Lexi peeked out. It was a young man, she guessed early twenties. She recognized him, turned back to Dick, and mouthed, "Caleb."

The young Caleb was already beginning to get a paunch, and his hair was thinning.

She considered how easy it would be to decapitate him right now and save herself a boatload of grief.

Dick sensed what she was thinking. He put a hand on her shoulder and gently pulled her back into the shadows.

"We'll see what your father has to say about this, big man." Devon ushered the young man back to the entrance.

When Devon was seeing Caleb off with a reminder of his threat, she walked over to see what Caleb had been peering at. "Look at this."

Devon joined her. "It's the spell to bind a demon to a person."

Dick looked over her shoulder. "It still shows the animal fat we changed it to last time." He shuddered.

Devon put his hands on his hips. "What do you want this time?"

Lexi rolled her eyes. She liked young Devon more. "You're the one who sent us back. You chose the time and the place."

Devon didn't have an answer for that, but he still didn't look pleased to see them again. "Where's the other one?"

"He's upstairs with—"

Dick interrupted, "Quentin Crisp."

Devon's face lit up. "Oh really? He's a delightful fellow. Do you know him?"

Dick smoothed an eyebrow. "Good heavens, yes. Quite well, in fact. We're here because you've had a delivery of historical documents from the Salem archive."

Devon nodded and started walking. "This way. I haven't been

through them properly yet, but I've already found one or two items of interest. What are you looking for?"

Lexi followed behind them. "You didn't tell us."

"That's a shame." Devon stopped in front of a mountain of scrolls.

Dick raised an eyebrow. "Which ones are the new ones?"

Devon spread out his arms. "All of them."

Lexi rolled up her sleeves. "How are we supposed to know when we've found it?"

Devon gave them a grim smile. "Don't ask me. Perhaps you should have asked me." He chuckled and left them to it.

Lexi grabbed a scroll, opened it, and read a few words. "Witch trials." She closed the scroll and put it to the side.

Dick did the same. "Witch trials."

After twenty minutes, the piles to the sides of them had grown.

Dick paused. "What if we're supposed to be looking at all this witch trial stuff? We could be missing something relevant." He read more deeply into the scroll in his hand, then grimaced. "Nope. Not reading that." He tossed it onto the pile and reached for the next one

Lexi grabbed the next. "This one's a spell." She read for a few seconds. "Know anyone with warts?"

Dick screwed up his face. "No."

"Know anyone who wants them?" Lexi quipped.

They both said, "Millicent," at the same time and laughed. She dropped it and continued the search. She grabbed the next and scrolled down a few inches. "Witch trials."

The pile was almost finished, and they'd found nothing of interest. Lexi threw another one over her shoulder but didn't hear it hit the pile. She turned.

"How's it going?" Scott held the scroll.

"About as well as it looks. Ninety percent of this stuff is about the witch trials. One gruesome account after the next. What remains can't possibly be what we're looking for."

Scott bent down and retrieved a scroll with green edges. He tapped it, and a smaller scroll slipped out. It had a wax seal. "How about this one?"

Lexi narrowed her eyes. She snatched the scroll from his hand and tried to open it. "It's broken."

Scott took the ring and pressed it to the scroll. The wax fell off.

Lexi snatched it back, narrowed her eyes suspiciously at Scott, and unrolled it.

"To alter the source of a mage's magicks." Lexi's jaw dropped. "No fucking way! How did you do that?"

Scott shrugged. "Just lucky, I guess. What is it?"

She narrowed her eyes at the mage. "I'm betting you could make an educated guess."

Dick dropped the scroll in his hand. "I can't. What is it?"

"It's instructions on how to create a shadow mage."

Dick narrowed his eyes. "This is what Azatoth has been looking for. Isn't this bad?"

Lexi barked a laugh. "Are you kidding? You might be perfectly fine with living forever. Me? Not so much. If we can reverse engineer this spell, it will make me normal again."

Dick shook his head slowly. "With this, she can make Alicia the perfect host and never have to leave. Then she can open the portal herself and make a bunch of shadow mage hosts from those lunatics on the council. More importantly, all the people she's been keeping alive as leverage against you, i.e., *us*, specifically *me*, are expendable."

Scott put a hand on Dick's shoulder. "What's your problem? We're not taking this out of here."

The vampire looked confused. "We're not?"

Scott shook his head. "No. Like the last one, I'll memorize it, and we can destroy it. You can do it yourself if you like."

"Fine. I don't want to know anything about the contents." Dick wandered away while Lexi and Scott spread out the scroll and read it.

A minute later, Dick was back. "Are you done?" He placed a brass trash can on the desk.

"You're serious about destroying it, aren't you? Okay." Lexi released the bottom of the scroll, and it rolled back up.

She dropped it into the can, and Scott pulled a little bottle out of his pocket. He handed it to Dick. "Sprinkle this over it and leave it. I'll be back to burn it. I just need to speak to Devon."

Scott headed back into the stacks.

Dick opened the jar and studied it. "What is it?"

Lexi shrugged. "Not a clue. I've never seen it before."

Dick sniffed at it and sneezed. The powder billowed out, and a cloud of it settled on the pile of scrolls.

Lexi and Dick both froze. Nothing happened.

Dick shrugged. "My bad." He dumped the rest of the powder on the scroll in the can, then nudged Lexi.

She stepped back. "What? He said he'd be back to burn it."

Dick shrugged. "Can't you just *incendio* or whatever?" He waved his fingers.

"No."

Dick waited two seconds, then pulled out a lighter and touched it to the corner of the scroll. A flame curled up and consumed the scroll.

Lexi rolled her eyes. "Happy?"

"I believe I am." Dick flashed Lexi a smug grin and led the way to the exit, where Scott and Devon were deep in discussion.

Lexi asked, "Are you ready to go?"

Scott frowned. "I need to destroy the scroll."

"No, we took care of it." Lexi turned to leave, and the others followed.

They headed back up to Dick's room.

Devon was waiting for them. He sighed sadly. "How did it go?"

Lexi gave him a thumbs up. "We found what we needed. Thank you."

"I imagine everything is progressing as expected." Devon shook his head. "I expect the alarm will sound shortly. We should go. The place is going to be filled with Kindred."

Lexi furrowed her brow. "Alarm?"

Devon frowned. "I assume it was underway when you left."

They looked at each other. No one knew what he was talking about.

The old man scowled, then drew a circle in the air and muttered. They saw the archives through the portal. They were ablaze.

Scott's jaw dropped. "Did we do that? How? I used the green powder. It should have turned to ash."

Lexi grimaced. "Dick used his lighter."

"Don't look at me," Dick protested. "You let me do it."

Scott looked from her to Devon. "Is that the famous archive fire? *We* started it?"

A flame shot out of the portal and singed the drapes in the room. Devon jumped back and closed the portal. "Time to go." He stepped to the bathroom door and waved his hand in a complicated configuration in the air, then turned to see them lined up behind him. "Your exit is downstairs, remember?"

"Right!" Scott grabbed Lexi and Dick and translocated them down to the exit and through the time portal in the back door.

Once they were on Twenty-second Street, they took a breath.

Scott looked at them. "I can't believe we started that fire."

Dick facepalmed. "I'm so sorry. I should have waited for you to come back."

Scott patted his back. "No, you shouldn't. That fire happened. If it hadn't, things would be worse now. A lot worse."

Lexi closed her eyes and checked the seeing ball in Alicia's dimensional pocket. "Ew!"

Scott and Dick asked, "What?"

"Azatoth's throwing up again. Every time I check on her, she's puking. What the hell's going on? I think I should see Alicia."

"I need to get Jesús out of Palm Springs." Dick tapped his cell phone.

Moments later, Dolores appeared with her fae door. "Your carriage awaits." She turned to Lexi. "What about you?"

"We're going to Phil's. I need to see Bryan and Alicia."

The fae woman nodded. "I'll meet you there."

They disappeared through the door.

CHAPTER THIRTY-ONE

L exi and Scott met Dolores at Phil's and were shown to his office without going through the restaurant. He opened the maze, and Bryan was waiting at the door.

Lexi dreaded seeing her sister. She couldn't imagine what condition she would be in after months with the demon inside her body.

Bryan pulled them into his dimensional pocket and opened the door to Alicia's.

She had her back to them, and to Lexi's shock, she was juggling three striped balls.

Bryan, Lexi, and Scott just stood there.

Bryan cleared his throat.

Alicia spun and her face became animated. "You're back!" She hugged her sister. "Thank God." She turned to face Scott. "Did you get word to your friends in time? It's in touch with the demon realm, or whatever it is. It told you this amazing story about where it came from but then had you counseled. And the weird experiments! I've been freaking out about being unable to warn people. Well, I warned the counselor, but that guy didn't make it out of the office alive. At least he didn't give me up to the demon."

Scott stared at the juggling balls. "Um, we've warned them."

"Shouldn't you be out protecting people, then?" Alicia sounded annoyed.

"We've got people working on it." Lexi was beginning to feel like her sister wasn't happy to see her.

Alicia put the balls down. "Did you know they were going to raid Phil's?"

Lexi blinked. "Actually, no. We didn't."

Outside in Phil's office, Lexi turned to the minotaur and relayed the message.

Phil rushed out of the room.

Lexi returned her attention to her sister. "Are you okay? Why is Azatoth puking everywhere?"

Alicia grinned. "It's great, isn't it? I've managed to take back control of my stomach. Watch this." She pointed at a screen that allowed her to see through her eyes. Then she reached out, balled her hand into a fist, and twisted it.

Azatoth leaped up from her desk and into the bathroom. She vomited into the toilet.

Bryan took her hand. "Why are you doing that?"

Alicia looked delighted. "I'm trying to kill it. I don't know how I'm still standing. We haven't kept a meal down for weeks."

Her husband was horrified. "You need to stop this. You're killing yourself!"

She shook her head. "No."

"What?" Bryan looked from the screen to Alicia.

Alicia's expression was resolute. "I'm going to do what you should have done. What all of you have failed to do."

Lexi shook her head. "Just give me some time. A day, give me a day. I met our dad, and I'm trying to release him from the demon realm."

Phil came back into the office. "I've emptied the restaurant. All staff and customers have gone."

A loud smash sounded. "It's started. They're in." He locked his office door.

Lexi, Bryan, Dolores, and Phil went into the maze.

Phil closed the door and twisted the doorknob in the opposite direction. The door disappeared, and the only thing left was the crystal doorknob.

Scott asked, "Can they get in here?"

"The question you should be asking isn't can they get in. It's can they get out?" Phil held up the doorknob.

Lexi remembered that Phil's was a dimensional pocket. "They're in that?"

Phil nodded. "And the answer is yes, eventually they'll get out."

Phil's face was slowly becoming more and more bull-like. "I'm slowing the process as much as I can, but we need to move."

He opened another door, and a putrid smell wafted out.

Bryan covered his nose. "What the hell is that?"

Phil grinned. "It's another dumpster realm. But this one is full, so it's officially closed."

Lexi grimaced. "I've never understood the point of those things."

"This is one way new realms are formed," Phil explained. "Think of it as a compost heap. Eventually, the conditions will be right for it to become its own bio environment."

Phil threw the doorknob in through the door and closed it. "It's going to take them a very long time to get out of there."

Scott blinked. "But that's your restaurant and your spa."

Phil laughed. "I'll have a new one in a couple of days. I've been thinking about giving the place a new look."

Lexi hadn't finished with Alicia. She felt strongly that her sister was hiding something from her. She turned back to her in Bryan's dimensional pocket. "Listen—"

Alicia put her hand up and looked at the screen. "Shh! Something's happening."

Azatoth left the office and went down in the elevator to the archive level but turned right toward the blank wall opposite. She drew a pattern in the air and muttered a word. The wall disappeared, and the elixir room appeared in front of her.

"What did she say?"

Alicia kept her eyes on the screen but answered, *"Ánoixe.* It's Greek. It uses a lot of Greek in spells and some other archaic languages I don't recognize."

Azatoth joined Eric. They stood together and watched Millicent as she laid out items on a tabletop. "She looks skittish."

Eric shook his head. "She'll be fine. It's just nerves. She's been on board since I told her I had feelings for her."

"And do you?"

"Don't you already know that?" Eric tapped his head.

Azatoth paused. "I'd say you're hoping that when I possess her, I will obliterate her vile personality."

Alicia tapped her head the same way Eric had. "Oh, I forgot to mention that Azatoth's consciousness is also renting space in Eric's brain right now."

Eric sneered. "Do you think she knows what's coming?"

Azatoth shook her head. "I doubt it. She'd be looking a sight more nervous if she did."

Lexi turned to Alicia and did a double-take when she saw her sister was eating popcorn. "What are they planning?"

"They're going to magically mummify Millicent to stop her from flying apart when Azatoth possesses her. Azatoth is only going to use her body to store her essence. It's already present in Eric's mind, the same way it was in Caleb's. It's a temporary solution until they can find a shadow mage, but the connection will be stronger once the essence is inside Millicent." Alicia turned back to Lexi. "I mean, she is vile, but I wouldn't wish that on anyone."

Bryan narrowed his eyes. "How is Azatoth planning to get out of you?"

"No idea." Alicia stepped in front of the screen. "You need to get to your friends and help them. The attacks are starting."

Lexi stepped up and put her arms out to her sister. When she was close enough, she clamped them onto her shoulders and moved her aside to see the screen. "What are you playing at?" She didn't need to wait for an answer from Alicia.

Eric had taken out a sword and was sharpening it. "I'll make it quick."

Bryan's jaw dropped. "No!"

Scott pulled out his cell phone. On the screen, Azatoth looked at her own. "Oh, look, it's Scott." She pressed the speaker icon. "Hi, Scotty. Let me guess; you can't come to work today because you're visiting friends in Palm Springs? New Orleans? Or perhaps you're at Emmersley House?"

Scott and Lexi grimaced. They hadn't thought of Emmersley. The elderly supes were unprotected. Dolores pulled out her cell phone and began texting furiously.

Scott continued his conversation. "What? No, I'm in the archives. I think the stern admonishment I gave the spirits worked. I'm finding all kinds of documents I've been looking for, including what I think is the ritual to release you from Alicia. I'll come up to your office."

Millicent approached and stared at the cell phone with a frown. "I need some things from the archives. I'll meet you there." She spun on her heel and marched out.

Eric smirked at Azatoth. "She even walks angrily. Honestly, I think you've got your work cut out for you when you get in there."

Lexi nodded. "So, the reason she's diverting our attention everywhere is to ensure there are no interruptions during this ritual."

Alicia shoved another handful of popcorn into her mouth.

She noticed Lexi was staring at her and offered the bucket to her. Lexi shook her head, more in disbelief at Alicia's nonchalant behavior than rejecting the offer of popcorn. She returned her attention to the screen.

In the maze, Phil was holding another doorknob. He pushed it into a wall, and a door appeared. "This is your exit. It's one way; you won't be able to return this way." He addressed Dolores. "I need your help for a moment."

The two went into the maze.

Bryan and Alicia said their goodbyes. Once again, they sealed the pathway between Bryan's and Alicia's dimensional pockets, then Lexi and Scott left Bryan's.

Dolores came out of the maze without Phil.

They stepped through the door into what looked like a building site.

A quick check behind them revealed a stone wall. The maze, the door, and Bryan were gone.

Lexi squinted into the light. "Where are we?"

Dolores put on a pair of sunglasses. "Crete, a Greek island. This is the palace of Knossos."

Scott pulled a piece of paper from his dimensional pocket. It was a copy of the sheet from the 1968 archives with added notes. "I had a panic attack. That place is a mess. I had to print it again."

Dolores' phone rang. She looked at the screen, then glanced at Scott in confusion, "Yes? Yes. I don't want—" She listened again. "Okay. Thank you for calling. I don't require the services of an injury lawyer, but someone I know might. I'll let you know."

Lexi narrowed her eyes at the fae woman. "There are apps to stop those calls."

Dolores rolled her eyes. "I should look into that."

Lexi smiled. "I need to get to the archives. Dolores, can you drop me in New York? I'll translocate from there to the archives."

Dolores called her door, and they walked through it onto a

New York street. Scott had disappeared again before Lexi was through the door.

Dolores looked worried. "I hope he's all right." She turned back to Lexi. "Well, I suppose I should go to Emmersley."

A shadow detached itself from the wall beside them.

"Dolores, it is not your destiny to go to Emmersley House today."

Lexi nearly jumped out of her skin. "Joseph?" She put a hand on her heart. "How does he do that?"

The New Orleans voodoo priest laughed. "My mother was a black cat." He walked heavily, leaning on his staff, but Lexi knew he didn't need it.

Joseph continued. "A half-spirit follows you, Lexi Braxton. A woman who straddles the veil. Even now she holds on, refusing to relinquish her grip on this earth. She has a message for you. 'You forgot something.'"

Lexi turned to Dolores. "Do you have any idea what he's talking about?" She turned back to Joseph. "Who is—"

He was gone.

"He's just showing off." Dolores pursed her lips and turned back to Lexi. "We don't need him for this anyway. The seer from Emmersley, Anne Lown, has called Scott maybe twenty times. 'Lexi forgot something, Lexi forgot something.' But she wouldn't say what. Doubtless, you are the one who needs to learn what it is."

"She called and said the same thing before I left for my off-world sabbatical." Lexi raised an eyebrow. "If it *is* a pair of socks, I won't be impressed."

She closed her eyes for a moment. "Azatoth and Eric are looking at the objects on the altar. There's no sign of Millicent or Scott yet."

Lexi translocated to Emmersley.

CHAPTER THIRTY-TWO

Scott appeared in the antiquities room. He went to the iron maiden, shivering as he opened its doors. The artifact brought back horrific memories. He removed the poison from the spikes. If he'd had time, he'd have removed the spikes, too.

Such a thing shouldn't exist.

He headed through the shelves, around the corner at the end of the room, and out of sight. He was nervous. He'd only seen this done once. He prayed to God it would work.

After focusing his mind on the year, he drew the sigil in the air. A few seconds went by, and he doubted he'd done it correctly. Then the pulsing began. He waited until the bright swirls cleared, then stepped through.

He was in the room with the elixir. The room was as it had been described to him, but this was hundreds of years ago. He realized the room in Kindred HQ wasn't in the same building. It was probably connected in some way to the archives. There wasn't the time to puzzle it out.

Voices startled him. He translocated to the walkway above the huge glass vial. A few more steps took him to a bookcase that hid him from anyone below.

The people belonging to the voices entered. He'd hoped to find the room empty in the middle of the night, but it wasn't to be.

Scott pulled a dark cloak from his dimensional pocket and threw it over his head, further obscuring himself as the conversation below continued.

"Woah! Would you look at that?"

"You haven't seen it before?"

"I've heard about it but not seen it. It's as pretty as they say. The future of Kindred and all of Otherkind."

"Well, I don't know about that. I wonder what it tastes like. Do you think it might be made with rum?"

Scott realized that the night watchmen were loaded.

"I wouldn't risk it for fear of turning into a wolf or a vampire."

Scott chanced a glance. They were settling down at a table off to the side of the room.

"But you've requested to be a legacy, haven't you?

"Yes, but I'm still not going to drink that stuff. You try it."

"If I dropped dead on the spot, you'd take my shoes."

"That I would."

They laughed uproariously.

Scott used the sound as cover as he moved along the platform to the glass cylinder and opened the top. He took a couple of water bottles from his pocket and unscrewed the lids. When he was ready to move, he waved a hand at the men and whispered, "Sleep."

The man facing him dropped his head and started snoring.

"Oh, fine company you are tonight." The other man tapped his companion's face. "Hey."

Dammit, the other one must have a protection spell.

This was the best chance Scott was going to get. It would have been much easier to do this from the bottom.

He filled the bottles and screwed the lids back on, then put them in his pocket and attempted to close the cylinder quietly. As he twisted it closed, it squealed, and the conscious man looked up.

"Hey, you!" The man ran to climb the steps.

Scott waited for him to get near the top, then translocated to the corner of the room, opened his portal, and dashed through. It closed behind him.

He put the bottles on the shelf opposite the iron maiden, then messaged Dolores and headed into the archives. He left the door open a crack and went to find Millicent.

He found her sitting on Devon's engraving desk with her cell phone to her ear.

She jumped when she saw him. "What are you doing? Sneaking up on people like that?"

"I thought you came here to meet me. What are you doing hiding..." Scott paused when he realized her eyes were red. "What's happened?"

She seemed to be struggling with whether or not to tell him something.

"If you don't tell me, I can't help."

Finally, she sighed. "Eric and the demon are up to something. I'm trying to find out what it is. I've bugged the room they're in."

Scott raised an eyebrow. "Ballsy move. Well? what are they saying?"

"They were talking about the ritual. They're planning to transfer Azatoth into me. Then you appear with your spell and mess up what I've got going on."

Scott almost felt sorry for her. "What you've got going on isn't as great as you think."

"What do you know?"

"They're planning to mummify you to stop you from exploding." He shrugged.

Millicent looked horrified. "That can't be true. Azatoth would be doing that to herself."

"She only plans to be inside you temporarily. Her essence will be inside you, but her consciousness will be inside Eric."

Millicent's lip curled in a snarl. "That two-faced bastard. Well, he's going to get more than he bargained for."

Scott wasn't sure he liked the sound of that. "What does that mean?"

She waved a hand. "Nothing. It means nothing. But I'm not taking even the chance of being mummified. I need to get out of here."

He led her to the aisle with the steps and whispered, "Go up and touch the thesaurus." She started up the steps, put her hand on the book, and disappeared.

CHAPTER THIRTY-THREE

L exi's heart was in her mouth as she crept through the front doors. Blood spatters trailed across the walls, floor, and ceiling of the entrance hall. The bloody trail of a dragged body went from the desk to the door leading to the lower floors.

As she followed the trail, she called her katana into her hand and moved silently to the steps. She followed the trail past the swimming pool, which she noted had been remodeled and was now filled for use. The trail stopped at the doors to the steam room.

Thoughts of the lovely elderly people she'd met flashed through her mind. She swallowed and opened the door.

The bodies of nine demonic legacies, slashed and savaged, lay on the benches and floor. Lexi closed the door and turned.

A brown and white pit bull sat in the hall, licking its red chops.

Lexi sighed in relief. "Hello, Phyllis. I'm relieved to see you're well."

The dog shifted. "Lexi, dear. Anne told us you were coming. Everyone's upstairs."

Lexi moved through the crowd of residents in the hallway outside Anne's room. Patrick was coming out with tears in his eyes as she reached the door. She gave him a quick hug and entered. Someone closed the door behind her.

She stood in the low light, watching Anne's chest rise and fall in jerky movements. Her wheelchair wasn't in its usual place. She probably hadn't left the bed in some time.

The old woman's eyes opened. She gazed at the ceiling and drew a sharp breath. "About time."

Lexi stepped to the side of the bed and took the woman's hand. "I hear you've been calling Scott. He thinks you're a sex pest."

Anne laughed, then wheezed, then coughed. "If I were fifty years younger." She pointed at the dresser. "No time. Bottom drawer. The box."

Lexi went to the dresser and opened the bottom drawer. She found the box at the back and pulled it out. She took it over and held it close to the old woman.

"Watch." Anne placed a hand on it and drew two fingers along the top in a wavy pattern. Something clicked.

Anne waved her hand, indicating that Lexi should open the box.

The hinged lid lifted, and Lexi found herself staring at a beating heart.

You forgot something.

The tower.

Her sister on an altar.

The shadow in the veil.

Azatoth.

Punching through, ripping out the heart of…not a demon, but a possessed shadow mage.

An immortal shadow mage.

The heart of the shadow.

Anne's eyes were closed, but she had a smile on her face. "Finally, I can get some rest."

Her eyes didn't open again.

Lexi left the room and closed the door behind her. The others knew Anne had passed.

"What happened downstairs?" she asked Patrick.

"They arrived yesterday, saying they were doing an audit for Kindred."

Lexi was confused. She hadn't heard of any action from the other locations. "When did they attack you?"

Patrick snarled. "We didn't wait. We attacked them."

"Oh. Probably for the best." Lexi closed her eyes and checked the seeing ball. Eric was looking at his watch. It had been about twenty minutes since Millicent had left to meet Scott.

Eric dangled the sword. "Should I put this away?"

Azatoth shrugged. "Maybe. It might be fun to do it this way in any case."

Eric grinned. "It would be good to take Alexa's sister. I owe her for taking my son."

Azatoth snorted. "Give it a rest, Eric. Warren gave *me* the heebie-jeebies, and I'm a demon."

Lexi's cell phone rang. "Scott, what's happening? Eric and Az are getting angsty."

He whispered, "I ran into Millicent. I told her about the mummifying thing, and she freaked out. I hid her in Devon's dimensional pocket."

Lexi winced. "What's your plan?"

"To give them the spell to get the demon out of Alicia without beheading her. Beyond that, no idea."

Lexi kept an eye on the seeing ball.

Eric kept checking his watch. "What's keeping that woman?" He frowned. "I can't sense her."

Azatoth walked across the room and turned to Eric. "Message the teams. They can begin their attacks."

Lexi warned Scott, "They're coming."

"Okay. Tell Dolores everything's in place." Scott disconnected.

Lexi messaged Dolores without taking her eyes off the demon.

Eric readied his sword. "We could start with Scott."

Azatoth shook her head. "Let's wait until we've finished the ritual. He might come in handy if we can't find Millicent."

Lexi snarled. "I need to go. Set some new protections around this place."

She watched as Scott approached Azatoth and Eric in the archives, then translocated herself there, remaining out of sight while she observed through Azatoth's eyes.

Eric eyed Scott suspiciously. "Have you seen Millicent?"

Scott furrowed his brow. "No. I thought you were sending her to meet me?"

Eric looked around. "She was definitely in here a moment ago."

Scott shrugged. "It's a big archive. Have you tried calling her?"

Eric just stared at him.

Azatoth asked, "What have you found?"

Scott showed them the copy of the document. "This must be the ritual Caleb used to put you in there. I'm guessing this part is how to get you back out."

Eric read over the sheet. "Say what you like about Millicent. She was spot on with this part. The extraction looks feasible."

Scott tried not to look shocked. "Millicent already found this?"

Azatoth nodded. "The possession, yes. But not the extraction."

Scott did a mental eye roll, realizing she must have found the spell in his dimensional pocket. For some reason, she was only interested in the possession part. She didn't even pass on the instructions to allow them to get the demon out of Alicia without killing her.

Scott thought he couldn't regret his decision to protect her more.

The sound of Millicent's stamping heels hit the floor for a few seconds before she rounded the corner.

"She's back." Millicent marched toward them with both pieces of stained glass in her hands as she pointed at Scott. "Alexa is back, and he knows it."

Lexi watched as dismay appeared on Scott's face.

CHAPTER THIRTY-FOUR

Dolores appeared in her apartment and collected a few things she wanted to keep. She felt a vibration in the walls. It was starting. She guessed they were going to bust their way in through both doors simultaneously, so she called her fae door. It appeared as a tall mirror on the wall. She grabbed a bottle, then stepped through the mirror.

She came out in Dick's Palm Springs home. She turned back to the fae door and watched as demonic legacies burst into her apartment and ransacked it. They tore up cushions and smashed crockery. The fae woman shook her head and tutted.

Dick stepped up beside her. "What's happening?"

"They're turning over my apartment." She held out the bottle to him. "Here, I saved this for you."

Dick took the bourbon. "My brother, Jack. Thank you." He looked back through the fae door. "Feckless thugs."

The leader was barking commands. "Empty out those drawers. Look under that."

After a minute, they gave up hope of finding anything of use. "There's nothing here." He pointed to a couple of legacies. "You two, stay here in case she comes back. The rest of you come with me." He took out his cell phone and tapped on it as he flung the front door open and walked out. At exactly the same time, the back door opened, and he walked into the room. He looked up. "What the hell?" He turned around, walked out again, and came in through the front. He stood still. "Can anyone translocate out of here?"

Several of them replied, "No."

Dick laughed. "Dolores, dear, that's evil."

"Let's go." She turned away, and they went down the hall. Most of the furniture was gone, and white sheets were draped over the few pieces. "How is it going here?"

"I arranged for Jesús to attend an apprentice program at Ralph Lauren, so he's safely out of the way. I spoke to Edward." Dick sighed. "He says Kindred's had spies floating around for the last few months, but there has been a recent influx. There are currently forty or fifty of them. Most turned up over the last few days. He says they smell funny. Where are we meeting?"

"Kate's bar. I'm ready to head over when you are." She called her door again, and they stepped through, this time to the shifter woman's bar.

Edward saw them enter. "Okay, shields up." He grinned at Dick. "I always wanted to say that."

The witches salted the window ledges and doorways.

The shifter passed a drink to Dick. "Kindred are everywhere. They started moving in a few minutes ago. They've got this place surrounded. I'm not sure what they're waiting for."

"Have you explained what's happening?" Dick asked.

Edward nodded.

Dick spoke to the assembled crowd. "I assume you've already been told they're planning this attack as a distraction. The demon usurper at the top of Kindred doesn't care how many of their own people die."

A voice from the back shouted, "Neither do we. They're monsters now."

"They were monsters before," someone else added.

A witch near the window shouted, "I think they're moving in."

Dick rubbed his hands together. "They think this attack will be a surprise, but we're going to disappoint them. We're going to move so fast they're not going to see it coming."

CHAPTER THIRTY-FIVE

Scott felt sick with betrayal. He knew he should never have trusted Millicent.

He felt his cheekbone crack as Eric's fist hit his face. He flew back several feet, hitting Devon's desk before crashing to the ground.

Millicent looked shocked. "Jesus, Eric. You better not have killed him. We might need him."

Azatoth went to Scott's side.

Scott mentally closed down his dimensional pocket. He was aware that he could only see through one eye.

Is the other eye gone? Is this the vision I had? Is this where my head comes off?

The demon put a hand on his cheek, and he groaned at the movement of his cheekbone crunching back into place. The vision in his eye returned, and he was relieved to realize there were still two of them. The demon put a hand on his head, and he lost consciousness. The last thing he saw was Eric, gazing in confusion at his own fist.

Scott came to in the elixir room. He remained slumped in the chair and kept his eyes closed.

Millicent was giddy with excitement. "This changes everything."

Eric was still looking at his fist. "I don't understand how I hit him so hard."

Azatoth was leaning against the cylinder of black elixir. "Oh, Scotty. I'm so disappointed in you."

Scott shook his head and sat up. "I'm sure you'll get over it."

"How about you call Lexi? Ask her to come over here, and we can all sit down and have a civilized chat about how things are going to go."

Scott snorted. "You're going to be disappointed."

Azatoth shook a finger at him. "Don't be too hasty, Scotty. I know what you're thinking. You think I want you to draw her into a trap, but that's not what I'm asking. I would like you to call her and tell her what the situation is. Let her make up her own mind."

Millicent busied herself at the makeshift altar, placing and rearranging items. She took the bowl containing the mixture designed to mark her as a vessel and sniffed it. She stirred it with a knife and poured some of it into the box beside it.

Eric walked over to watch her. "What are you doing?"

"There's more than enough of the anointing oil here. It sounds like we're going to have to keep some for the other Braxton woman."

Azatoth spoke from behind her, making her jump. "It looks like I'll just be borrowing your body temporarily, Millicent."

Millicent glanced at Scott. "If he's not going to be of any use, can we get him out of here? I don't want him messing this up."

"Good point." Eric called in two demon legacies. "Get him out of here."

They grabbed Scott by the tops of his arms. One of them asked, "Where do you want him?"

"Um…" Eric frowned.

Millicent gave Scott a wink and a smile. "Put him in the iron maiden."

Scott struggled. "No. I'm not going back there. Don't put me back there."

They dragged him out of the room.

CHAPTER THIRTY-SIX

A zatoth rubbed her hands together. "Come on, then, Eric. Get your sword out. Let's get moving."

"Excuse me?" Millicent looked confused. "Surely, if we've got the right spell to get you out of there, it's safer to do it that way? We don't know what the results will be if you just lop her head off."

Eric stepped up beside Millicent and brought the hilt of his sword down on her head.

She crumpled to the floor.

Lexi sat up in her dimensional pocket and rubbed her head. She hadn't seen that coming.

"What the hell? You said if I let you skinwalk, no harm would come to me." Millicent's consciousness was sitting on the floor with her hands over her head.

"I think Eric killed you. No, wait, you're still here. It's okay; you're not dead." Lexi frowned. "Why would he try to kill you right before a ritual he wants you to take part in?"

"He didn't. He's just stronger than he realizes." Millicent stood up and turned back to the screen. "It's weird seeing out of Azatoth's eyes like this."

Lexi viewed the seeing ball.

Azatoth was staring at Eric. "First you nearly killed Scott, then Millicent. I feel like you might have your own agenda, but I can't for the life of me work out what it is."

"If we're not using magic to get you out, we don't need her. I'm sick of the sound of her voice." He lifted the bowl from the altar and splashed the contents on Millicent's face. "There, she's ready."

Azatoth sulked. "I was thinking about her suggestion. She might be right."

"We could get Scott back here."

Azatoth shook her head. "Just wake her up."

In her dimensional pocket, Lexi opened her eyes. "They're going to wake you up. They need you to do the spell to release Azatoth."

"You think it's okay to send me back in there to be mummified?"

"That's not what's going to happen. I'll be there in a minute."

Lexi sent Millicent back to her body. She had a quick look at Azatoth's view.

Eric was gazing at his hands again. "Could it be that having you in my head has made me stronger?"

Azatoth sighed. "Maybe. I don't know. Let's get on with this. You're taking all the fun out of it."

CHAPTER THIRTY-SEVEN

The two legacies dragged Scott, wearing magic dampening cuffs, through the archives into the antiquities room.

One of them grinned, revealing pointed teeth. "I've never seen an iron maiden in real life. This is going to be great."

He opened the doors of the device. "Is it supposed to look like that?"

The other shrugged. "I guess. Just throw him in and see what happens."

"Wait." The first one picked up a water bottle from the shelf behind them. "Purple stuff. Doesn't look important." He shrugged and tossed it in.

The bottle disappeared into the blackness. Scott's jaw dropped. *It was all for nothing.*

The guy turned to his friend. "Right, let's just throw him in—"

A full tequila bottle came flying out of the blackness at speed. It hit the guy in the temple, and he dropped.

Scott caught the bottle before it could hit the ground. The other legacy stared at him and growled, "Don't look at me. I didn't throw it."

The black surface shimmered, drawing the demon thug's attention. He narrowed his eyes and leaned in, jerking as though expecting another bottle to fly out.

No bottle flew out, but a huge wolf did. It hit the guy in the chest.

He went down and found himself on the floor staring at a much more impressive set of pointy teeth than his.

Scott grinned. "Hi, Edward. Long time no see. Don't eat him. I need to try something."

Sebastian came through the portal with blood streaming down his face from his nose. "Who threw this fucking bottle?"

Scott grimaced and pointed at the unconscious guy. "That was a hell of a shot back, by the way."

Kate came out of the inky blackness. "That was me."

Sebastian noticed the cuffs and shook his head. "Dude."

"It went mostly to plan, except Millicent double-crossed me, and I don't know if Alicia's still alive." Scott put his hands up, and Sebastian released him.

Dick came through the door with his cell phone in his hand. "Albin's not picking up. I hope he's okay."

Dolores stepped through and put a folded piece of paper in Scott's hand. "Pop this into your pocket for later. Don't look at it now."

Scott opened the bottle and poured a drop of the thick purple liquid onto both legacies' foreheads. They began writhing on the floor and spitting out pointed teeth. Their eyes returned to normal, and they sat up, confused.

More people flooded through the portal.

When Kira, the witch from Palm Springs, arrived, she passed a box of little atomizers to Scott. "I hear you need these. We use them to make our lavender perfume."

Scott took the box gratefully. "Thanks. You won't remember me, but we've met."

Kira winked. "Oh, I remember, handsome. Caleb's spell to make us forget him stopped working when he died."

Sebastian took a water bottle and transferred the elixir into the fifty atomizer bottles with a quick spell. They handed the bottles out.

"We were only attacked by legacies. Where are all the mages?"

"Asleep all over the building."

The supes continued spilling out into the archive. By the time the bottles were filled, so was the room.

Dolores disappeared through the door and came back. "The New Orleans contingent is coming through."

Geraldine and her wolf pack came through, followed by Anne Bird with James and Sam. They were armed to the teeth with hex bags.

Rosa and Ruby were the last people through.

Ruby looked exhilarated. "There's a hundred or so disappointed pointy-toothed demon legacies about to break through the last barrier, and they're going to be bursting through here any moment."

"Everyone take an atomizer," Sebastian called. "Remember, they've been altered and don't know what they're doing. If we can avoid killing them, we should."

Jess called to Dolores, "Can you let them through twenty at a time so we've got time to move the bodies or unconscious ones out of the way?"

Dolores nodded. "I'll do my best, dear. Here they come."

A demon legacy came into the antiquities room. Anne Bird sprayed her in the face, then Jess yanked her aside for the next one.

One of the shifters complained, "You promised us a fight. This is like a production line."

They came through in a steady stream until Anne went to spray and nothing came out. The legacy snarled at Anne and lunged for her. She was taken out of the air by Ruby, who punched her in the face.

"The elixir, dear," Dolores reminded her.

"Oh, right. Sorry." Ruby took an atomizer from her sister and squirted the legacy in the eye.

"I'll look after her." Anne got up and dragged the legacy, who was spitting blood and howling with a hand over her eye, to where the group of legacies was recovering in the corner.

Someone else had taken over the atomizer welcome party, but Scott had the feeling they were forgetting to swap out the sprays a little too frequently, looking for excuses to fight.

Lexi appeared at the door. "Scott, are you here?"

Scott made his way through the crowd. "Is Alicia okay?"

Lexi nodded. "I'm watching them. Eric nearly killed Millicent."

Scott narrowed his eyes. "Good. She double-crossed me and ratted us out to Azatoth. She knows you're back."

"That wasn't Millicent. That was me," Lexi corrected.

Scott's scowl faded. "No, it was Millicent. She told them you're back and sent me to the iron maiden."

Lexi shook her head. "No, that was me. I winked so you'd know it was me."

"How would that tell me it was you? Eric nearly killed me."

"Yeah, sorry about that. I didn't see it coming. Hang on." She put up a hand to silence him.

The whole room went silent, and everyone looked at her.

"Eric's telling Azatoth he can't get through to the team at Emmersley, and the team at New Orleans has found an empty room. I think the jig's up. He's calling them back. I need to get over there. Things are about to get nasty."

"Well, about time." There was a group whoop.

"Keep the noise down." Lexi left.

Sebastian went to the recovering legacies. "Are you ready to move? We're taking Kindred back. I need you to lead these folks through the building." He pointed at the witches, shifters, and vampires.

Scott joined them. "Get your IDs out." He started tapping them with his own. "You're an assistant curator, you're an assistant curator. Hell, you know where I'm going with this."

"Right, you can all translocate out of the archives. Take two guests each." Sebastian turned to the shifters. "Elixir first!"

CHAPTER THIRTY-EIGHT

L exi watched the room through the seeing ball as she tried to remember the sigil and the word Azatoth had used to enter it. She waved her arms a couple of times but messed up the pronunciation of the Ancient Greek.

Millicent was preparing for the spell. She'd done a good job of delaying it.

Azatoth waved a hand. "Millicent, forget it. This is taking too long. Eric, Plan B."

Eric took out his sword as his cell phone rang. He looked at Azatoth.

The demon rolled her eyes. "Just take the fucking call. I'll be chopping my own head off at this rate."

Eric listened for a few seconds. "The Palm Springs team has just reported in. The targets have gone, and so have most of our people."

Azatoth scowled. "Where the hell are they?"

Lexi huffed in frustration as the portal remained closed. "This isn't working for me." She slashed her arm through the air and the wall exploded, revealing the portal and the room beyond.

"Take a guess," Lexi stated as she entered the elixir room.

"Sister. I've been waiting for you." Azatoth pulled the sword from Eric's hand.

Lexi took out her katana.

The demon raised an eyebrow. "What, no magic sword today?"

"My dad's using it to finish off your buddies in the demon realm." Lexi was rewarded with a scowl.

Azatoth threw a blast of energy at Lexi.

Lexi dived behind the giant glass elixir canister as the lightning bolt shot from Azatoth's hands. The glass smashed, and the elixir flooded across the floor.

Lexi smirked. "Oh, no! You broke your evil army juice."

"I've got enough of an army. I know where your Order friends are. I know where *all* your friends are. And I've got Scott. What's the point of this, Lexi? You're not going to kill your sister. We both know it." Azatoth flicked a finger at Lexi.

Everything went black. It was the same spell the demon had used on her when she trained her. Intuition told her to duck and roll, so she did. She muttered a word, and the blackness disappeared. Her vision returned in time for her to translocate away as the floor erupted from another blast.

The blackness hit her again and again. Each time she shook off the illusion easily and translocated to avoid the inevitable blow, but finally, enough was enough. She closed her eyes.

Azatoth snorted. "Don't tell me you're using the force. This is going to be fun."

Lexi looked through the seeing ball. Viewing through the demon's eyes, she saw the back of her own head. She translocated to behind Azatoth.

Azatoth spun, and Lexi punched her in the face. The demon staggered.

Lexi glanced up to see Eric taking a step toward her. She tightened her grip on the katana.

Millicent put a hand on Eric's arm to stop him. "Let's see how this plays out."

Eric nodded once and stepped back.

"Go, Lexi!" Alicia called from the dimensional pocket.

Lexi froze as she heard her sister's voice through the seeing ball and nearly paid for it. She translocated and saw a blade swipe the air where she had been standing.

The demon translocated again, and Lexi moved to counter.

"Take her head off, Lexi," Alicia screamed at the screen.

Lexi wanted her sister to know she could hear her. "Maybe I should take your head off."

Azatoth scoffed. "You'd do that to your sister's body?"

Lexi's eyes stung. She prayed it wouldn't come to that. "I've got a feeling she'd approve."

"It doesn't matter. You know she's gone." The demon flashed a cruel grin.

Lexi smirked. "She's gone, is she? It would be terrible if you felt nauseous right now."

The demon's eyes widened as she gripped her stomach. She translocated and swept the box containing the anointing oil off the table and over Lexi. As the box fell to the floor, she turned away, bent over, and vomited.

Eric cried in a strangled voice, "No! You promised the power to me."

Lexi translocated behind Azatoth as the demon heaved and brought the *tsuka* of her katana down on her head. The demon dropped limply to the ground.

"Sorry, sis."

Eric growled at Millicent, "We have to end her. The power was supposed to be mine. Ours."

Millicent sneered. "You have only to ask, my beloved."

Light poured from Millicent's hands, and she spoke the spell.

Dark mist containing Azatoth's demonic essence floated up from Alicia's unconscious body. Lexi stared slack-jawed at the ritual oil dripping down her.

That was not good.

The box lay closed at her feet. She bent down and flipped the lid open, hoping it would be enough.

When Lexi looked back up, the mist had disappeared. Her heart hammered. Had Azatoth entered her unseen, or was the demon in the heart?

Lexi paused with her katana, ready for an enemy that could well be herself. Nothing happened.

She looked at Millicent, then back at the heart.

"Behind you," Alicia croaked.

Lexi spun and brought her sword up to fight the new threat.

Eric's right eye was flashing between its natural color and the yellow and black of Azatoth's. His left eye remained white.

Eric shook his head. "How? I don't understand."

Millicent purred, "You wanted Azatoth's power so badly, Eric. Now you've got it. But you won't need to be mummified to hold yourself together. Just don't take the ring and watch off, or the mere presence of the demon will tear you to pieces."

Eric snarled at Millicent. "The aftershave. Very clever."

Millicent raised her chin. "I thought the smell of sadness and disappointment suited you, and it had the added benefit of hiding the odor of tallow. The anointing oil I used on myself was never meant to prepare my body for Azatoth. It was a barrier to stop the demon's essence from coming anywhere near me."

Lexi wanted to slap Millicent for not telling her about this plan.

I poured that useless oil all over the heart.

She had to admit to herself it had been a good thing the oil was fake since Azatoth had just splashed her with it.

Eric's expression was murderous. He took a step toward Millicent but stopped. His eyes flashed, and his voice became soft and calm. It was Azatoth. "Don't mind him, Millicent. Everything has worked out fine." Eric shook his head as he regained control of his body.

Azatoth continued, "But you have made yourself somewhat redundant."

Millicent started to fade but froze in mid-translocation. She gritted her teeth and groaned as she fought the spell that pinned her in place. Finally, she sagged and became solid. She stared contemptuously at Eric.

The white-eyed legacy slashed his arm through the air, and Millicent's body split from the left shoulder to the right hip. The top half of her body slid off ungracefully and landed with a sickening thud.

Eric's eyes flashed black and yellow, indicating that the demon had once again taken control. He stared at Millicent's gory body as his hand went to his stomach. A moment later, the demon grinned. "Marvelous! It seems I'm not going to hurl. This is a definite upgrade, Eric, but we're going to have to chat about who's in charge around here." He flew backward as a bolt of energy from Lexi's outstretched hand hit him square in the stomach.

Lexi smirked. "While you possessed my sister, I tried at all costs to avoid harming her. But now, you've made the mistake of possessing the one human I have no compunction about killing."

Azatoth scrambled to his feet and threw a freezing spell at where Lexi appeared to be standing. The image faded.

Lexi laughed from the other side of the room.

Scott shouted from the hallway, "Lexi!"

Eric's face grinned. He looked up and held out his arms. "Come to me, my children."

Lexi couldn't figure out which one was in control. The legacy was such an evil shit that it was difficult to separate his actions from the demon's. Either way, the face gave away the intention. He was going after Scott.

Lexi translocated her sister to the hallway and put a wall of ice between them, leaving Scott outside.

CHAPTER THIRTY-NINE

H is heart skipping, Scott recognized Azatoth no longer possessed Alicia. He didn't need to ask the question.

Alicia shook her head. "Eric."

Scott raised an eyebrow. "I didn't see that coming."

He stepped back from the portal and blasted the ice wall to no avail. Nothing could get through it. He tried to translocate through but reappeared in the same place.

Alicia punched the wall in frustration. Her enormous strength had not returned.

Scott noticed that her movements were jerky. "Are you okay?"

She nodded. "This is the first time I've used my own body in months. It feels weird. Also, I've been on a starvation diet for weeks. I'm sort of regretting that now."

Three sets of elevator doors simultaneously appeared in the wall and opened.

Demonic legacies streamed out, and their all-black eyes turned to Scott. He tried to translocate back into the archives, but it didn't work. He surmised it was due to his proximity to Lexi's barrier.

He called the atomizer from his pocket. Ten squirts of elixir weren't going to cut it when he was faced with at least thirty pointy-toothed demons. "I don't suppose you'd consider forming an orderly line?"

Scott didn't want to kill these legacies, knowing they were compromised by the tainted elixir. He froze the first few with a wave of his hand, then managed to spray three of them before the rest pushed toward him.

The archive doors at the other end of the hallway opened with a bang as they hit the walls. Most of the legacies turned to face the new threat, but the hall was so full he couldn't see. A moment later, he heard Dolores.

The fae shouted, "Fire in the hole!" and threw something into the middle of the crowd. Everyone dived to the ground, expecting an explosion, including Scott and Alicia.

There was no explosion, but something happened. A figure unfurled, quickly growing and spreading in the middle of the floor. The shape of a man with the head of a bull and long, lethal horns became clear. He towered over the legacies, displacing the ceiling tiles.

Scott's jaw dropped. "Phil?"

In reply, the minotaur bellowed and whipped his horns from side to side. The demon legacies were tossed like rag-dolls. As the unfortunates flew in Scott's direction, he squirted the elixir at them until he ran out.

He considered that he and Alicia might be able to make their way to the other end of the hall when the elevators opened again and the corridor filled with demonic legacies again. The second influx hit Phil with a spell that made him dizzy. He shook his head, sending several of them flying before crashing to the floor. Scott raised a shield around him and Alicia as the legacies advanced.

They were backed up against the barrier when the elevator doors opened a third time, not smoothly as before but with a squeal of resistance like they were being wrenched open. They were.

Two arms reached out of the darkness of the elevator shaft, and a woman crawled out. The hall was suddenly filled with a sickening, pungent smell.

To Scott's disbelief, it was Nora...and she wasn't alone. The former cabal member was in better shape than most of the dead who followed her, staggering to their feet after dragging themselves out of the elevator shaft. If not an army of the dead, they were a decent-sized squadron. They milled among the demonic legacies.

Scott mentally flicked through the spells he knew, wracking his brain to find one that would deal with all the undead at once, but they were still crawling out, and the hallway was full.

I have to do something.

He raised his arms, thinking it might just be safer to blast the place with flames. Before he could act, the undead fell upon the legacies.

"Ye of little faith."

Scott jumped. He found Joseph standing beside him. "They're with you?"

The voodoo priest laughed.

Phil sat up and groaned. He got to his feet and staggered before leaning against the wall with an impaled legacy dangling from one of his horns.

Scott pointed. "Um... You've got a little something."

Phil bent over and shook his head. The body slipped off.

The doors to the archive opened and John Braxton stepped through, followed by Lexi's unit brother Isaac.

The demonic legacies were getting over their horror and fighting back against the dead. The Braxtons were followed by Dolores, members of the Order of the Shadows, and some of the recovering legacies. All armed with weapons and spray bottles, they moved swiftly through the melee, ignoring the dead and distributing squirts of the elixir.

Scott turned to Joseph and pointed at the zombies. "They're not going to cause an epidemic, are they?"

Joseph shook his staff and the dead shuffled back to the elevator shaft, stepping in without complaint. "No, they were just a distraction, but they need to be safely disposed of. It's unsanitary and disrespectful to leave them down there."

The mage grimaced. "Yeah, I don't think we'd pass a Health and Safety assessment."

When the zombies were gone, the legacies and Order members piled into the elevators to find the mages.

Dolores stepped past the legacies, who were spitting out pointed teeth and groaning on the floor. She took a doorknob from her purse and handed it to Phil.

The minotaur pushed it into a wall, and the shape of a door appeared. Phil turned the knob and opened the door to reveal the maze…and Bryan's concerned face.

The mage walked into the hall, then ran to Alicia, scooped her up, and kissed her. "You are so thin."

Dolores put a hand on his arm. "Take her out of here and get her some food."

Alicia shook her head and pointed at the wall of ice. "Lexi's alone in there with Azatoth. We need to find a way through."

Scott sagged. "I've tried everything. I can't get through."

"I think I can help with that." Dick walked through the archive door with Limpet following him.

The thinner demon put his hands and feet on the barrier, and it wavered.

The moment the portal was completed, Scott dived through.

CHAPTER FORTY

Lexi was losing. The fight had been raging between her and Azatoth and Eric for over half an hour. They'd been throwing energy balls and lightning bolts at each other, using swords and anything else at hand to try to best each other. A fight of equal ferocity was going on between Azatoth and his new host. The demon was trying to beat her without damaging her too much since he still wanted to possess her. Eric wanted her dead, or, given that she was immortal, in pieces. He didn't want to give Azatoth up.

And so they fought.

Except they didn't.

Scott appeared through the barrier, followed by Dick, the Braxtons, and Limpet.

Lexi spoke softly to them without taking her focus off Azatoth. "I've glamoured him. He thinks he's strangling me right now."

Scott sounded puzzled. "Why didn't you just kill him?"

Lexi shrugged. "I really wanted to. But I don't know where the essence might go next if I just lop off his head. Best to use the spell, I think."

She pointed at the box on the floor. "The heart has been soaked in an oil designed to stop Azatoth from transferring into it. Can you rinse it off or something? Then get him out of Eric and into the heart. If we're quick, he could be trapped before he realizes he's in a glamour."

Scott went over to the box, which put him in full view of Millicent's body. Lexi saw the look of shock on his face in her peripheral vision. He stumbled backward and stepped into a pool of Millicent's blood.

Reaching out as he slipped, he grabbed Lexi, bringing her down with him. His foot slid out and kicked the box, sending it flying into Eric's leg, which pulled him out of the illusion.

Azatoth blinked in confusion, looked down at the box, then scowled as he realized he'd been played. The demon disappeared.

Lexi turned to Scott who's face was horrified by what he'd done. She scrambled to her feet. "Where would either of them go?"

"I don't know where Eric lives." Scott thought about it for a moment. "Azatoth has been living in Caleb's apartment by the river."

John Braxton stepped up to Lexi. "The last I heard, Eric was living in Denver."

Dick walked around the blood and gore in the middle of the room. He toed the box. "Where's the heart?"

All eyes turned to the empty box on the floor.

Lexi swore under her breath. "The demon gate." She turned to her unit brother and father. "We have to follow him."

John Braxton shook his head. "I'll head upstairs. But it's time you got the backing from your family you deserve." He turned to his son. "Zac?"

Isaac nodded his agreement and loaded a bolt into his crossbow pistol.

When they arrived at the demon gate outside Las Vegas, the portal was open and the shadow mages were fighting to hold it.

Akeem and Philippe had their arms outstretched, light shimmering and pulsing from their palms as they forced back the gray mist of the Darkness and the solid shapes of possessed shadow mages moving within it.

Jonathan clashed swords with Azatoth.

The demon parried blows with one hand while throwing lightning at the two shadow mages blocking the portal, but the bolts were fizzling out.

Azatoth's voice rang out over sounds of the battle, "Eric. Stop this."

Lexi smirked. Eric was putting up a fight with the demon, but she wasn't sure why.

Jonathan flicked a glance at Lexi. "Nice of you to join us."

Lexi studied the ground. "Where's the heart?"

Philippe made a face. "The what?"

Lexi guessed it might be in Eric's dimensional pocket. They'd never get it at this rate.

Scott joined the two shadow mages, adding his power to their shield. "Lexi. Use an ice barrier like you did earlier."

She cast the spell, and an ice wall appeared over the portal. It gave a loud whine and cracked, then burst into icy splinters.

The mages redoubled their previous efforts, but they were sweating profusely.

Akeem shook his head. "They seem to have their foot in the door."

Isaac put a hand on Lexi's shoulder. "What can I do?"

She thought, then turned to Philippe. "Would a bolt go through this?"

The Frenchman nodded. "From this side, yes."

Lexi turned back to her brother. "Yes…"

Isaac shot a bolt through the portal and was rewarded with a high-pitched howl.

Lexi shrugged. "That's what I was going to say."

Jonathan lunged at Azatoth, who faded to mist to stop Harpe from touching him.

Jonathan wiped sweat from his brow. "We can't keep this up. What the hell are we going to do?"

Scott sighed. "I think we need to go back to where it all started." He pulled Lexi and Dick away to speak.

"Where it began? You don't mean Atlantis, do you?" Lexi blinked.

"Can we do that?" Dick frowned. "Does anyone even know where it was? Or *when* it was?"

Lexi smiled. "The fae would. Dolores could get it for us."

Scott's shoulders sagged. "You know what she's like about timelines. Do you really think she'd say yes?"

Dick shrugged. "Let's go back to her and ask."

Lexi shook her head. "She's got her hands full at HQ."

Scott's brow wrinkled as the thought. "We could go back to just before it all kicked off."

Dick asked, "Could we go to Albin's place? I tried to call him, but he didn't pick up. I'm a little distracted about that."

Scott nodded. "That's fine with me." He drew sigils in the air, and moments later, a portal appeared.

They stepped through into the lobby of Albin's building. Scott dropped onto a couch and pulled out his cell phone. He dialed and put it on speakerphone.

Dolores answered, "Yes?"

"Hi, Dolores. It's Scott...from the future."

Lexi rolled her eyes.

There was a pause and a slight groan. "Yes."

"We need some information."

Dolores muttered, "I don't want—"

Scott interrupted, "This is super urgent. We need to know the exact location of Atlantis and the exact date it sank. Can you get that?"

Dick leaned closer to the cell phone. "But you have to give him the information without him knowing what it is."

Lexi grinned. "Dolores, could you write it on a piece of paper and tell Scott not to look at it until later?"

Scott pulled the paper out of his back pocket. "Oh, wait, she did that in the antiquities room. Thanks, Dolores."

Dolores sighed. "Okay. Thank you for calling. I don't require the services of an injury lawyer, but someone I know might. I'll let you know." She disconnected.

The three of them stared at the cell phone.

Dick grinned. "My mind is blown."

Scott opened the little sheet of paper. "She's given us the exact location of Atlantis, but she says that due to different calendars being used over the years and slight time slippages between Earth and Faerie, we could arrive up to ten years either side of our target. And there's a note at the bottom."

He held it up for them to see.

Remember, you can't save them. Not one.

Dick looked concerned. "If we arrive ten years after the earth-quake, we'll appear in an empty ocean."

Lexi put a hand on Scott's arm. "Then let's try not to do that."

Scott raised an eyebrow. "No pressure."

The desk phone in the lobby rang, and a desk clerk called to the doorman, "We're getting complaints of a fight upstairs."

Lexi grabbed the two of them and translocated up to Albin's floor. They were met by the sounds of smashing glass and breaking furniture.

Dick growled, "I'll tear them apart." He raced to the other end of the hallway at vamp speed and booted open the door. He didn't move. He just stared into the apartment. He covered his mouth and stepped back, turning his face away.

A chill came over Lexi. "Oh, no." She translocated the short distance to his side.

She found herself facing a tangled heap of bodies in the middle of Albin's apartment. They were contorted and twisted yet still moving.

Scott approached, but before he reached the scene, Lexi put a hand on his chest. "You stay there."

A woman's face appeared among the body parts. "Albin, you've got visitors."

A hand came out of the pile at the other end and shifted a bare leg to reveal another woman's face. "Oh, hi."

Albin came out of his bedroom with a book in his hand. "Oh, dear. These are my friends Lucinda and Janine. They're succubi."

Lexi returned her gaze to the people-mound. She counted four men with glazed eyes and pointed teeth. "I can see that. You party pretty hard, Albin."

Albin put his book down. "Azatoth sent some heterosexual, manly men who I wouldn't be able to distract from killing me. I figured she'd do that, so I brought in reinforcements."

Scott tried to look again, but Lexi still had a hand on his chest. "Not gonna happen."

The mage rolled his eyes.

Dick cleared his throat. "I called you. You didn't pick up. I was worried."

"You did? I didn't hear it ring." Albin glanced around his apartment.

A woman's muffled voice asked, "Do you want us to finish them off?"

Dick grimaced. "Ew!"

"I mean, do you want them dead or alive?" she clarified.

Albin shrugged and looked at Lexi.

Lexi considered it. "Call Dolores and ask her to bring you an elixir spray. One squirt for each."

"Ew!" Dick repeated.

Lexi groaned. "For the love of—"

"Ooh!" Lucinda squealed. "I'm getting vibrations."

Lexi grabbed Dick's arm. "Okay, we need to leave."

"It's your cell phone, Albin." She looked at the screen. "Someone called Dick."

Albin narrowed his eyes at the vampire.

A smile spread across Dick's face. "There I am. If you answer it, I won't have to come here, and I'll never have seen…" He pointed at the heap without looking at it. "This."

Lexi and Scott said, "No!" in unison.

Dick rolled his eyes. "Fine. Don't answer it. Anything in the refrigerator?"

"Hang on." Albin ran to the kitchen.

Lexi heard doors opening and closing as she locked eyes with Lucinda, who gave her a cheerful smile from the weird sex pile. Lexi smiled back and swiveled her eyes away. No one spoke.

Albin ran to the door with a cooler. "There are four bags inside." He and Dick kissed.

Dick turned away, then quickly turned back. "Oh, how's Marcel?"

Albin smiled. "Asleep on my bed."

"Lucky him." Dick sighed as he put the bag over his shoulder.

Lexi grabbed the vampire's jacket. "Come on. We're in a hurry."

Dick frowned. "How can we possibly be in a hurry?" He turned back to the door as Lexi pulled it closed. "I love you."

Albin called back. "I love you, too."

The elevator doors opened, and the doorman stepped out.

Scott touched his arm. "Oh, excuse me."

The man turned to face him.

Scott looked him in the eyes. "It was just a loud TV. There's nothing to see here. You should go back down to the lobby."

The man turned and went back into the elevator.

Scott looked at the instructions from Dolores. "Let's start the time journey closer to the destination. I want to reduce the margin for error."

Lexi nodded. "Good idea. Where?"

Scott thought about it. "Gibraltar, I think."

Lexi held on to the two of them and translocated to Newfoundland.

Dick shook himself. "Urgh! Can I sit on your revolting green couch instead?"

"Oh, you want to travel in first class? Fine." She pulled him into her dimensional pocket and continued with Scott to Iceland and then Gibraltar.

They emerged under a brooding sky, and high waves smashed into the wall around the harbor. From the isolated hillside above, the boats looked like toys as they bounced around in the wind.

Scott tensed.

Lexi took his hand and squeezed it. "Are you sure you can do this?"

"Yes. I'll get us there... Or then." He paused for a moment. "What if we run straight into Azatoth and she recognizes us?"

Lexi shook her head. "Thousands of years later? That's a hell of a memory."

"Not just our faces, our clothes. We're going to stick out. I think we should disguise ourselves."

Lexi agreed, "I think you're right. Let me do it so they won't see through it. I guess we can use our Shaun and Lena identities again. It worked well enough at Emmersley. How about you, Dick?"

The vampire shrugged. "Let's use Johnny. Everyone loves me as Johnny."

Scott smirked. "Didn't you die at the end of that one?"

Dick narrowed his eyes. "You know I did."

Lexi drew a glamour around each of them. She gave herself the face of a woman who worked at a supermarket near the condo. She did the same to Scott but paused at Dick. "Did Azatoth or Caleb ever see Albin?"

"No."

She gave him Albin's face. "There."

Dick stroked his face. "What a jawline!"

Scott rolled his eyes. "Come on, then." He drew the sigil in the air to create the portal. He took Lexi's hand, and they stepped through into a wooded area. Scott collapsed.

Lexi dropped to his side. "Scott? *Scott!*"

Dick called from the dimensional pocket, "What's happening?"

Lexi pulled the vampire out. "He just keeled over. He won't wake up."

Dick crouched down. "His heartbeat is faint, but it's there. You could try waking him up with magic."

"I don't know what's happening. I don't think blundering in with magic going to be the best idea."

Dick stood back up and did a three-sixty. "Put us back into your pocket. We need to find people."

Lexi did as Dick suggested. She walked for the best part of the day. "How is he?"

"He's the same as he was when you asked two minutes ago and two minutes before that."

"I hear people." Lexi quickened her steps. She found a trail and saw a horse and cart approaching with a man and woman in the front.

She ran out and waved. "Help."

The cart stopped, and the couple stared at her. They were sorcerers, she realized. "Please help me. My friend is injured."

They didn't respond, just stared at her.

She had been about to pull Dick and Scott out but considered they might never have seen a dimensional pocket. She put up her hands palms out. "Please wait?" She pointed at the ground. "Please wait here." Then she ran back into the woods.

CHAPTER FORTY-ONE

Lexi pulled Scott and Dick out of her dimensional pocket, and between them, she and Dick carried Scott to the road. She sighed with relief to see the couple had not moved on.

When the sorcerors saw them carrying Scott, the man jumped down and ran to meet them. Dick tried speaking to them in several languages, but they did not understand.

After an hour of riding, they crested a hill, and a beautiful walled city was revealed on the next hill.

Lexi looked down into the valley to see small villages sparsely laid out. They were denser close to the city's walls.

Dicks face was rapt. "Good heavens, those buildings are beautiful. How can this be nine thousand years ago?"

The woman turned to him and smiled shyly. She had been doing so repeatedly throughout the journey.

Dick whispered to Lexi, "I wish she'd stop doing that. I don't want to wind up in a fight with her husband."

Lexi decided not to tell the vampire the old man was looking at Dick in the same way his wife was in case it made him more uncomfortable than he already was.

Unfortunately, by the time they had ridden through the first village, there was no hiding it from him. Everyone on the streets they passed gazed up at Dick with reverence.

The vampire muttered. "Lexi, what's going on?"

"I haven't a clue."

Lexi absently stroked Scott's hand as they journeyed on. When they reached the third village, which looked more like a town, the cart stopped.

The old woman knocked on a door, and a man stepped out. He moved to the back of the cart and climbed up to look at Scott. He turned to Lexi and spoke to her in a language she couldn't understand. All she could do was shake her head. "I don't understand."

The old man turned to Dick and froze. He opened and closed his mouth several times as though unable to speak.

Dick put his hand on his friend's shoulder. "Can you help him?"

The man shook himself and called to someone.

Three men appeared and helped Dick to carry Scott inside the little sandstone building. They put him on a bed, and the other men were shooed outside.

Over the next few days, the old man worked ceaselessly to try to wake Scott. He wafted foul-smelling ointments under the sleeping man's nose, put leaves under his tongue, and searched gently for signs of trauma.

Dick paced in the room. "Scott's sick. What if the earthquake happens tomorrow and we can't get out of here? We just go down with the ship?"

Lexi shook her head. "I'll be able to translocate us to Spain or Africa."

Dick looked relieved. "Oh, right. Thank goodness."

Lexi glanced at him. "You're going stir-crazy. Go for a walk."

She wouldn't leave Scott's side, but Dick followed her suggestion and went for walks in the area. He returned with information about the town. While he couldn't understand the people, he observed that they had running water from wells in little squares dotted around the town.

"I can't believe how advanced they are. It's remarkable. Everywhere I go, I'm treated with deference. I haven't experienced this kind of behavior since the old days in Hollywood, but that was nothing compared to this."

The next day, Lexi heard the front door open. A fae entered the room. She was tiny and did nothing to hide her nature. Gossamer wings fluttered gently behind her as she spoke in the unfathomable language to Lexi, who shook her head to indicate that she did not understand.

Lexi tried speaking to her, but it was clear the fae did not understand her either.

Finally, the woman sighed and drew her thumb across Lexi's forehead. She felt a warm tingle. The woman stood back and stared intently at Lexi. "Do you understand me now?"

Lexi couldn't control her relief. "Yes. Yes, I understand you. Do you understand me?"

The woman smiled and nodded. "Tell me what happened to your friend and from where you have traveled."

Lexi paused. She knew better than to interfere with the timeline. She felt certain that if she shared that they had come from nine thousand years in the future, she was going to do exactly that. "We have traveled a great distance. My friend collapsed the moment we arrived. I think it was too much for him."

"And what of the god?" the fae woman asked. "Is he here?"

"The god?" Lexi was confused. Why was this woman speaking to her of gods?

The fae nodded. "I am told that the god of the afterlife travels with you."

Lexi furrowed her brow. "The god of... Wait, they think Dick is a god? Please don't tell him that. I'll never hear the end of it."

The fae smiled. "I am Pearl."

Lexi smiled, although she felt bad. She was finally able to communicate, but all she could do was lie. "I'm Lena, this is Shaun, and our friend is Johnny."

Pearl looked at Lexi for longer than necessary. She had the impression the fae was telling her she knew that wasn't true, but she was going to let it pass.

Pearl leaned over Scott. She busied herself around the unconscious mage for a few minutes then turned back to Lexi. "Your friend extinguished his magical energy and used his life force to complete the journey you spoke of."

Lexi's heart hammered. "His life force? Is he—"

"No, fear not. He has used some years, but not all. One must wonder why you did not take this burden upon yourself. You are as the people here, yet ageless. I haven't seen such as you before."

Lexi shook her head. "I don't know how to do what he did. He didn't show me. We didn't have the time."

The fae pursed her lips. "Time. Hmm."

It was abundantly clear that the fae knew they had traveled through time, but Lexi still didn't want to share too much. She sighed. "It is as you suspect. I hope you understand that I can't say anymore. Please don't ask me."

The fae's wings fluttered, and she nodded in acquiescence. "It shall be as you have asked."

"I didn't realize you had such an ear for linguistics." Dick stood at the door.

Pearl jumped up and buzzed to the far corner of the room, staring at Dick in shock. "What is this that walks and yet lives not? Is this the god of the world beyond?"

Dick stared at her and blinked, then looked at Lexi. "I assume she doesn't like the look of me."

"This is my friend, Johnny. He is most certainly not a god, but I suppose you could say he has a foot in both worlds. I don't know if it means anything, but I can vouch for him."

Pearl drew her thumb across Dick's forehead and waited.

For a few moments, Dick was silent. "I don't know what to say."

Lexi snorted. "Well, that's a first."

Pearl smiled. "Welcome to Atlantis, Johnny of Two Worlds."

"Finally. Would you believe I'm proficient in several languages? Being unable to communicate with the people around me has been most disquieting." Dick turned to face the doctor's wife in the other room. "Varna, your hospitality is deeply appreciated. I feel I have offended you by not accepting the food you've offered me. I do not eat, but if you happen to have wine, I would be delighted to help you with that."

Varna gave Dick a big smile and dashed into the pantry.

Dick returned his attention to Pearl. "Will you be able to awaken our friend?"

Pearl turned to Lexi. "I cannot, but you can. Share your life force with him."

Dick became animated. "Of course! That must be what you did to Adele."

Lexi frowned. "But Adele died. Eric killed her."

"No, he didn't." Dick paused. "Well, yes. She was dead, and Eric killed her again. But you un-undeaded her. What's more, whatever you did, it brought her back to life. The last I heard from her, she and Raj were getting married."

Lexi blinked. "I didn't know. Why didn't anyone tell me?"

Dick shrugged. "There has been a lot going on."

Pearl left the room.

Lexi leaned over Scott and put her hands on his chest. She closed her eyes and breathed slow, deliberate breaths to counter the speed her heart was beating. "Come on, Scott. Time to wake up." As she breathed out, she drew on the boundless life force within her and pushed it into him.

When she opened her eyes, Scott was staring at her with a confused expression. "Where am I?"

Dick sniffled.

Lexi looked up at the vampire, ready to make a snarky remark about him crying until she felt her own eyes sting with relief. She held Scott's hand. "The question isn't just where, but when."

CHAPTER FORTY-TWO

Lexi and Scott were sitting on a hillside, eating honey-covered bread and looking down on the quiet town.

Scott suggested, "The problem with arriving early is that we don't know how early we are."

Lexi nibbled on her bread. "I wish we'd thought to ask more questions before we left. I must have seen books at the Seelie Court that would've helped. We don't know when the signs began to show the island was in trouble."

Scott turned to her. "Are we going to see Dick tonight?"

Lexi flopped back onto the grass. "Again? Do we have to?"

Scott grinned. "He's enjoying himself."

Lexi raised an eyebrow. "Rewriting the works of William Shakespeare and passing them off as his own."

Scott's eyes widened. "Isn't that risky? What if someone writes it down and takes it to fae?"

Lexi shrugged. "I think he changed it enough to be safe. I'm sure Dolores would have told us if anything remained of this place. The people, their arts, science, and magic; all disappeared into myth." She took another bite of her bread. "This stuff is so nice. I wonder if I could get the recipe before…" She stopped speaking.

Scott lay back. "It's horrible knowing it's going to happen. Knowing we can't warn them or save them. We've been here three months. Every day knowing what's coming gets harder. These are our friends."

Lexi sighed. "What else can we do? We've experienced five tremors here in the last few months. Three in the last month alone. I think it's getting closer."

Scott rolled over onto his stomach and propped himself up onto his elbows. "I could just go forward a month at a time or a week at a time."

"No." Her tone left no room for argument.

Still, Scott tried. "Small jumps aren't going to kill me."

Lexi sat up. "Still no."

Scott sat up next to her. "Then what are we going to do?"

Lexi grinned. "I've got an idea for something we could do. But I'm not sure if you'd agree it would be a good use of our time?"

Scott narrowed his eyes. "What?"

Lexi grabbed the front of his shirt and kissed him.

When they finally broke apart, Scott was grinning.

"Still want to go see Dick perform *Thirteenth Night?*" Lexi asked.

Scott reached for her. "No, I think your idea was better."

The tremors were coming every day by their third year in Atlantis.

Dick nudged Scott. "It's been two weeks. Can I visit my magic blood supply?"

"Sure." Scott put a hand on the vampire's shoulder, and they went into his dimensional pocket.

Scott walked over to where Lexi was writing on the whiteboard, recording the tsunamis and earthquakes, while Dick went to his cooler and took out one of the four full blood bags.

He drained it and threw the empty into the cooler, then closed it. He started walking back to the others but turned and tiptoed back to the bag. He opened it again.

The empty blood bag was still there. "Damn. I never catch it refilling. That would be interesting to see."

Scott laughed. "Ha! One day." He sent Dick out of the dimensional pocket and walked over to the cooler. He slowly translocated a pint of blood from his veins to the bag.

Lexi walked up behind him and wrapped her arms around his waist. "Does he still think he's getting magically-refilling blood?"

Scott grinned. "Yes. Don't you dare spoil it for him."

Lexi laughed. "Of course not. It would be like telling a kid there's no Santa Claus."

Scott put the full bag under the others and closed the cooler bag.

Lexi took his hand. "Let's go and rehydrate you."

They walked out of their little room in the back of the doctor's office, where Scott had been assisting the doctor for the past three years.

Varna was preparing dinner. "Lena, would you like to take the cart to the bakery? We're running low on honey bread." She looked sideways at Scott.

Lexi chuckled. "It's not just Shaun. I've been eating it, too. We'd be happy to replenish your stocks."

They climbed onto the cart and rode to the well, where they found Dick regaling a crowd of young men with a highly doctored tale from his life in Hollywood.

Scott filled a carafe with water, drank the whole thing, and filled it again.

Dick appeared at Lexi's side. "You've got the cart. Where are you heading?"

"High Village to get some bread and flour for Varna. Finally, my opportunity to see if I can get the recipe."

Dick looked speculatively at Lexi. "Did you bake before you came here?"

Lexi shook her head. "Not once. I never even wondered what a simple human life might be like."

Scott put an arm around Lexi. "Maybe when all this is over, we could come back here a hundred years earlier and grow old and die here."

She kissed his cheek. "There could be worse ways to live."

Dick climbed into the cart. "I'll just nap in the back."

As the wheels left dirt and hit cobbles, Dick sat up. "That was a rude awakening."

The cart slowed as Lexi spoke to a woman walking with a basket of bread. "Could you direct us to the bakery?"

The woman pointed. "Straight ahead to the square and left. Then follow your nose."

As they moved on, Dick mused, "Do you remember when we first arrived and you thought you'd never speak a word of Atlantean?"

They all smiled.

They stopped the cart a little way down the street from the bakery behind another cart and walked in.

"Dear God, that smell. I've died and gone to heaven." Lexi followed her nose into the store.

She ordered the bread and flour and paid for it, then asked the woman, "Who do I have to bribe to get the recipe for the honey bread? This stuff has changed my life."

Dick muttered, "It's changed your hips."

She punched his arm.

"I'll go see if I can talk the people in the winery into building a still." Dick left quickly.

The woman laughed. "Thank you for your kind words. I'm

afraid the only person with the recipe is my husband, the baker. He won't even tell me."

Lexi didn't believe that for a minute.

They left the shop with their arms full and put the bread and flour on the back of the cart.

The woman followed them into the street. "You're welcome to ask him. He'll say no, but he'll be pleased you asked." She pointed across the street to a man with a tray of little honey buns. "He gives them out to the children just before we close up. It's his favorite part of the day."

The baker sang, "Sweet treats for sweet smiles."

The children surrounded him.

He held up a glaze topped bun. "This is a big honey bun. I'm sure it's bigger than the others."

The children chorused, "No, it's the same size."

"No, I think it's bigger. Who's got the sweetest smile?" He surveyed the crowd of little faces, then handed the bun to a little girl, who squealed with delight.

Then he let the rest of the children converge on the tray and take a bun each.

Lexi and Scott watched as the children dashed away, but two remained, clinging onto the baker's apron.

"They are our little treasures." She called out, "These people want to meet you and steal your honey bun recipe."

The baker waved.

"Hurry, Azatoth. They need to get back before dark." The woman didn't see the smiles slip off Lexi's and Scott's faces.

The baker crossed the street and handed the tray to his wife. "So, you want to steal my honey bun recipe?"

Lexi hoped her face was smiling. She felt detached from it. She just nodded.

He didn't seem to notice anything strange about her. "They're made with a little magic and a lot of love." He picked up the little girl. She looked to be five or six years old. "What do you think, princess? Should we let the lady steal our honey bun recipe?"

The little girl looked scandalized. "No, never. They're your buns, Daddy. They'll always be yours." She threw her arms around his neck and kissed his cheek.

He smiled at them. "I'm afraid the princess has spoken."

Lexi found her voice. "That's okay. We need to get back."

Beside Lexi, the horse whinnied. A flock of birds flew over them, then a rumble sounded as the earth beneath them groaned and shifted. Trays clattered and fell to the floor inside the bakery. The horse panicked and neighed. Azatoth's son pitched forward, and Scott caught him before he hit the ground.

The street buckled in front of the cart, and the wheel of the baker's cart slipped into the crack. The cart tipped over, and the wheel broke in half. Luckily, there was no horse tethered to the cart. Azatoth reached out and touched the doctor's horse. It was calmed down.

Moments later, the quake was over.

Dick came out of the winery with the owner following him.

"Wait, you can't escape that easily."

Azatoth asked, "Is everything all right?"

The owner of the winery nodded, smiling at Dick. "This is a useful man to have around. I was able to keep most of the barrels in the wall steady. I was expecting to lose the carafes, but he was so fast. He caught them all and laid them down safely. It was a marvelous thing to witness."

Dick inclined his head. "It was no trouble."

The man pushed a carafe into Dick's hand. "Here. Take this with my thanks."

Dick nodded at the man and took the earthenware carafe. He approached his friends. "Are you okay? That wasn't a light one, and it might be signaling a worse one. We should get back."

Scott turned to Dick. "Johnny, come and meet the baker. This is Azatoth and his lovely family."

Dick dropped the carafe and remained frozen as it hit the ground and smashed, spilling wine onto the street.

Azatoth held his little girl close as he assessed Dick. "Are you all right?"

The vampire recovered. "I think it must have been damaged. Hairline fracture or something."

The baker looked at the sky. "I think you're right that we have another one on the way. The augurs in the city say as much. They say we've angered the gods, and a big one is coming. They have a plan to appease them. I'm not convinced, but how would I know? I'm just a simple baker, and when did a baker ever change the course of history?" He turned to his son. "Go get Daddy a package of buns."

The little boy ran into the bakery on chubby legs and came out with a basketful of buns.

Azatoth handed them to Scott. "Thank you for catching my boy."

His wife came out. "You're going to be short a basket for the augurs gathering tonight."

"I'll bake more." Azatoth kissed his wife's forehead.

She frowned. "How are you going to get there?"

Scott stepped over to Azatoth. "We'd be happy to give you a ride to the city. If the augurs are doing something special, it might be exciting to see."

Azatoth smiled. "Then we are fortunate indeed to have met new friends."

Lexi asked, "When do you need to leave?"

"When the shadow of the sun is at my door." Azatoth put a hand on his heart. "Thank you so much for your kindness."

Scott looked at the position of the sun. "We'll see you then. We have a few errands to run first."

Azatoth waved as they drove away in the cart. No one spoke until they were at the edge of town.

Finally, Lexi whispered, "I'm not ready. It's too soon." Scott hugged her.

They stopped the cart on the quiet trail just out of town, and Scott jumped down and paced. "What should we do? We didn't plan how this would work if we were out of town."

Lexi asked. "Should we just go to Varna's house and get her first?"

Dick jumped down. "You planned to use a shield, right? Stick to that plan. I'll stay at the house."

They translocated. Dick gathered his things, then met Lexi in her room. "Varna's outside hanging out the washing. I don't know why I said that."

The earth grumbled again.

Lexi put a shield over the room, then Scott did the same.

They translocated back to the cart and drove back to the bakery.

Scott sighed. "If they are truly the ancestors of sorcerers, it's such a shame these people won't live to see the progression of their race. This is the dawn of magic."

They helped Azatoth load the buns. He sat in the back of the cart as they drove to the city.

The guards stopped the cart. "Azatoth. Do you have anything for us?"

"Of course." He handed out buns.

"Who are these people?" a guard asked.

Azatoth smiled. "My cart broke in the last quake. These are my kind customers, helping me out."

"All of your customers are kind. I think we're all under your spell." The other guards laughed. "You had best be on your way. They're waiting for you. We've had a lot of important visitors today for the dinner after their important ritual. Apparently, it's going to change all our lives. You might find your list of customers growing after tonight."

Lexi and Scott shared a glance.

Azatoth directed them where to stop. "I'm going to take these into the kitchens. Are you religious, folks? If you want to attend the ritual, we can stay for it."

"We'd love to. Thank you." Lexi looked at the building. People were crowding outside the doors. "I don't think we're going to see much, though."

"Lucky for you, I'm connected." Azatoth smiled. "Grab some baskets and follow me." He walked around the side of the building. "It's not really my thing. I'll wait for you at the cart. He dropped a bun into Lexi's hand. "In case you get peckish. Just come back the same way." He led them into the kitchens. "These are my friends. Could they get a good view of proceedings? There'll be a basket of buns in it for you tomorrow."

"I shouldn't, but come on." A chef led them through a side door and up a staircase that came out to a balcony with a small window looking out onto the room. "Stay here and don't make a sound."

The hall below them was filled with people. A small rumble caused dust and tiny fragments of stone to fall from the vaulted ceilings. The gathered people muttered and wept.

Lexi stuffed the bun into her pocket and watched as the ritual took place. She listened to the impassioned prayers, the promises of purity to their gods.

As she and Scott held onto each other, Lexi whispered into his ear. "I want to scream. I want to warn them."

Scott pulled her closer.

Lexi created her shield, and Scott created his, both unseen by the people below.

Then the spell. A ball of energy floating above them. A tear in the veil. The casting of everything but goodness and innocence into the void. The tiniest speck of mist rising from each person and floating into the ball. As the specks flying in through the doors and window grew in numbers, the cloud darkened and poured through. With the last of the dark mist, the ball slipped all the way into the void, and the tear in the veil closed.

The silence was deafening. The gathered people stared emptily. Not moving.

They made their way through the kitchens and past the chef who had shown them in, who was sitting on the floor.

When they reached the cart, they found Azatoth slumped over, staring at nothing.

The wails of children carried on the breeze. It was more than Lexi could stand.

Scott translocated them to the doctor's home.

Lexi opened the door to their little room and found Dick red-eyed. Her heart skipped a beat. "Is she all right?"

A brown-haired toddler sat up in the crib beside the bed. She put out her chubby arms. "Mama."

"Mama's here." Lexi pulled her daughter into her arms.

The ground shifted, and loud crashes sounded around them.

"It's time to go." Lexi put her daughter in Dick's arms and moved him into her dimensional pocket.

Scott held her hand. "Gibraltar first?"

"No, straight back. We've got this."

Lexi took care of the distance while Scott handled the time. Lexi flooded him with shadow mage life force as he led them through the portal.

CHAPTER FORTY-THREE

Lexi and Scott stepped out of the time portal just as Dolores, Alicia, and Bryan appeared.

"If you're going somewhere, hurry up." Jonathan glanced over his shoulder, then stared at them. The three of them wore simple peasant clothes, Scott had a beard, and Lexi was holding a toddler. She passed the little girl to Dolores.

The little fae was almost apoplectic. "I told you, you couldn't save even one of them."

Scott grinned. "We made that one."

Isaac called from the portal, "We're starting to struggle here."

Bryan ran over and pushed on the portal.

With Jonathan distracted, Azatoth solidified.

Lexi shouted, "Watch out."

But Azatoth wasn't intending to attack Jonathan. He translocated behind Alicia and held a knife to her throat. "If any of you vanishes, I'll assume you're behind me and cut her throat. Get back from the portal. Let them through."

"You don't have to do this, Azatoth. I've got something you won't have seen for a long time." Lexi pulled the honey bun from her pocket.

Azatoth blinked. "What's that?"

Scott added, "This is how a baker can change the course of history."

Lexi threw the bun to him. He reached out to catch it, and Alicia pulled away from him. He didn't notice. He caught the bun and fell to his knees. "My babies. I lost my babies."

Lexi couldn't hate him anymore. "Your babies were probably saved by the fae. Nearly all of them were. They were the beginning of the mages."

Akeem shouted, "They're pushing us back!"

Lexi walked to the portal. "Stand back. We know what to do."

Akeem, Isaac, and Philippe stood back, gasping with exhaustion, while Lexi and Scott stood in front of the portal. Scott removed the shield the others had been holding in place, and they stepped back.

Philippe squeaked, "What are you doing?"

The Darkness flooded through the portal and spread into the air above them, creating a shadow above the people on the ground.

Lexi began to doubt that she'd done the right thing, but the Darkness faded, dissipating on the wind. "They are the souls of hundreds of sorcerers. Let them find their peace."

Azatoth wept, still cradling the bun like a tiny precious thing. He looked up as the dark mist dispersed and the sun shone on them again. He stared at Eric's body. "It seems I have made myself another prison." He frowned as he noticed Dolores holding the child. "Reveal."

The air shimmered, and Kenneth was revealed to be standing next to them with his evil rictus grin and a crossbow bolt in his fist.

Jonathan appeared behind him and stabbed him with Harpe. "That's the last of them."

Scott spoke the spell to release Azatoth.

The demon's mouth opened, and he screamed. It was Eric; he wasn't letting Azatoth go.

Lexi raced to him. "Dick. Get his watch."

Lexi grabbed one arm, and Dick grabbed the other. They pulled off the ring and the watch.

Eric gazed at his hands in horror. "No."

His face became calm. Azatoth again. "Thank you."

Lexi translocated away, but Dick didn't know what was coming.

Eric exploded, and Dick screamed, "My suit! This will never come out."

Azatoth's essence swirled upward and dispersed.

Philippe pointed to the portal. "We still need to get rid of this."

Lexi shook her head. "If only we could have found that heart."

Limpet burped.

Lexi narrowed her eyes at the thinner demon. "You didn't."

Limpet shrugged.

Lexi grabbed Limpet by the leg and slapped his back. "Hoik that thing up right this minute, Limpet, or I'll reach down your throat and…"

Limpet threw up the heart. *You only had to ask.*

They stared at the goop-covered heart. No one wanted to touch it.

"Oh, for goodness sake." Dick picked up the heart and threw it through the portal, which faded. "I need a drink." The vampire walked down the hill toward Las Vegas, and everyone followed.

Bryan called, "Actually, there are still some demonic legacies running around Kindred HQ."

Dick didn't break stride or turn back. "Not my circus, not my monkeys."

EPILOGUE

L exi turned away from the view of New York in the executive conference room and faced her father. "Are you sure about this?"

"Positive." Jonathan nodded. "I've been alive for two hundred and twenty-eight years. If it goes wrong, it doesn't matter. I have a hankering to see your mother again."

Alicia leaned toward him. "We don't know how this is going to work. You could have the rest of your natural life, or the spell could turn you to dust."

Jonathan hugged his daughters. "I'm ready, whatever happens."

Philippe looked up from his quiet conversation with Maria. She was showing him photographs of his wife and the generations of children who came after them. "I too am ready. I am satisfied to see that my family has endured and blossomed, but eternal life is a burden."

Scott raised an eyebrow. "Azatoth said as much."

Akeem gave her a smile and a nod. "I'm ready." The big man strode into the middle of the room and laid down on the floor.

Jonathan and Philippe joined him. They leaned back so their heads were almost touching.

Scott, Bryan, and Maggie stood at the feet of the prone men. They raised their arms and sent beams of light into the center and in a triangle surrounding them. Scott spoke the words of the spell.

Lexi stood at the edge of the room with Alicia. "Nothing's happening. What if they don't wake up?"

A glow appeared around the men on the floor.

"Um, Lexi?" Alicia sounded concerned. "You're glowing."

Lexi turned to her sister as she was overcome with dizziness. She rubbed her forehead. "I feel weird." She went weak at the knees, then dropped to the floor.

She opened her eyes. "What happened?"

"You might have been too close. The spell seems to have worked on you too." Scott was kneeling beside her.

Lexi sat up and felt something tumble down on her. She grabbed it and opened her hand to find a yellow stone. "It's a piece of sulfur."

Akeem sat up. "See, old friends? It appears that we're not dead yet. I'm pleased. I wasn't really ready."

Philippe grinned. "But one day, we will be. Thank God."

Lexi's cell phone rang. "Hi, Dick."

Dick's voice was high-pitched. "Don't panic. I mean, she's perfectly fine, but Amelia just glowed up, then went to sleep, and a yellow stone appeared on her chest."

She looked at Scott. "I don't think it was my proximity to the spell. It happened to Amelia, too."

Scott frowned. "Is she all right?"

Lexi nodded. "Dick says she's fine. He sounds like he needs some bourbon, though."

Dick's voice came from the cell phone. "Darling, Uncle Dick always needs a bourbon."

A tiny voice shouted, "Horsey!"

Dick's mouth moved away from the cell phone. "As her majesty commands. But just to be clear, the Queen Mother will be buying me a new suit." He neighed as he disconnected.

Lexi smiled at her father. "Still with us?"

"It seems *my* Amelia will have to wait a little longer." Jonathan closed his eyes for a few moments, then looked at Scott. "I checked the box in my dimensional pocket. The chalky remains I carried from the other world have turned to ash, and this was on top of the pile." He opened his hand to reveal a yellow stone.

"So, this spell undid the original one." Scott put out a hand to help Jonathan off the floor. "I'm sorry your friends won't be coming back."

"It's for the best. It would have been torturous. I have a vague memory of it from Azatoth's mind." Alicia turned to Bryan. "That's another memory I could do without."

Bryan nodded and pulled his wife into a hug. She had been in counseling to remove the more horrific memories.

Though Lexi felt counseling had been misused in Kindred, she had to admit it did have its benefits.

Akeem asked, "What of the future of Kindred? While it has had a rotten element, someone needs to run the place."

Bryan took his wife's hand. "Azatoth's council of inmates is back in the Hollows."

Alicia shrugged. "Is there anyone remaining who's senior enough to run it? We need someone who would make the changes Kindred really needs."

Bryan asked, "Like what?"

Alicia counted off on her fingers. "The elixir is gone. We're only going to have a limited number of natural legacies. We need to rebuild our relationship with the community and bring the supes in. Instead of us policing them, they should be learning to police their own communities, and we should absolutely outlaw forced bondings of any kind. In fact, the whole concept of family units in the community needs to be reassessed."

A quiet knock on the door drew their attention to a young man entering hesitantly. "I'm sorry to interrupt." He walked over to Alicia and handed her a clipboard. "The expense report needs to be signed off."

As Alicia took the clipboard and pen, she continued to talk. "The Grandfathers are probably next in line, but most of them are too much like Eric." She flicked through the sheets and circled several figures. "That's wrong, and that. Get the latest figures from Sebastian's team and run the numbers again."

The young man turned white. "I'm so sorry."

Alicia smiled. "It's fine. Just fix it."

The man nodded and left.

When she turned back, everyone was staring at her. "Oh no. Don't look at me. Did you see the way that guy looked at me? He was practically peeing his pants."

"Why not you? You're already in the office. You can make all those changes you were talking about, and as long as they keep looking at you like that, they'll make those changes." Jonathan smiled. "You won't be alone. We'll be around for a few years."

Alicia's gaze flew to Lexi. "I think out of the two of us—"

"Sorry." Lexi dangled her ID. "I'm already the Archive Curator."

Scott put up a hand. "Assistant Curator. Speaking of which, I've got curator things to do." He disappeared.

Lexi looked at her wrist like she was wearing a watch, which she wasn't. "I should—"

Alicia's eyes narrowed. "Don't you dare."

"I should...sit here. That's what I was going to say." She sat at the conference table and called Scott, muttering into the phone, "Come back, you sneaky asshole."

Scott chuckled. "I can't. I'm in the archives, putting books away."

"You're spinning the puzzle on Devon's desk. I can hear it."

"I'm just looking at the painting of Devon outside the Chelsea Hotel. I can't believe it's all over."

Lexi sighed. "I hope Devon is at rest now."

The words had barely left her mouth when Scott yelped, "Son of a bitch."

"What's wrong?

"A book just hit me on the head."

"Maybe it's Devon telling you he's not at peace." Lexi frowned at the sad thought. "What book was it?"

She waited while he groaned and picked up the book. *"The Fifth Ward."*

Lexi furrowed her brow. "Devon mentioned that book to me. Bring it up, would you?"

Scott appeared in the conference room and passed it to Lexi.

"While you're here, take a seat." She smirked.

The front of the book showed a diner that had been styled to look like a railway car.

Lexi flicked through the pages from front to back. "That's strange. It doesn't mention the words Fifth Ward anywhere."

Scott frowned. "How can you know that?"

Lexi shrugged. "I don't know. It must be a curator thing."

Scott snatched the book and flipped through it. Then he did it again, then again. "Apparently, it's not an assistant curator thing."

Akeem looked at the book over Scott's shoulder and pointed at a woman sitting in the window of the diner. "Jonathan. Who does that look like?"

Lexi's father crossed the room and took the proffered book. "My Amelia." He smiled and stroked the cover.

———

Lexi straightened her wine-colored uniform and pinned on her Alexa nametag.

Alicia pushed her sister out of the way to check her own uniform and pin on her "Alicia" nametag.

It had taken weeks to find the place. They'd spent a significant amount of time searching Las Vegas, assuming that since the city had four magical wards, there could be a hidden fifth ward. Then they'd trawled every city that had anything called Fifth Ward.

Finally, they found it in Los Angeles: a diner called the Fifth Ward that had closed twenty years before. All the clues were in the cover. The newspaper vending machine outside the diner bore the date. The clock on the wall inside the diner showed the time.

"Is everyone ready?" Scott stood in front of the portal.

Lexi, Alicia, and Jonathan lined up, and the four of them walked through.

"Well, about time." The woman behind the counter pulled off her apron. "The coffee's made." She shooed Scott behind the counter.

A man walked out and handed Scott an apron, then stood near the exit.

The woman gave Lexi and Alicia a pad and pen each. "Write the orders on there and pass them through to the kitchen." She snapped her fingers in front of Lexi's face. "What are you looking at? They haven't sent me a simpleton, have they?"

"No. Sorry. I was looking to see if any tables need to be wiped." Lexi smiled.

"Well, good." The woman picked up her purse. "We'll be back in two hours." She pointed at a man reading a newspaper. "He's been served. Give him a few minutes, then see if he wants a refill." She pointed at Jonathan. "There's your first customer." She disappeared through the door.

Alicia was staring at a table near the window where Lexi had been looking. "That's where she was in the picture. Could we have missed her?"

Jonathan sat at the table across the aisle opposite the seat where Amelia had been sitting in the cover picture.

Lexi shrugged. "Coffee?"

Her father smiled. "Yes, please."

Alicia brought the mug, and Lexi poured the coffee. "Cream and sugar?"

He shook his head.

Lexi was just going to offer a refill to the man behind the newspaper when a bell chimed. They all turned to the door.

A beautiful heavily pregnant woman entered and took a seat near the window.

Lexi took a step, but Alicia moved in first.

She handed the woman a menu. "Can I get you a drink?"

The woman smiled. "Could I just have a coffee to go, please?"

Alicia wrote Coffee on her pad. "Of course. What name?"

"My name?" The woman frowned.

Alicia didn't look certain of herself. "It's a new thing we're trying out."

"Oh, I see. The name's Liz."

While Lexi poured the coffee, she whispered to her sister. "What was that about?"

"I don't know. That's what they do in Starbucks." Alicia shrugged.

Lexi noticed that Jonathan was glancing at the woman with a haunted look in his eyes every few seconds.

Lexi put the coffee down on the table. "Coffee for Liz." She glared at her sister. Then turned back to the woman. "Congratulations. Do you have long to go?"

Liz looked up and did a double-take. She looked at Alicia, then at Lexi. "Good heavens, identical twins." She put a hand on her belly. "I'm expecting twin girls."

"I'm sure they'll be as amazing as we are," Alicia called across the room.

Liz laughed and looked at the name tags. "Alexa and Alicia.

You have such lovely names. I'll have to remember them when the time comes."

The man in the corner shuffled his newspaper.

Lexi had forgotten about him. She grabbed the coffee carafe and took it to his table. "Would you like a refill?"

He folded down the newspaper. It was Devon. He was around the age he had been in Dick's room at the Chelsea.

Lexi shrugged. "Honestly, I'm not surprised."

Devon chuckled.

She gave him a lopsided grin. "So, you knew everything would turn out okay."

Devon shook his head. "Not me. I'm living this moment in real-time."

Lexi raised an eyebrow. "I mean, later you."

"I can't answer for him. Who's the man staring at her? Wait, don't tell me. I'll just have that refill." Devon's jaw dropped as he stared across the room. "He's not going to…"

Jonathan had joined Amelia at her table. "I'm sorry to bother you."

Lexi and Alicia exchanged panicked looks as Scott stepped through from the kitchen.

Jonathan continued, "I wonder if you could help me. I'm trying to compose my thoughts. I want to tell someone how I feel about my wife, but it seems like there's so much to say. I can't quite find the words." He waved a pen and a blank scrap of paper. "I'm sorry, I shouldn't bother you, but you have very kind eyes."

Liz smiled. "What do you want to tell her?"

Jonathan didn't miss a beat. "That from the moment we were parted all those years ago, there isn't a moment I haven't missed her. Since then, I've lived every day without hope. I hardened my heart for the bleak future of an eternity without her, but her face was always there when I closed my eyes. Although I became but a shadow through my loss of her, I never gave in to the darkness because my heart was always hers. I want to tell her, 'You are, and have always been, the Heart of the Shadow.'"

Amelia blinked tears from her eyes. "What's her name?"

Jonathan struggled to speak. "Amelia."

"That's a beautiful name." She reached out and laid her hand on his. "You don't need to write it down. You said it perfectly." She took out her coin purse.

Jonathan shook his head. "Please, allow me to buy your coffee. You've been so kind."

She smiled. "Thank you." She got to her feet and picked up the coffee. "Good luck."

Amelia walked to the door, turned, and looked at Lexi, Alicia, and Jonathan. A thoughtful expression crossed her face, followed by a warm smile like something somewhere had just slipped into place. She smiled again and left.

Scott put his arms around Lexi. "Let's go rescue Uncle Dick from Princess Amelia."

She gave him a mischievous grin. "Nah. Let's go to Phil's."

THE END

I can't believe we got to the last book in the series. I hope you enjoyed it. I'm going to miss Lexi, Scott and Dick. I know we're not supposed to have favorites, but I'm going to miss Dick the most.

I finished the book at the end of September. Since then, I've been pondering what to do next. I've had a couple of short stories in anthologies that could be new series, but I had a great meeting with Michael at the 20Booksto50k Vegas conference, where we hashed out an idea for our next project. I'm super excited about it and can't wait to get started.

Vegas was great fun. I took my husband Phil (the minotaur) to Jessie Rae's for bbq. He said it was the best food of the whole trip, and while I'd also eaten at two top notch French restaurants and a Gordon Ramsey's restaurant, I have to agree.

On the subject of food, I don't know if any of you live in Vegas, but seriously, machines that dispense cake? What's that about? Sadly, I didn't find one while I was hungry, I kept walking past them after I'd just eaten. Maybe next year.

Hi to those of you I saw at the author signing event. That was a fun day and I'm sure you came to my table just for the signing and it had nothing to do with the pile of Rocky Road treats that Phil made.

Vegas was a lot of fun, I mean work, it was a lot of work. It was great to spend time with my LMBPN family; Michael, Craig Martelle, Sarah Noffke, Martha Carr, Charles Tillman, and Kevin McLaughlin to name but a few. And those of you who are in the Facebook groups will know Micky and Kelly. It's like a huge family gathering. I missed my lovely Natale so much but feel I may have consumed less alcohol as a result.

ps: If Michael says anything about catching me on Facebook all.the.time, don't believe him. He's an author. He makes shit up for a living

Thank you for not only reading this story but these author notes as well.

Many of you know what 20Booksto50k® is, and many do not. In a nutshell, it's a not-for-profit group I started where authors who have found business strategies that work share that information (and encouragement) with other authors who write and release their stories on Amazon, Apple, Google, and other platforms.

One of my best friends, Craig Martelle, decided to head up a 20Booksto50K® conference (also not-for-profit), and in the four short conferences (over five years), it has grown to become one of the top ten author conferences around and arguably the top for Indie Authors.

A lot of people from LMBPN (my company) come to help (out of their own time and pocket), so many of us find ourselves together during this week.

It's a bit of work, a bit of sleep, a lot of learning, and perhaps a bit too much laughing and having a good time.

I mean, *it's a lot of work.*

(Editor's note: but SO much fun! And good food. And candy. And fun people)

I find it astonishing that so many of the people I met over the internet (often on the Facebook group) to talk about this author profession will travel from all over the United States and the world to meet in this little town of glitz and glamour called Las Vegas...

But we do.

Close to 2,000 will be involved in the event next year in 2022. If you have any thoughts about writing stories and selling them, go check out this year's videos, which were put up for free on YouTube: https://www.youtube.com/results?search_query=20booksto50k+vegas+2021

For those fans who came to the book signing event, it was a smash. We thoroughly enjoyed you being with us on Friday of the event.

For those who are asking, "Why don't I know about it?" please look for the 20Books event being held next November at Bally's on the Strip in Las Vegas.

Do think about joining us. We would love to see you there!

Have a good week or weekend. Talk to you in the next story!

Ad Aeternitatem,

Michael Anderle

ACKNOWLEDGMENTS

This book could not have been written without the love and support of my family, my LMBPN family, and my Coronita family.

Thank you to Natale Roberts for the wonderful editing job (and the bbq brisket), to Moonchild for the wonderful cover, and to the LMBPN JIT team for the epic work they do.

Huge thanks to my partner in crime, Michael Anderle.

Sursum ad astra.

OTHER BOOKS FROM E.G. BATEMAN

The Faders Trilogy

Fade

The Network

Portal

Unseen – Free with newsletter signup at https://www.
subscribepage.com/s5f7q8

By E. G. Bateman and Michael Anderle

Legacy of the Shadow's Blood (Book 1)

The Bound Legacy (Book 2)

The Rising Legacy (Book 3)

Dawn Of The Shadow (Book 4)

Order Of The Shadow (Book 5)

Heart Of The Shadow (Book 6)

Sign up for E.G. Bateman's newsletter and receive The Fugitive Legacy!